KATHARINE, THE VIRGIN WIDOW

The young Spanish widow, Katharine of Aragon, has become the pawn between two powerful monarchies. After less than a year as the wife of the frail Prince Arthur, the question of whether the marriage was ever consummated will decide both her fate and England's.

But whilst England and Spain dispute her dowry, in the wings awaits her unexpected escape from poverty: Henry, Arthur's younger, more handsome brother—the future King of England. He alone has the power to restore her position, but at what sacrifice?

KATHARINE, THE VIRGIN WIDOW

Jean Plaidy

WINDSOR
PARAGON

First published 1961
by
Robert Hale Limited
This Large Print edition published 2006
by
BBC Audiobooks Ltd by arrangement with
The Random House Group Limited

Hardcover ISBN 10: 1 4056 1474 9
           ISBN 13: 978 1 405 61474 0
Softcover   ISBN 10: 1 4056 1475 7
           ISBN 13: 978 1 405 61475 7

British Library Cataloguing in Publication Data available

Printed and bound in Great Britain by
Antony Rowe Ltd., Chippenham, Wiltshire

CONTENTS

CHAPTER I

THE ARENA

The sun picked out sharp flints in the grey walls of the towers so that they glinted like diamonds. The heat was great, and the courtiers sweated beneath their stomachers over which their doublets were elegantly laced; they did not move even to throw back their long loose-sleeved gowns. Each man and woman among them was intent on what was going on in the arena before them, where a lion—one of the finest and fiercest in the King's menagerie—was engaged in a bloody fight with four English mastiffs. The dogs were sturdy and game; but this lion had never been beaten. He roared his contempt of the four dogs, and the spectators cheered him.

'Now, Rex, get to work,' shouted a boy who was seated among the royal party. His cheeks were ruddy, his hair gleamed reddish gold in the sunlight; and his voice was shrill with excitement.

The girl who sat beside him, and who was a few years older, laid a restraining hand on his arm; and several people let their attention stray from the animals to the children. Many found themselves catching the boy's excitement, for there was something infectious about the vitality and gaiety of young Prince Henry.

As for Henry, he was aware of nothing but the fight in the arena. He wanted the mastiffs to win, yet he did not believe they could. Rex was the finest lion in the world, which was why he had been

1

called Rex.

The King from his seat of honour was watchful. He sat erect, not so magnificently attired as many of his subjects, for he was a man who resented wasting money on outward show. Money, in his opinion, should be used to create more money. It had been his policy ever since Bosworth Field. And the result? A depleted treasury was now a full one, carefully watched over by the King's miserly eye, continually augmented by his clever schemes; although he would be the first to admit that he owed a great deal to those two able ministers of his—Richard Empson and Edmund Dudley—who now sat near the royal party, their lawyers' eyes alert.

The King's gaze rested briefly on his Queen—a beautiful woman of whom he was secretly proud. But he was not a man to show his feelings and would never allow Elizabeth of York to know how much he esteemed her. When a man's claim to the throne was doubtful, when there was the hint of bastardy among his forbears, he must be careful. Henry VII was a careful man.

Elizabeth had been a good wife and he had never regretted the marriage, even when he considered his early love for Maud Herbert and his more mature passion for Katherine Lee. He was not a man who would allow his emotions to interfere with his ambitions.

Once Richard III had been defeated, once Henry knew that the great ambition was about to be realised, he had ceased to think of Katherine Lee; he had known there was only one suitable bride for him, and that was Elizabeth of York, that the Houses of York and Lancaster might thus be

2

united and bring peace to England. Henry VII would never wage war if he could help it, for to him it represented the loss of gold.

He looked at his family and allowed his feeling of pleasure temporarily to turn up the corners of his stern mouth. Two sons and two daughters.

'Fair enough, fair enough,' he murmured to himself.

Elizabeth had been six times pregnant and they had lost only two so far, which, considering the fate of most children, was good fortune indeed.

It was true that Arthur, the eldest and Prince of Wales, who was not quite fifteen, was a sickly boy. He was handsome enough with his pretty pink and white complexion, but that was not in his case the sign of health. Arthur coughed too much; there were occasions when he spat blood; yet he lived.

Perhaps there would have been cause for anxiety if Arthur had not possessed such a brother as Henry. There was a Prince to delight the eyes of any parent. Glances were even now straying to this ten-year-old boy. It was the same when they went among the people. It was young Henry whom the people called for. It was for him they had their smiles. Fortunately, Arthur had the sweetest temper and knew no envy. But perhaps he was too tired to feel envy; perhaps he was grateful to this robust, vital brother who could appear so fresh at the end of a day's riding, who always knew how to respond to the people's applause.

Between the two boys sat Margaret, a dignified Princess, looking older than twelve, keeping a watchful eye on her exuberant brother Henry who, strangely, did not seem to resent this. It was pleasant to see such affection between a brother

3

and sister. And on the other side of Henry sat Mary, an enchanting creature of five years, a little wilful, because she was so pretty perhaps and doubtless over-pampered because of it.

Four children, mused the King, and Arthur the only one whose health gives cause for anxiety. Edward's daughter has done her duty well.

The Queen turned to him and was smiling. She read his thoughts. She knew that he was studying the children and had been thinking: There's time for more.

Elizabeth of York stilled the sudden resentment which rose within her. The only real desire her husband would feel would be for the aggrandisement of the throne. She was dear to him, she knew, not because of any beauty or talents she might possess, but because she was the daughter of Edward IV, and when she married him the union had brought peace to England; she had also given him children, four of whom were living.

There was tension among the spectators, and the King's attention was now on the arena, where the battle was not going according to expectations. Rex was lying on his back while one of the mastiffs had him by the throat; the others were leaping on him, tearing his flesh, their jaws bloody.

Prince Henry had risen to his feet.

'They have beaten Rex,' he cried. 'Oh, bravo . . . bravo!'

The cry was taken up among the spectators, as the body of Rex lay lifeless and the dogs continued to worry it.

The Queen leaned slightly towards the King.

'I would not have believed that the dogs could defeat the lion.'

The King did not answer, but beckoned to one of the keepers of his menagerie.

'Take the dogs away,' he said; 'remove the carcass of the lion and then return to me.'

As the man bowed low and went off to obey the King's command, an excited chatter broke out among the children.

Henry was shouting: 'Did you *see*? Arthur, did you see . . . ?'

Arthur was pale. He murmured: 'I like not these sports.'

Henry laughed at him. 'I like sport better than anything in the world, and never have I seen such a battle.'

Mary asked: 'What has happened to the lion?' But no one took any notice of her.

Margaret gripped Henry's arm. 'Be silent,' she whispered. 'Do you not see that our father is displeased?'

Henry turned to stare at the King. 'But why . . .' he began. 'I should have thought it was good sport. I . . .'

The King's stern eyes rested on his son. 'Henry,' he said, 'one day you will learn that what *you* think is of far more interest to yourself than to others.'

Henry looked puzzled, but it was impossible to check his exuberance.

The King signed to one of the keepers. 'Let the bears and the ban-dogs be brought on,' he said.

*   *   *

The company stared aghast.

Before them in the arena scaffolds had been set up and on these hung the bodies of the four

5

English mastiffs, the dogs which, but half an hour before, had conducted themselves so valiantly against the King's fiercest lion.

The King silently watched the assembly. His chief counsellors, Dudley and Empson, watched also.

The farce was ended, but everyone should have learned the lesson it was intended to convey.

The dogs had been sentenced to death for treason. They had dared to destroy Rex the lion. They were traitors.

The King had ordered the sentence to be read before the ropes were put about the animals' necks. Then he had said in his low sombre voice: 'So perish all traitors!'

His subjects stared at the writhing dogs, but it was of the King they were thinking.

Indeed he must be a man beset by fears since he could not resist pointing out to them the fate of those who attempted to overcome the power of kings.

Henry rose suddenly and, as he left his seat, his family and immediate circle prepared to follow him.

The games were over for that day.

* * *

The children had escaped to the privy garden. It was pleasant out of doors because a breeze was beginning to blow off the river.

They were unusually silent, for the hanging of the four mastiffs had subdued them. Here in this pleasant garden, in which the scent of roses was very strong, they often gathered when their parents were in residence at the Palace of the Tower of London. They delighted now in its familiarity because the scene they had witnessed had been unexpected, and it was comforting to be in a place they knew so well. This they looked upon as their own little garden; here they felt shut away from the ceremony which was such a large part of their lives. The great walls of the Cradle Tower and the Well Tower formed a bastion against too curious eyes. Here they could forget they were Princes and Princesses and be children.

Henry broke the silence. 'But why!' he demanded. 'Those four brave mastiffs . . . traitors! How could they be traitors?'

Mary began to cry. She loved dogs and she had been delighted when the four had beaten the cruel lion. Had she not been told so often that Princesses do not cry in public she would have burst into tears when she saw the ropes being put about their necks.

'Hush, Mary,' said Margaret, stern Margaret, who kept them in order as though she were the eldest. Someone, Margaret often pointed out, had to keep the family in order, and Arthur was useless in that respect.

Mary obediently stopped crying, but it was clear that she could not forget the mastiffs.

Arthur turned to Henry. He looked almost as old as his father in that moment. 'It is all so easy to understand,' he said.

'But *I* do not understand,' cried Henry hotly.

'That is because you are but a boy for all your arrogance,' Margaret retorted.

'Do not call me a boy. I am as tall as Arthur.'

'So you may be, but that does not make you

7

grown up,' Margaret told him.

Arthur said almost wearily: 'Our father had the dogs hanged because they had used their strength against Rex. Rex was the king of my father's beasts, and Rex means King. Our father was showing all those people what happens to those who pit their strength against kings.'

'But the dogs were sent into the arena to fight,' persisted Henry. 'It makes no sense.'

'The ways of kings do not always appear to make sense,' answered Arthur.

'But *I* would have good sense prevail always.'

'I . . . I . . . I!' murmured Margaret. 'You use that word more than any other, I do declare.'

'Should not a King show his subjects that he is a man of good sense then?' Henry persisted.

'No,' answered Arthur, 'only that he is a King to be feared.'

'I do not want the dogs to be dead,' cried Mary, and began to sob loudly.

Margaret knelt down and, taking a kerchief from her pocket, wiped Mary's tears away. 'Have you not been told that it is unseemly for a Princess to cry like a peasant?'

'But they killed the dogs. They put ropes round their necks. They killed . . .'

'I see,' said Henry in his resonant voice, 'that all traitors should be hanged, but . . .'

'Let us talk of something else,' commanded Margaret. 'I must stop this child making such a noise. Now, Mary, what will your new sister say when she comes here and finds you such a cry-baby?'

Mary stopped crying; it was obvious that she had forgotten the death of the dogs and was thinking of

8

her new sister.

'Just think,' went on Margaret, 'she is coming all the way across the sea to be our sister. So instead of four of us there'll be five.'

Arthur turned away from the group, pretending to examine one of the roses. He was embarrassed by this talk of his imminent marriage. He was a great deal more uneasy about it than he cared to admit.

'Will she be big like you?' asked Mary peering into Margaret's face.

'Bigger. She is older.'

'As old as our father?'

'Do not be foolish. But she is older than Arthur.'

'Then she must be very old.'

'Arthur is not really very old,' put in Henry. 'I am nearly as old as Arthur.'

'Nonsense,' said Margaret, 'you're five years younger.'

'In five years then *I* shall have a marriage.'

Margaret said sharply: '*You* are destined for the Church, Henry. That means that you'll have no marriage.'

'I shall if I want one,' retorted Henry; his small eyes narrowed suddenly in his plump, dimpled face.

'Don't talk so foolishly.'

'Arthur may not either,' went on Henry, who did not like the idea of his brother's having something which he could not. 'It seems to me that his Spaniard is a long time coming.'

Arthur turned to face them all. He said: 'Her ships have met with disaster. It is a long and hazardous journey she has to make.'

'Still,' said Henry, 'we heard a long time ago that

9

she had set out . . . and still she does not come.'

'There are storms in the Bay of Biscay,' Margaret put in.

'Perhaps,' cried Henry spitefully, 'she'll be drowned. Then *you* won't have a marriage either.'

Arthur nodded in his mild way; but he did not look in the least perturbed by this possibility.

Poor Arthur, thought the wise Margaret, he is not looking forward with any great pleasure to being a husband.

It occurred to her that the subject of the Spanish marriage was not really a very much happier topic than that of the mastiffs.

'I'm going to have a game of tennis,' said Henry suddenly. That meant that he was leaving the family party—because Arthur was not good enough to play with him. Henry would go and find the sprightliest of young boys, and doubtless he would win, not only because he hated to lose and his opponents knew this, but because he really did excel at all games. Arthur would shut himself into his own apartments to read or brood. Margaret would hand Mary over to her nurses, and she herself would do a little embroidery with some chosen companions, chatting lightly but thinking of Arthur's marriage with the Infanta of Spain and wondering what further marriages were being arranged. It was almost certain that her own would be the next. She would not be as fortunate as Arthur, who at least would stay at home. She believed she would have to go into the wild country beyond the border.

*　　　*　　　*

10

The Queen took an early opportunity of retiring to her own apartments. The spectacle had disgusted and alarmed her. She was shocked that her husband should have so betrayed himself. She had not dared to glance at him, sitting there stonily staring ahead at those struggling bodies, but she knew exactly how he would be looking. His lips would be tightly compressed; his eyes narrow and calculating. She understood more of his nature than he would have believed possible. She had seen much, during her lifetime, of the terrible fascination a crown had for some men and women; she had seen them face disaster and death to win and then retain it.

Yet Henry, her husband, did not understand this. He did not understand her at all; he made no attempt to. He was a man shut in with his emotions, and shared them with none. For two things only did he betray an overwhelming passion: for the crown and for gold; and these she knew he loved with an intensity he would never feel for anything or anyone else.

She herself was no longer young, having last February passed her thirty-fifth birthday; and during those thirty-five years what she had lacked most was security.

Her handsome father had doted on her; he had planned a grand marriage for her, and when she was nine years old she had been affianced to Charles, who was the eldest son of Louis XI, and she remembered how at that time everyone had called her Madame la Dauphine. She remembered the French lessons she had taken at that time. It was imperative, her father had said, that she speak fluently the language of the country which would

11

one day be her home. She had also learned to write and speak Spanish.

Thinking of those early days, she said to herself: 'The latter will be useful when the Infanta arrives ... if the Infanta ever does arrive.'

Royal marriages! How could one be sure they would ever take place until one witnessed the actual ceremony itself! Her marriage to the Dauphin had certainly not; she remembered the occasion when the news had arrived at the Palace of Westminster that Louis was seeking the hand of Margaret of Austria for his son.

Elizabeth could recall her father's rage; the hot red blood rushing to his face and the whites of his eyes. He had died soon after—some said of the rage this news had aroused in him.

She had been afraid of such emotion ever since. For that was the beginning of trouble. Her father dead, her uncle taking the crown, herself with her mother and some other members of the family taking refuge in sanctuary, where her little brothers were taken from them to be lodged in the Tower—this Tower in which she now sat. Somewhere in this place were buried the bodies of those two young princes who had disappeared mysteriously from their lodgings. She could remember them so well, her little brothers whom she had loved so dearly. What had happened to them? They had stood in the way to the throne. In the way of her uncle Richard? In the way of her husband, Henry?

She dared not think of their fate.

It had all happened so long ago. Her uncle Richard, who had once thought of marrying her, had met his death at Bosworth Field; the Tudor dynasty had begun.

It was this matter of hanging the mastiffs which had made her brood on the past. It was this betrayal of her husband's fear, of his determination to show all those who might rise against him what they could expect at his hands.

It was thus that Henry found her. He had come to her, she knew, to discover her feelings regarding the affair in the arena, though he would not ask. He never asked her advice or opinion. He was determined that she should remain his consort only. This desire to preserve his own supremacy was always present. Elizabeth knew it for a weakness which he attempted to hide by a show of arrogance.

'You are resting?' he asked.

He had come to her unheralded. She, who remembered the pageantry of royalty with which her father had surrounded himself, even now was a little surprised by this.

She gave him her hand which he kissed without much grace.

'The heat in the arena was overpowering,' she said. 'At one time I was afraid Arthur would be overcome by it.'

The King frowned. 'The boy's health leaves much to be desired,' he said.

The Queen agreed. She murmured: 'But young Henry grows more and more like my father every day.'

The King was not displeased; he liked to be reminded that his son's maternal grandfather was Edward IV. But he did not wish Elizabeth to realise the extent of his pride, so he said: 'Let us hope he does not inherit your father's vices.'

'He had many virtues,' Elizabeth said quietly.

'His virtues gave him the strength to fight for the throne; they brought men rallying to his side; but it was his vices which killed him. Let us hope young Henry will not be so fond of good food and wine, and most of all, women.'

'Henry will take care of himself. It is Arthur on whose account I am so concerned.'

'Soon the Infanta will be here, the marriage celebrated.' Henry rubbed his hands together and his grave face was illumined suddenly by a smile.

Elizabeth knew that he was contemplating the Infanta's dowry and congratulating himself that there could not have been a more advantageous match than this one with Spain.

Henry turned to his Queen. 'I must be watchful of Ferdinand. I am not sure that he is to be trusted. He will try to arrange that all the advantages are on his side.'

'You too are shrewd,' his wife reminded him.

Henry nodded. 'It has been very necessary for me to foster shrewdness. I shall be very pleased when the dowry is in my possession and the marriage ceremony has been performed.'

'It would seem that what is delaying our Infanta is not her father's diplomacy but the weather.'

'Ah, the weather. The winds of the Bay of Biscay are unaccountable, even in summer.'

'What is the latest news of her journey?'

The King hesitated. He did not share such information with any, even his ministers. But there could be no harm in telling her of the Infanta's progress.

'I have heard that her squadron is still at Laredo to which port she was forced to return on account

14

of the storms. It seems to me that Ferdinand and Isabella are deliberately keeping her there to delay her arrival in England.'

'No doubt the Queen finds it hard for a mother to part with her daughter.'

The King grunted impatiently. 'This is a girl who is to become Princess of Wales. I should have thought they would have been as distressed by the delay as we are.'

There was a great deal he did not understand, thought Elizabeth; and never would. This husband of hers was without emotions except those of ambition.

'Yet,' murmured the Queen, 'I have heard that Queen Isabella is loth to lose her daughter.'

'And she is said to be a great Queen!'

Henry was thoughtful; he was recalling the rumours he had heard concerning the relationship of the Spanish King and Queen with whom his own family would soon be linked in marriage. It was said that Isabella never forgot that she was the Queen of Castile and the senior in the royal partnership. Henry, glancing swiftly at his Queen, was once more grateful to the fate which had given him such a woman.

In an unguarded moment he said: 'I think some of our subjects were a little shocked by the hanging of the traitors.'

'The four dogs? I think many were.'

'And you?'

He so rarely allowed a personal note to creep into their relationship that she was momentarily startled.

'I . . . I was surprised.'

'It is not a pleasant death,' said the King. 'It is

well to remind ambitious men of this now and then.'

He was smiling but his smile was cold. He had been on the verge of telling her that he intended to send an English sailor to Laredo—a Devon pilot who could lead the fleet of the Spanish Infanta to England without delay; but he changed his mind.

Elizabeth was critical of his conduct and he would endure no criticisms from any man or woman living.

He said: 'Matters of state demand my attention. Tonight I shall visit you.'

She bowed her head in acquiescence, but she was afraid. Must there be another pregnancy, another child who, it was more than likely, would never grow to maturity?

It seemed such a short time ago that little Edmund had died. It was heart-breaking when they lived a little while and one grew to love them.

A pretty child, Edmund, but to suffer such discomfort, such pain, and then to give birth to a sickly child over whom one watched with anxiety until one suffered yet another loss!

I am too old, too weak for more childbearing, she thought. But she said nothing. What use would it have been to complain to him—to say: I have given you six children, four of whom are living. Do they not suffice?

His answer would be cool and to the point. A Queen must go on bearing children as long as possible. It is her duty.

Did he, she wondered, ever give a thought to Katherine Lee, her own maid of honour? If he did, not even Katherine would know it. She doubted whether Henry was ever unfaithful to herself even in thought.

She had married a strange man, a cold man; but at least she had a faithful husband. Henry would indulge in a sexual relationship for only one purpose: the procreation of children; and to procreate children with any other partner than his wife would in his opinion be an unnecessary act.

There were times when the Queen of England wanted to cast aside her dignity and laugh aloud; but that would be hysterical laughter and the Queen was no more given to hysterical outbursts than her husband was.

So she bowed her head and told herself that she must inform her women that this would be one of the nights which the King would spend in her bed.

CHAPTER II

THE MARRIAGE OF ARTHUR, PRINCE OF WALES

The Infanta stood on deck and watched the Spanish coastline fade from view.

When would she see it again? she wondered.

Doña Elvira Manuel, the stern and even formidable duenna whom Queen Isabella had put in charge of the Infanta and her maids of honour, was also gazing at the land she was leaving; but Elvira did not share the Infanta's sorrow. When she left Spain her authority began, and Elvira was a woman who dearly loved power.

She laid her hand on the Infanta's arm and said: 'You should not grieve. You are going to a new land whose Queen you will surely be one day.'

The Infanta did not answer. How could she expect Elvira Manuel to understand. She was praying silently, praying for courage, that she would not disgrace her family, that she would be able to remember all that her mother had taught her.

It had been a mistake to think of her mother. The thought had conjured up an image of that stern yet loving face which had changed in recent years. The Infanta remembered Queen Isabella, always full of quiet dignity but at the same time possessed of a purposeful energy. Sorrow had changed her—that sorrow which had come to her through her great love for her children.

In Spain I was dearly loved, thought the Infanta.

18

What will happen to me in England? Who will love me there? I am not even beautiful as my maids of honour are. I shall look plainer than ever, compared with them. It was not kind of my father-in-law to stipulate that my maids of honour should all be handsome.

'All will be different,' she whispered.

Elvira Manuel said quickly: 'Your Highness spoke?'

'I merely said that nothing will be the same, in this new land, as it has been in Spain. Even my name will be different. From now on I am no longer Catalina; I am Katharine. And they say there is little summer in England.'

'It cannot be colder there than it is in some parts of Spain.'

'But we shall miss the sun.'

'When you have children of your own you will not care whether or not the sun shines.'

The Infanta turned away and looked at the heaving waters. Yes, she thought, a son. Children would make her happy; she knew that. And she would have children. Her very device was the pomegranate, which to the Arabs signified fruitfulness. It reminded her of the pomegranate trees which grew so profusely, with the myrtle, in the gardens of the Alhambra. Whenever she saw her device, and she knew it would throughout her life be constantly with her, she would always remember the *patios* of Granada and the glistening waters in the fountains. She would think of her childhood, her parents and her brother and sisters. Would she always think of them with this deep yearning? Perhaps when she had children of her own she would overcome this desire to be back in

19

her own childhood.

But it was long before she could expect children; and in the meantime she could only yearn for home.

'Oh, Mother,' she whispered, 'I would give everything I have to be with you now.'

In the royal apartments in the Alhambra Queen Isabella would be thinking of her now. She could be certain of that. The Queen would pray for her daughter's safety at sea until she reached England; then she would pray that her Catalina's marriage with her English Prince might be fruitful, that Catalina might achieve a happiness which had been denied her sisters, Isabella and Juana, her brother Juan.

The Infanta shivered and Elvira said sharply: 'A breeze is rising, Highness. You should retire to your cabin.'

'I am warm enough,' was the answer. She was unaware of the wind. She was thinking of early days in the nursery when they were all together. She felt almost unbearably sad to recall those days when she had sat at her mother's knee while her sisters, Isabella and Maria, had worked at their tapestry and Juan read aloud to them. Her sister Juana had neither sat at her needlework nor read, nor nestled quietly at their mother's feet—restless Juana who gave them all cause for such anxiety!

Her sister Isabella and her brother Juan were tragically dead; Maria had gone into Portugal recently to marry Isabella's widower, Emanuel, King of Portugal. She would be happy there, for Emanuel was a kindly gentle man and would cherish Maria for the sake of her sister whom he had dearly loved. And Juana? Who could say what

20

was happening to Juana? Her life would never run smoothly. There had been rumours that all was not well with her marriage to the handsome Archduke Philip and that in the Brussels court there was many a stormy scene of jealousy which ended in outbursts of strange conduct on Juana's part.

All her life the Infanta had realised what a deep shadow her sister Juana cast over her mother's happiness.

But that was the family she was leaving. What of the new one to which she was going?

'Arthur, Margaret, Henry, Mary.' She whispered their names. They would be her companions now; and to them she would be Katharine . . . no longer Catalina.

She was going into a new country. The King and Queen of England would be her father and mother now. 'We shall regard the Infanta as our own daughter, and her happiness shall be our main concern . . .' Thus wrote the King of England to her mother, who had shown her those words.

'You see,' the Queen had said, 'you will have a new family, so perhaps you will soon forget us all at home.'

At that she had been unable to preserve the dignity which was considered necessary to an Infanta of Spain, and had flung herself into her mother's arms and sobbed: 'I shall never forget you. I shall never cease to long for my return.'

Her mother had wept with her. Only we, her children, know how gentle she is, thought the Infanta. Only we know that she is the best mother in the world and that necessarily our hearts must break to leave her.

It was different, saying goodbye to her father.

He embraced her affectionately, kissed her fondly, but his eyes gleamed, not with tears at the parting but with satisfaction at the marriage. If he had had his way she would have been despatched to England long before. He needed the friendship of England; he was eager for this marriage. He was fond of her, but the great loves of his life were power and money, and his feeling for his children was always second to the advantages they could bring him.

He had not attempted to hide his delight at the parting. There was little that was subtle about Ferdinand.

'Why, daughter,' he had said, 'you'll be Princess of Wales, and I'll warrant it won't be long before you're Queen of England. You'll not forget your home, my child?'

His meaning was different from that of her mother. The Queen meant: You will remember the love we bear each other, the happiness we have had together, all that I have taught you which will help you to bear your trials with fortitude. Ferdinand meant: Do not forget that you are a Spaniard. When you are at the Court of England be continually on the alert for the advantages of Spain.

'Write often,' Ferdinand had said, putting his lips close to her ear. 'You know the channels through which any secret information should be sent to me.'

She closed her eyes now and looked at the grey waters.

It was true, a storm was rising. The hazards of the sea were all about her. What if she should never reach England?

She gripped the rail and thought of Isabella and Juan, both of whom had finished with earthly trials. How long would it be before her mother joined them?

Such thoughts were wicked. She, not yet sixteen, to long for death!

Only in that moment had she realised the depth of her fear.

This is cowardice, she told herself sharply. How do I know what awaits me in England?

*   *   *

Sick from the rocking of the ship, cold and drenched with sea water, Katharine stood on deck watching the land which grew more and more distinct as she stood there.

England! The land in which she was destined to be Queen.

Elvira was at her side. 'Highness, you should prepare yourself to meet the King.'

'Do you think he will be at Plymouth to greet me?'

'Surely he will, and the Prince with him. Come! We must make you ready to receive them.'

They went to her cabin where her maids of honour clustered round her. All so much prettier than I, she thought; and she imagined Arthur, looking at them and being disappointed because she was the Infanta and his bride.

'We are far from London,' said Elvira. 'I have heard that the journey to the capital will last three weeks.'

Katharine thought: Three weeks! What did it matter what discomfort she had to endure if it

23

meant postponing the ceremony for three weeks!

When she was ready to go on deck the ship already lay at anchor. A beautiful sight met her eyes; the sun had come out and was discovering brilliants on the blue water. Stretched before her was the lovely coast of Devon, the grass of which was greener than any she had ever seen; and the gorse was golden.

Before her was Plymouth Hoe, and she saw that many people had gathered there and that they carried banners on which were the words—she knew little English but they were translated for her: 'Welcome to the Princess of Wales!' 'God bless the Infanta of Spain!'

There was the sound of cheering as she came on deck with her ladies, and she found that her spirits were lifted. Then she heard the bells ringing out and she saw a small boat approaching the ship; in it was a company of splendidly dressed men.

The English pilot who had brought them safely to England came to Katharine's side and bowing to the veiled figure said: 'Your Highness, you are safe from the sea. This is Plymouth Sound and the people of Devon are eager to show you how glad they are to have you with them. Here come the Mayor and his aldermen to give you formal welcome.'

She turned to an interpreter who stood beside her and told him to ask whether the King and Prince of Wales were in Plymouth.

'I doubt they could make the journey to Plymouth, Your Highness,' was the answer. 'We are three weeks' journey from London. But they will have sent orders that all are to welcome you right royally until they can do so themselves.'

24

She had a feeling that this was an apology for the absence of his King and Prince. It need not have been made to her. She was relieved that she could have a little respite before she met them.

She received the Mayor and his aldermen as graciously as even her mother could have wished.

'Tell them I am happy to be with them,' she said. 'I am grateful that I have escaped the perils of the sea. I see a church steeple there. I would first like to go to church and give thanks for my safe arrival.'

'It shall be as Her Highness commands,' was the Mayor's answer.

Then Katharine came ashore and the people of Plymouth crowded about her.

'Why,' they said, 'she is naught but a child.' For although her face was veiled there was no doubt that she was young, and there was many a mother in the crowd who wiped her eyes to think of a young girl's leaving her home and going to a strange land.

How brave she was! She gave no sign of her disquiet. 'She's a Princess,' they said, 'every inch a Princess. God bless her.'

Thus Katharine of Aragon rode through the streets of Plymouth to give thanks for her safe arrival in England and to pray that she might give no offence to the people of her new country, but please them in every way.

Her spirits rose a little as she went through those streets in which the tang of the sea was evident. She smiled at the fresh faces which pressed forward to glimpse her. Their free and easy manners were strange to her; but they were showing her that they were pleased to see her, and that gave infinite comfort to a lonely girl.

25

The journey towards London had begun; it was inevitably a slow one, for the people of England had been commanded by their King to show a hearty welcome to the Princess from Spain. They needed no such injunctions; they were ever ready to accept an excuse for gaiety.

In the villages and towns through which the cavalcade passed the people halted its progress. The Princess must see their folk dances, must admire the floral decorations and the bonfires which were all in her honour.

They were attracted by this quiet Princess. She was such a child, such a shy, dignified young girl.

It was a pleasant journey indeed from Plymouth to Exeter, and Katharine was astonished by the warmth and brilliance of the sun. She had been told to expect mists and fog, but this was as pleasant as the Spanish sunshine; and never before had she seen such cool green grass.

At Exeter the nature of the journey changed. In that noble city she found more ceremony awaiting her than she had received in Plymouth, and she realised that thus it would be as she drew nearer to the capital.

Waiting to receive her was Lord Willoughby de Broke, who told her that he was High Steward of the King's household and that it was the express command of His Majesty that all should be done for her comfort.

She assured him that nothing more could be done for her than had been done already; but he bowed and smiled gravely as though he believed she could have no notion of the extent of English hospitality.

Now about her lodgings were ranged the men at arms and yeomen, all in the royal green and white liveries—and a pleasant sight they were.

She made the acquaintance of her father's ambassador to England and Scotland, Don Pedro de Ayala, an amusing and very witty man, whose stay in England seemed to have robbed him of his Spanish dignity. There was also Dr de Puebla, a man whom she had been most anxious to meet because Ferdinand had warned her that if she had any secret matter to impart to him she might do it through Puebla.

Both these men, she realised, were to some extent her father's spies, as most ambassadors were for their own countries. And how different were these two: Don Pedro de Ayala was an aristocrat who had received the title of Bishop of the Canaries. Handsome, elegant, he knew how to charm Katharine with his courtly manners. Puebla was of humble origin, a lawyer who had reached his present position through his own ingenuity. He was highly educated and despised all those who were not; and Ayala he put into this category, for the Bishop had spent his youth in riotous living and, since he came of a noble family, had not thought it necessary to achieve scholarship.

Puebla's manner was a little sullen, for he told himself that if all had gone as he had wished he should have greeted the Infanta without the help of Ayala. As for Ayala, he was fully aware of Puebla's feelings towards him and did everything he could to aggravate them.

As they left Exeter, Don Pedro de Ayala rode

beside Katharine, and Lord Willoughby de Broke was on her other side, while Puebla was jostled into the background and fumed with rage because of this.

Ayala talked to Katharine in rapid Castilian which he knew Willoughby de Broke could not understand.

'I trust Your Highness has not been put out by this outrageous fellow, Puebla.'

'Indeed no,' replied Katharine. 'I found him most attentive.'

'Beware of him. The fellow's an adventurer and a Jew at that.'

'He is in the service of the Sovereigns of Spain,' she answered.

'Yes, Highness, but your noble father is fully aware that the fellow serves the King of England more faithfully than he does the King and Queen of Spain.'

'Then why is he not recalled and another given his position?'

'Because, Highness, he understands the King of England and the King of England understands him. He has been long in England. In London he follows the profession of lawyer; he lives like an Englishman. Ah, I could tell you some tales of him. He is parsimonious—so much so that he brings disgrace to our country. He has his lodgings in a house of ill-fame and I have heard that when he does not dine at the King's table he dines at this disreputable house at the cost of two pence a day. This, Highness, is a very small sum for a man in his position to spend, and I have heard it said that the landlord of this house is glad to accommodate him in exchange for certain favours.'

'What favours?' demanded Katharine.

'The man is a lawyer and practises as such; he is on good terms with the King of England. He protects his landlord against the law, Highness.'

'It seems strange that my father should employ the man if he is all you say he is.'

'His Highness believes him to have his uses. It is but a few years ago that the English King offered him a bishopric, which would have brought him good revenues.'

'And he did not accept?'

'He longed to accept, Highness, but could not do so without the consent of your royal parents. This was withheld.'

'Then it would seem that they value his services.'

'Oh, he has wriggled his way into the King's confidence. But beware of the man, Highness. He is a Jew, and he bears his grudges like the rest.'

Katharine was silent, contemplating the unpleasantness of having to meet two ambassadors who clearly disliked each other; and she was not surprised when Puebla seized his opportunity to warn her against Ayala.

'A coxcomb, Highness. Do not put your trust in such a one. A Bishop! He knows nothing of law and has never mastered Latin. His manner of living is a disgrace to Spain and his cloth. Bishop indeed! He should be in Scotland now. It was for this purpose that he was sent to this country.'

'It would not please my parents if they knew of this discord between their two ambassadors.'

'Highness, they know of it. I should be neglectful of my duty if I did not inform them. And inform them I have.'

Katharine looked with faint dislike at Puebla.

Not only did he lack the charming manners of Ayala but she found him pompous, and she thought that his petty meanness, which was noticed by many of those who travelled with them, was humiliating for Spain.

'I used the fellow in Scotland,' went on Puebla. 'He was useful there in cementing English and Scottish relations which, Highness, was the desire of your noble father. War between England and Scotland would have been an embarrassment to him at this time, and James IV was harbouring the pretender, Perkin Warbeck, and seemed likely to support him.'

'Warbeck has now paid the price of presumption,' said Katharine.

'Your Highness most wisely has become informed of English politics, I see.'

'Her Highness, my mother, insisted that I should know something of the country to which I was going.'

Puebla shook his head. 'There are bound to be such impostors when two young Princes disappear. So we had our Perkin Warbeck claiming to be Richard, Duke of York.'

'How very sad for the Queen of England,' said Katharine. 'Does she still mourn for her two brothers who disappeared so mysteriously in the Tower of London?'

'The Queen is not one to show her feelings. She has children of her own, a good husband and a crown. The last certainly could not be hers had her brothers lived.'

'Still she must mourn,' said Katharine; and she thought of her own brother, Juan, who had died, young and beautiful, a few months after his wedding. She believed she would never forget Juan and the shock and tragedy of his death.

'Well, quite rightly Warbeck has been hanged at Tyburn,' went on Puebla, 'and that little matter has been settled. That would be satisfactory if it did not mean that Ayala has left the Scottish Court for that of England. London suits him better than Edinburgh. He is a soft liver. He did not like the northern climate nor the rough Scottish castles. So . . . we have him with us.'

Ayala rode up beside them.

His smile was mischievous. 'Dr de Puebla,' he said, 'I do declare your doublet is torn. Is that the way to appear in the presence of our Infanta! Oh, he's a close-fisted fellow, Highness. If you would know why, look at the shape of his nose.'

Katharine was horrified at the gibe and did not look at Ayala.

'Highness,' cried Puebla, 'I would ask you to consider this: Don Pedro de Ayala may have the nose of a Castilian but the bags under his eyes are a revelation of the life he leads. One is born with one's nose; that is not a result of dissipation, evil living . . .'

Ayala brought his horse closer to Katharine's. 'Let us heed him not, Highness,' he murmured. 'He is a low fellow; I have heard that he follows the trade of usurer in London. But what can one expect of a Jew?'

Katharine touched her horse's flanks and rode forward to join Lord Willoughby de Broke.

She was alarmed. These two men, who could not control their hatred of each other, were the two whom her parents had selected to be her guides and counsellors during her first months in this strange land.

*　　　*　　　*

Yet as the journey progressed she was attracted by the gaiety of Ayala.

She had discovered that he was amusing and witty, that he was ready to answer all her questions about the customs of the country and, what was more interesting, to give her little snippets of gossip about the family to which she would soon belong.

For much of the journey Katharine travelled in a horse litter, although occasionally she rode on a mule or a palfrey. October in the West country was by no means cold, but there was a dampness in the air and often Katharine would see the sun only as a red ball through the mist. Occasionally there were rain showers, but they were generally brief and then the sun would break through the clouds and Katharine would enjoy its gentle warmth. In the villages through which they passed the people came out to see them, and they were entertained in the houses of the local squires.

Here there was food in plenty; Katharine discovered that her new countrymen set great store by eating; in the great fireplaces enormous fires blazed; even the servants in the houses crowded round to see her—plump, rosy-cheeked young men and women, who shouted to each other and seemed to laugh a good deal. These people were as different from the Spaniards as a people could be. They appeared to have little dignity and little respect for the dignity of others. They were a vigorous people; and, having taken Katharine to

32

their hearts, they did not hesitate to let her know this.

But for the ordeal she knew to be awaiting her at the end of the journey, she would have enjoyed her progress through this land of mists and pale sunshine and rosy-cheeked, exuberant people.

Ayala often rode beside her litter and she would ask him questions which he would be only too ready to answer. She had turned from the pompous Puebla in his musty clothes to the gay cleric, and Ayala was determined to exploit the situation to the full.

He made her feel that there was a conspiracy between them, which to some extent there was. For she knew that, when he rattled on in the Castilian tongue, none of those who were near could understand what was said.

His talk was gay and scandalous, but Katharine felt it was what she needed, and she looked forward to these conversations.

'You must be wary of the King,' he told her. 'Have no fear of Arthur. Arthur is as mild as milk. You will be able to mould that one to your way . . . have no fear of that. Now, had it been Henry, that might have been another matter. But, praise be to the saints, Henry is the second son and it is Arthur for Your Highness.'

'Tell me about Arthur.'

Ayala lifted his shoulders. 'Imagine a young boy, a little nervous, pink and white and golden-haired. He is half a head shorter than you are. He will be your slave.'

'Is it true that he does not enjoy good health?'

'It is. But he will grow out of that. And he seems the weaker because he is compared with robust

33

young Henry.'

Katharine was relieved; she was delighted with the idea of a gentle young husband. She had already begun to think of him as her brother Juan, who had been as fair as an angel and gentle in his manner.

'You said I must beware of the King.'

'The King is quiet and ruthless. If he does not like you he will have no compunction in sending you back to Spain.'

'That would not greatly distress me.'

'It would distress your royal parents. And think of the disgrace to Your Highness and the House of Spain.'

'Is the King very formidable?'

'He will be gracious to you but he will never cease to watch. Do not be deceived by his mild manners. He fears all the time that some claimant to the throne will appear, and that there will be supporters to say such a claimant has a greater right. It is not always comfortable to wear the crown.'

Katharine nodded; she thought of the strife which had marred the earlier years of her parents' life together, when Isabella had been engaged in the bitter War of the Succession.

'There is a mystery surrounding the death of the Queen's two young brothers, the elder of whom was King Edward V and the younger the Duke of York. Many say they were murdered in the Tower of London by their wicked uncle, the crook-backed Richard, but their bodies were never discovered and there are many rumours concerning those deaths of which it would be unwise even to think, Highness.'

Katharine shivered. 'Poor children,' she murmured.

'They are now past all earthly pain, and there is a wise King sitting on the throne of England. He married the Princes' sister, and so joined the two warring factions. It might be wise not to dwell on the past, Highness. There have been two pretenders to the throne: Perkin Warbeck and Lambert Simnel. Simnel, who pretended he was Edward Plantagenet, Earl of Warwick and nephew of Richard III, is now serving as a scullion in the King's household. He was obviously an impostor; therefore the King sent him to the kitchens—a sign of the King's contempt—but Warbeck was hanged at Tyburn. This King is fond of showing examples to his people, because he lives in perpetual terror that someone will try to overthrow him.'

'I hope I shall find favour in his sight.'

'Your dowry has already found favour with him, Highness. As for yourself, you will please him too.'

'And the Queen?'

'Have no fear of the Queen. She will receive you kindly. She has no influence with the King, who is eager to show her that he owes no part of the throne to her. He is a man who takes counsel of none, but if he could be said to be under the influence of any, that one is his mother. You must please Margaret Beaufort Countess of Richmond if you will please the King—and all you need do is to provide the royal house with heirs, and all will go merrily.'

'I pray that God will make me fruitful. That, it seems, is the prayer of all Princes.'

'If there is aught else Your Highness wishes to know at any time, I pray you ask of me and ignore

35

the Jew.'

Katharine bowed her head. And so the journey progressed.

*   *   *

The King set out from Richmond Palace. He had become impatient. He was all eagerness to see the Spanish Infanta who had taken so long in reaching his country.

Arthur had been on pilgrimage to Wales—as Prince of Wales he was warmly greeted there and the King wished his son to show himself now and then in the Principality. Arthur had received word from his father that he was to come with all speed to East Hampstead, where he would greet his bride.

Henry disliked journeys, for he was not a man of action and they seemed to him an unnecessary expense.

'But on the occasion of my son's wedding,' he grumbled to Empson, 'I daresay we are expected to lay out a little.'

'That is so, Sire,' was the answer.

'Let us hope that we shall have the revenues to meet this occasion,' sighed the King; and Empson decided that he would raise certain fines to meet the extra expense.

Henry smiled wryly, but he was in fact delighted because his son was acquiring one of the richest Princesses in Europe. It was a good thing that this little island should be allied to the greatest power in the world, and what better tie could there be than through marriage?

Heirs were what were needed and, once this girl

36

provided them, all well and good. But he was a little anxious about her. Her brother, the heir of Spain, had died shortly after his marriage. Exhausted by being a husband, it was said in some quarters. He hoped Katharine was of stronger health. And if *she* were . . . what of his own Arthur? Arthur's cough and spitting of blood denoted weakness. They would have to take great care of Arthur, and he was not yet fifteen. Was it too young to tax his strength with a bride?

He had not consulted his physicians; he consulted no one; he and he alone would decide whether the marriage should be consummated immediately, or whether the royal couple should wait for a few months, or perhaps a year.

Young people, he mused, might indulge unwisely in the act of love. They might have no restraint. Not that he believed this would be the case with Arthur. Had it been Henry, it would have been another matter; but then there would have been no cause for anxiety on that account where Henry was concerned. But what of the Infanta? Was she a lusty young woman? Or was she sickly like her elder sister who had recently died in childbirth?

The more the King pondered this matter, the more eager he was to meet the Infanta.

*   *   *

There was consternation in the Infanta's party.

A message had been brought to Ayala stating that the King was on his way to meet his son's bride, who had stayed that night at the residence of the Bishop of Bath in Dogmersfield and was some fifteen leagues from London Bridge.

Ayala did not pass on the news to Puebla. Indeed he was determined to keep it from the man—not only because he disliked him and never lost an opportunity of insulting him, but because he really did believe that Puebla was more ready to serve Henry VII of England than Isabella and Ferdinand of Spain.

Instead he sought out Elvira Manuel.

'The King is on his way to meet us,' he told her abruptly. 'He wishes to see the Infanta.'

'That is quite impossible,' retorted Elvira. 'You know the instructions of their Highnesses.'

'I do. The Infanta is not to be seen by her bridegroom or anyone at the English Court until she is a wife. She is to remain veiled until after the ceremony.'

'I am determined,' said Elvira, 'to obey the commands of the King and Queen of Spain, no matter what are the wishes of the King of England.'

'I wonder what Henry will say to that.' Ayala smiled somewhat mischievously, for he found the situation piquant and amusing.

'There is one thing that must be done,' said Elvira. 'To prevent discord, you should go ahead and explain to the King.'

'I will leave at once,' Ayala told her. 'In the meantime you should warn the Infanta.'

Ayala set out on the road to East Hampstead; and Elvira, her lips pursed with determination, prepared herself to do battle.

She went to Katharine and told her that the King would make an attempt to see her, and that on no account must he succeed.

Katharine was disturbed. She was afraid that the King of England might consider her extremely discourteous if she refused to receive him.

*   *   *

When Arthur joined his father at East Hampstead, Henry noticed that his son looked wan and worried.

No, the King decided, the marriage shall not be consummated for a year. In any case I doubt whether Arthur would be capable of consummating it.

'Put your shoulders back, boy,' he said. 'You stoop too much.'

Arthur obediently straightened his shoulders. There was no resentment. How differently young Henry would have behaved! But of course there would have been no necessity to criticise Henry's deportment.

We should get more sons, thought the King anxiously.

'Well, my son,' he said, 'very soon now you will be face to face with your bride.'

'Yes, Father.'

'You must not let her think that you are a child, you know. She is almost a year older than you are.'

'I know it, Father.'

'Very well. Prepare yourself to meet her.'

Arthur asked leave to retire and was glad when he reached his own apartment. He felt sick with anxiety. What should he say to his bride? What must he do with her? His brother Henry had talked slyly of these matters. Henry knew a great deal about them already. Henry ought to have been the elder son.

He would have made a good king, thought Arthur. I should have done better in the Church.

He let himself brood on the peace of monastic life. What relief! To be alone, to read, to meditate, not to have to take a prominent part in ceremonies, not to have to suffer continual reproach because a few hours in the saddle tired him, because he could never learn to joust and play the games at which Henry excelled.

'If only,' he murmured to himself, 'I were not the first-born. If only I could miraculously change places with my brother Henry, how happy I could be!'

*   *   *

The next morning the King, with the Prince beside him, set out on the journey to Dogmersfield.

Almost immediately it began to rain, and the King looked uneasily at his son while Arthur squirmed in the saddle. His cough would almost certainly come back if he suffered a wetting, and although the rain was fine it was penetrating.

Arthur always felt that it was his fault that he had not been born strong. He tried to smile and look as though there was nothing he enjoyed so much as a ride in the rain.

When they were within a few miles of the Bishop's Palace the King saw a rider galloping towards his party, and in a very short time he recognised the Spanish Ambassador Ayala.

Ayala drew up before Henry and sweeping off his hat bowed gracefully.

'News has been brought to me that Your Grace

is on the way to see the Infanta.'

'That news is now confirmed,' answered the King. 'So impatient was our young bridegroom that, having heard that the Infanta was at Dogmersfield, he could wait no longer. He himself has come hot-foot from Wales. He yearns to see his bride.'

Arthur tried to force his wet face into an expression which would confirm his father's words as the Spanish Ambassador threw a sly smile in his direction which clearly conveyed his knowledge of the boy's nervousness.

'Alas,' said Ayala, 'Your Grace will be unable to see the bride.'

'I . . . unable to see the bride!' said the King in a cold, quiet voice.

'The King and Queen of Spain insist that their daughter should observe the customs of a high-born Spanish lady. She will be veiled until after the ceremony, and not even her bridegroom may see her face until then.'

The King was silent. A terrible suspicion had come into his mind; he was the most suspicious of men. Why should he not look on the face of the Infanta? What had the Spanish Sovereigns to hide? Was this some deformed creature they were sending him? 'Not until after the ceremony.' The words sounded ominous.

'This seems a strange condition,' said Henry slowly.

'Sire, it is a Spanish custom.'

'I like it not.'

He turned his head slightly and said over his shoulder: 'We will form a council, my lords. Here is an urgent matter to discuss. Ambassador, you will excuse us. It will take us but a short time to come to a decision, I imagine.'

Ayala bowed his head and drew his horse to the side of the road while the King waved a hand towards a nearby field.

'Come with us, Arthur,' he said. 'You must join our council.'

Henry placed himself and his son in the centre of the field and his followers ranged themselves about him. Then he addressed them:

'I like this not. I am denied admittance to my son's bride although she is in my territory. I would not wish to go against the law in this matter. Therefore, the council must decide what should be done. The Infanta has been married to the Prince by proxy. What we must decide is whether she is now my subject; and, if she is my subject, what law could prevent my seeing her if I wished. I pray you, gentlemen, consider this matter, but make it quick for the rain shows no sign of abating and we shall be wet to the skin by the time we reach Dogmersfield.'

There was whispering among those gathered in the field. Henry watched them covertly. He had as usual conveyed his wishes and he expected his councillors to obey them. If any one of them raised objections to what he wished, that man would doubtless find himself guilty of some offence later on; he would not be sent to prison; he would merely have to pay a handsome fine.

All knew this. Many of them had paid their fines for small offences. The King thought no worse of them, once they had paid. It was their money which placated him.

In a few seconds the council had made its

decision.

'In the King's realm the King is absolute master. He need not consider any foreign law or customs. All the King's subjects should obey his wishes, and the Infanta, having married the Prince of Wales, albeit by proxy, is the King's subject.'

Henry's eyes gleamed with satisfaction which held a faint tinge of regret. He could not, with justice, extract a fine from one of them.

'Your answer is the only one I expected from you,' he said. 'It is not to be thought of that the King should be denied access to any of his subjects.'

He led the way out of the field to where Ayala was waiting for him.

'The decision is made,' he said. Then he turned to Arthur. 'You may ride on to Dogmersfield at the head of the cavalcade. I go on ahead.'

He spurred his horse and galloped off; and Ayala, laughing inwardly, closely followed him.

The Sovereigns of Spain would learn that this Henry of England was not a man to take orders, thought the ambassador. He wondered what Doña Elvira was going to say when she was confronted by the King of England.

*   *   *

Katharine was sitting with her maids of honour when they heard the commotion in the hall below. It had been too miserable a day for them to leave the Bishop's Palace and it had been decided that they should remain there until the rain stopped.

Elvira burst on them, and never had Katharine seen her so agitated.

43

'The King is below,' she said.

Katharine stood up in alarm.

'He insists on seeing you. He declares he *will* see you. I cannot imagine what their Highnesses will say when this reaches their ears.'

'But does not the King of England know of my parents' wishes?'

'It would seem there is only one whose wishes are considered in this place and that is the King of England.'

'What is happening below?'

'The Count of Cabra is telling the King that you are not to be seen until after the wedding, and the King is saying that he will not wait.'

'There is only one thing to be done,' said Katharine quietly. 'This is England and when we are in the King's country we must obey the King. Let there be no more protests. We must forget our own customs and learn theirs. Go and tell them that I am ready to receive the King.'

Elvira stared at her in astonishment; in that moment Katharine looked very like her mother, and it was as impossible for even Elvira to disobey her as it would have been to disobey Isabella of Castile.

*   *   *

She stood facing the light, her veil thrown back.

She saw her father-in-law, a man a little above medium height, so thin that his somewhat sombre garments hung loosely on him; his sparse fair hair, which fell almost to his shoulders, was lank and wet; his long gown which covered his doublet was trimmed with ermine about the neck and wide sleeves. There was mud on his clothes and even on his face. He had clearly travelled far on horseback in this inclement weather and had not thought it necessary to remove the stains of travel before confronting her.

Katharine smiled and the alert, crafty eyes studied her intently, looking for some defect, some deformity which would make her parents desirous of hiding her from him; he could see none.

Henry could not speak Spanish and he had no Latin. Katharine had learned a little French from her brother Juan's wife, Margaret of Austria, but Margaret's stay in Spain had been short and, when she had gone, there had been no one with whom Katharine could converse in that language. Henry spoke in English: 'Welcome to England, my lady Infanta. My son and I have eagerly awaited your coming these many months. If we have rudely thrust aside the customs of your country we ask pardon. You must understand that it was our great desire to welcome you that made us do so.'

Katharine attempted to reply in French but slipped into Spanish. She curtseyed before the King while his little eyes took in the details of her figure. She was healthy, this Spanish Infanta, more so than his frail Arthur. She was a good deal taller than Arthur; her eyes were clear; so was her skin. Her body was sturdy, and if not voluptuous it was strong. She was no beauty, but she was healthy and she was young; it was merely custom which had made her parents wish to hide her from him. Her only real claim to beauty was that abundant hair— thick, healthy hair with a touch of red in its colour.

Henry was well satisfied.

She was talking to him now in her own tongue,

45

and, although he could not understand her, he knew that she was replying to his welcome with grace and charm.

He took her hand and led her to the window.

Then he signed to Ayala who had at that moment entered the apartment.

'Tell the Infanta,' said Henry, 'that I am a happy man this day.'

Ayala translated, and Katharine replied that the King's kindness made her very happy too.

'Tell her,' said the King, 'that in a few minutes her bridegroom will be riding to the palace at the head of a cavalcade. They cannot be much more than half an hour after me.'

Ayala told Katharine this; and she smiled.

She was standing between the King and Ayala, they in their wet garments, when she first saw her bridegroom.

He looked very small, riding at the head of that cavalcade, and her first feeling for him was: He is so young—he is younger than I am. He looks frightened. He is more frightened than I am.

And in that moment she felt less resentful of her fate.

She determined that she and Arthur were going to be happy together.

*   *   *

It was later that evening. Katharine looked almost pretty in candlelight; her cheeks were faintly flushed; her grey eyes alight with excitement. Her maids of honour, all chosen for their beauty, were very lovely indeed. Only Doña Elvira Manuel sat aloof, displeased. She could not forget that the wishes of her Sovereigns had been ignored.

The Infanta had invited the King and the Prince to supper in her apartments in the Bishop's Palace; and in the gallery the minstrels were playing. The supper had been a prolonged meal; Katharine was continually being astonished at the amount that was eaten in England. At tonight's feast there had been sucking pigs and capons, peacocks, chickens, mutton and beef, savoury pies, deer, fish and wild fowl, all washed down with malmsey, romney and muscadell.

The English smacked their lips and showed their appreciation of the food; even the King's eyes glistened with pleasure and only those who knew him well guessed that he was calculating how much the feast had cost, and that if the Bishop could afford such lavish entertainment he might be expected to contribute with equal bounty to the ever hungry exchequer.

The Prince sat beside Katharine. He was an elegant boy, for he was fastidious in his ways and his lawn shirt was spotlessly clean as was the fine silk at collar and wristbands; his long gown was trimmed with fur as was his father's, and his fair hair hung about his face, shining like gold from its recent rain-wash.

His skin was milk-white but there was a delicate rose-flush in his cheeks and his blue eyes seemed to have sunk too far into their sockets; but his smile was very sweet and a little shy, and Katharine warmed to him. He was not in the least like his father, nor like her own father. Her mother had once told her of her first meeting with her father and how she had thought him the handsomest man in the world. Katharine would never think that of

Arthur; but then before she had seen him Isabella of Castile had determined to marry Ferdinand of Aragon, and she had gone to great pains to avoid all the marriages which others had attempted to thrust upon her.

All marriages could not be like that of Isabella and Ferdinand, and even that marriage had had its dangerous moments. Katharine remembered the conflict for power between those two. She knew that she had brothers and sisters who were her father's children but not her mother's.

As she looked at gentle Arthur she was sure that their marriage would be quite different from that of her parents.

Arthur spoke to her in Latin because he had no Spanish and she had no English.

That would soon be remedied, he told her. She should teach him her language; he would teach her his. He thanked her for the letters she had written him and she thanked him for his.

They had been formal little notes, those letters in Latin, written at the instigation of their parents, giving no hint of the reluctance both felt towards their marriage; and now that they had seen each other they felt comforted.

'I long to meet your brother and sisters,' she told him.

'You shall do so ere long.'

'You must be happy to have them with you. All mine have gone away now. Every one of them.'

'I am sorry for the sadness you have suffered.'

She bowed her head.

He went on: 'You will grow fond of them. Margaret is full of good sense. She will help you to understand our ways. Mary is little more than a baby—a little pampered, I fear, but charming withal. As for Henry, when you see him you will wish that he had been born my father's elder son.'

'But why should I wish that?'

'Because you will see how far he excels me in all things and, had he been my father's elder son, he would have been your husband.'

'He is but a boy, I believe.'

'He is ten years old, but already as tall as I. He is full of vitality and the people's cheers are all for him. I believe that everyone wishes that he had been my father's elder son. Whereas now he will doubtless be Archbishop of Canterbury and I shall wear the crown.'

'Would you have preferred to be Archbishop of Canterbury?'

Arthur smiled at her. He felt it would have sounded churlish to have admitted this, for that would mean that he could not marry her. He said rather shyly: 'I did wish so; now I believe I have changed my mind.'

Katharine smiled. It was all so much easier than she had believed possible.

Elvira had approached her and was whispering: 'The King would like to see some of our Spanish dances. He would like to see you dance. You must do so only with one of your maids of honour.'

'I should enjoy that,' cried Katharine.

She rose and selected two maids of honour. They would show the English, she said, one of the stateliest of the Spanish dances; and she signed to the minstrels to play.

The three graceful girls, dancing solemnly in the candlelit apartment, were a charming sight.

Arthur watched, his pale eyes lighting with

pleasure. How graceful was his Infanta! How wonderful to be able to dance and not become breathless as he did!

The King's eyes were speculative. The girl was healthy, he was thinking. She would bear many children. There was nothing to fear. Moreover Arthur was attracted by her, and had seemed to grow a little more mature in the last hour. Was he ready? What a problem! To put them to bed together might terrify this oversensitive boy, might disclose that he was impotent. On the other hand, if he proved not to be impotent, might he not tax his strength by too much indulgence?

What to do? Wait? There could be no harm in waiting. Six months perhaps. A year. They would still be little more than children.

If Henry had only been the elder son!

Ayala was at the King's elbow, sly, subtle, guessing his thoughts.

'The Infanta says that she does not wish Your Grace to think that only solemn dances are danced in Spain; she and her ladies will show you something in a different mood.'

'Let it be done,' answered the King.

And there was the Infanta, graceful still, dignified, charming, yet as gay as a gipsy girl, her full skirts twirling in the dance, her white hands as expressive as her feet. Katharine of Aragon could dance well.

The King clapped his hands and the Prince echoed his father's applause.

'We are grateful to the ladies of Spain for giving us such enjoyment,' said Henry. 'I fancy our English dances are not without merit; and since the Infanta has danced for the Prince, the Prince

50

should dance for the Infanta. The Prince of Wales will now partner the Lady Guildford in one of our English dances.'

Arthur felt a sudden panic. How could he match Katharine in the dance? She would despise him. She would see how small he was, how weak; he was terrified that he would be out of breath and, if he began to cough, as he often did at such times, his father would be displeased.

Lady Guildford was smiling at him; he knew her well, for she was his sisters' governess and they often practised dancing together. The touch of her cool fingers comforted him, and as he danced his eyes met the grave ones of the watching Infanta, and he thought: She is kind. She will understand. There is nothing to fear.

The dance over he came to sit beside her once more. He was a little breathless, but he felt very happy.

*   *   *

This was her wedding day. She was waiting in the Bishop's Palace of St Paul's to be escorted to the Cathedral for the ceremony. She would be led to the altar by the Duke of York, whom she had already met and who disturbed her faintly. There was something so bold and arrogant about her young brother-in-law, and an expression which she could not understand appeared on his face when he looked at her. It was an almost peevish, sullen expression; she felt as though she were some delicious sweetmeat which he desired and which had been snatched from him to be presented to someone else.

51

That seemed ridiculous. She was no sweetmeat. And why should a boy of ten be peevish because his elder brother was about to be married?

She had imagined this; but all the same she felt an unaccountable excitement at the prospect of seeing the Duke of York again.

She had ridden into London from Lambeth to Southwark by way of London Bridge, and her young brother-in-law had come to escort her.

He was certainly handsome, this young boy. He swept into the apartment as though he were the King himself, magnificently attired in a doublet of satin the sleeves of which were slashed and ruched somewhat extravagantly; there were rubies at his throat. His face was broad and dimpled; his mouth thin, his eyes blue and fierce, but so small that when he smiled they seemed to disappear into the smooth pink flesh. His complexion was clear, bright and glowing with health; his hair was shining, vital and reddish gold in colour. There could be no mistaking him for anyone but a Prince. She found it hard to believe that he was merely ten years old, for he seemed older than Arthur, and she wondered fleetingly how she would have felt if this boy had been her bridegroom instead of his brother.

They would not have married her to a boy of ten. But why not? There had been more incongruous royal marriages.

He had taken off his feathered hat to bow to her.

'Madam, your servant,' he had said; but his looks belied the humility of his words.

He had explained in Latin that he had come to escort her into London. 'It is my father's command,' he said. 'But had it not been I should have come.'

She did not believe that, and she suspected him of being a braggart; but she was conscious of the fascination he had for her and she realised that she was not the only one who was conscious of his power.

He had stared at her thick hair which she was to wear loose for the journey into London, and had put out a plump finger to touch it.

'It is very soft,' he had said, and his little eyes gleamed.

She had been aware that she seemed strange to him, with her hair flowing thus under the hat which was tied on her head with a gold lace; beneath the hat she wore a headdress of scarlet.

'Your hat,' he had told her, 'reminds me of that which Cardinals wear.'

And he had laughed, seeming but a boy of ten in that moment.

He had ridden on one side of her as they came through the streets while on the other side was the Legate of Rome. The people had lined the streets to see the procession and she had noticed that, although many curious glances came her way, eyes continually strayed to the young Prince riding beside her. He had been aware of this and she had noticed that he lost no opportunity of acknowledging his popularity and, she suspected, doing all he could to add to it.

The citizens of London had organised a pageant to show their welcome for the Spanish Princess whom they regarded as their future Queen, and in the centre of this pageant had been Saint Katharine surrounded by a company of virgins all singing the praises of the Princess of Wales.

She had smiled graciously at the people and they had cheered calling: 'Long live the Princess of Wales! God bless the Infanta of Spain! Long live the Prince of Wales! Long live the Duke of York!'

And the young Duke of York had lifted his bonnet high so that the light caught his golden hair, and Katharine admitted that he was indeed a handsome Prince.

When they had reached the Bishop's Palace, which was adjacent to the Cathedral, it had been the young Duke of York who took her hand and led her in.

That had happened some days before, and now this was her wedding day; and once again that young boy would walk beside her and lead her to the altar where his brother would be waiting for her.

She stood still in her elaborate wedding finery; indeed she found it not easy to move. Her gown stood out over the hoops beneath it, and on her head she wore the mantilla of gold, pearls and precious stones. The veil cascaded over her head and shielded her face. She was dressed as a Spanish Princess and the style was new to England.

Henry came to her and looked at her in blank admiration.

Then he spoke: 'Why, you are beautiful!'

'And you are kind,' she answered.

'I am truthful,' he said. 'That is not kindness, sister.'

'I am glad that I please you.'

His eyes narrowed suddenly in a manner which she already knew was a habit with him. 'It is not I whom you wish to please,' he said sullenly. 'Is that not so? It is my brother.'

'I wish to please every member of my new family.'

'You please Arthur,' he said, 'and you please Henry. It is of no importance that you please the girls.'

'Oh, but it is . . . it is of the greatest importance.'

'You will please Margaret if you embroider.' He snapped his fingers. 'Your eyes are too beautiful to strain with needlework. As for Mary, she is pleased by everyone who makes much of her. But you please me because you are beautiful. Is that not a better reason?'

'To embroider means to have learned how to do so. There is great credit in that. But if I should be beautiful—which I do not think I am—that would be no credit to me.'

'You will find that people in England admire your beauty more than your embroidery,' he told her. He frowned. He wished that he could think of something clever to say, the sort of remark which his tutor, John Skelton, would have made had he been present. Henry admired Skelton as much as anyone he knew. Skelton had taught his pupil a great deal—and not only from lesson books. Henry liked Skelton's bold, swaggering speech, his quick wit, and had absorbed all that he had taught him about the way a gentleman should live and a good deal else besides; Skelton was not averse to repeating Court gossip and tales of the scandalous habits of some of the courtiers. Often certain information passed between them which was to be secret; Skelton had said: 'You have to be a man, my Prince, as well as an Archbishop, and if by ill fate you should be forced to enter the Church then you will do well to sow your wild oats early.' Henry knew a great deal about the kind of wild oats which could be sown and was longing to sow some. He pitied poor Arthur under the tutelage of Dr Linacre, a solemn, wise old man who thought—and endeavoured to make Arthur agree with him—that the main object in life should be the mastery of Greek and Latin.

He wanted to tell Katharine now that although he was young he would doubtless make a better husband for her even at this stage than Arthur. But the precocious child did not know how to express such thoughts.

So he took her by the hand, this wondrously apparelled bride of his brother's, and led her from the Palace to the Cathedral; and the people cheered and said: 'What a handsome bridegroom our Prince Henry will make when his time comes!'

Henry heard and was pleased; yet he was angry at the same time. Life had given him all but one important thing, he believed. Good health, handsome looks, vitality, the power to excel—and then had made him the second son.

In the Cathedral a stage had been erected; it was circular in shape and large enough to contain eight people, including Katharine in her voluminous wedding dress. It was covered with scarlet cloth and about it a rail had been set up.

To this dais Henry led Katharine; and there waiting for her was Arthur, dazzling in white satin adorned with jewels.

Henry VII and his Queen, Elizabeth of York, watched the ceremony from a box at the side of the dais.

The King thought how small Arthur looked

beside his bride and wondered whether the unhealthy whiteness of his skin was made more obvious by the hectic flush on his cheeks. He was still undecided. To consummate or not consummate? To make an effort to get a grandson quickly and perhaps endanger his heir's health, or to let the pair wait a year or so? He had half the bride's dowry already; he could scarcely wait to get his hands on the other half. He would have to watch Ferdinand. Ferdinand was continually planning wars; he wanted to see the Italian states under Spanish control; he would make all sorts of excuses about that second half of the dowry.

But I'll keep him to it, thought Henry. If there were a child, that would make him realise the need to pay the second half quickly. He would be doubly pleased with the marriage if his daughter conceived and bore quickly.

And yet . . .

Elizabeth was conscious of her husband's thoughts. They are too young, she considered. Arthur at least is too young. Over-excitement weakens him. If only Henry would talk to me about this matter! But what is the use of wishing that, when he never consults anyone. There will be one person to decide whether the young Infanta is to lose her virginity this night—and that will be the King of England. And as yet he is undecided.

The Archbishop of Canterbury with nineteen bishops and abbots was preparing to take part in the ceremony. Now he was demanding of the young couple that they repeat their vows; their voices were only just audible in the hushed Cathedral. The Infanta's was firm enough; Arthur's sounded feeble.

57

I trust, his mother thought uneasily, that he is not going to faint. It would be construed as an evil omen.

Her eyes rested long on her white-clad firstborn and she remembered that September day in Winchester Castle when she had first heard the feeble cries of her son.

She had been brought to bed in her chamber which had been hung with a rich arras; but she had insisted that one window should not be covered because she could not endure the thought of having all light and air shut out. Her mother-in-law, Margaret Beaufort, Countess of Richmond, had been with her, and she had been grateful for her presence. Before this she had been considerably in awe of this formidable lady, for she knew that she was the only woman who had any real influence with the King.

The birth had been painful and she had been glad that she had only women to attend to her. Margaret had agreed with her that the delivery of babies was women's work; so she had said farewell to all the gentlemen of the Court when her pains had begun and retired to her chamber, with her mother-in-law in charge of the female attendants.

How ill she had been! Arthur had arrived a month before he was expected, and afterwards she had suffered cruelly from the ague; but she had recovered and had tried not to dread the next confinement, which she knew was inevitable. A Queen must fight, even to the death, if necessary, to give her King and country heirs. It was her mission in life.

And there he was now—that fair, fragile baby, her firstborn—having lived precariously enough through a delicate childhood, preparing now to repeat the pattern with this young girl from Spain.

There was a tear in her eye and her lips were moving. She realised she was praying: 'Preserve my son. Give him strength to serve his country. Give him happiness, long life and fruitful marriage.'

Elizabeth of York feared that she was praying for a miracle.

*   *   *

After mass had been celebrated, the young bride and groom stood at the door of the Cathedral, and there the crowds were able to see them kneel while Arthur declared that he endowed his bride with a third of his property.

The people cheered.

'Long live the Prince and Princess of Wales!'

The couple rose, and there beside the bride was young Prince Henry as though determined not to be shut out from the centre of attraction. He took the bride's hand and walked with her and his brother to the banqueting hall in the Bishop's Palace where a feast of great magnificence had been set out for them.

There Katharine was served on gold plate which was studded with precious gems; but as she ate she was thinking with trepidation of the night which lay before her, and she knew that her bridegroom shared her fears. She felt that she wanted to hold back the night; she was so frightened that she longed for her mother, longed to hear that calm, serene voice telling her that there was nothing to fear.

The feasting went on for several hours. How the

English enjoyed their food! How many dishes there were! What quantities of wine!

The King was watching them. Was he aware of their fear? Katharine was beginning to believe that there was little the King did not understand.

The Queen was smiling too. How kind she was—or would have been if she had been allowed to be. The Queen would always be what her husband wished, thought Katharine; and there might be times when he wished her to be cruel.

Katharine had heard of the ceremony of putting the bride to bed. In England it was riotous and ribald . . . even among royalty. It could never have been so for her mother, she was sure. But these people were not dignified Spaniards; they were the lusty English.

She turned to Arthur who was trying to smile at her reassuringly, but she was sure his teeth were chattering.

*   *   *

The moment had come and they were in the bedchamber. There was the bed, and the curtains were drawn back, while it was being blessed; Katharine knew enough English now to recognise the word fruitful.

She dared not look at Arthur, but she guessed how he was feeling.

The room was illuminated by many candles and their light shone on the scarlet arras, on the silk bed curtains and the many faces of those who had crowded into the bedchamber.

The King came to them and, laying a hand on the shoulder of each, he drew them towards him.

60

He said: 'You are very young. Your lives lie before you. You are not yet ready for marriage, but this ceremony shall be a symbol, and when you are of an age to consummate the marriage then shall it be consummated.'

Katharine saw the relief in Arthur's face and she herself felt as though she wanted to weep for joy. She was no longer afraid; nor was Arthur.

They were led to the bed and the curtains were drawn while their attendants stripped them of their clothes; and when there was nothing to cover their white naked bodies and they knelt side by side, still they were not afraid.

They prayed that they might do their duty; they prayed as all married people were expected to pray on the night of their nuptials. But this was no ordinary wedding night because it was the King's express command that they were too young to consummate the marriage.

A cup of warm, sweet wine was brought to them and they drank as commanded. Then an attendant came and wrapped their robes about them. The ceremony was over.

The people who had crowded into the bedchamber departed; the servants of Katharine and Arthur—Spanish and English—remained in the ante-chamber; the door of the nuptial chamber was locked, and the bride and bridegroom were together.

Arthur said to her: 'There is nothing to fear.'

'I heard the King's command,' she answered.

Then he kissed her brow, and said: 'In time I shall be your husband in truth.'

'In time,' she answered.

Then she lay down in the marriage bed still

wearing the robe which her attendant had wrapped about her. The bed was big. Arthur lay down beside her in his robe.

'I am so tired,' said Katharine. 'There was so much noise.'

Arthur said: 'I am often tired, Katharine.'

'Goodnight, Arthur.'

'Goodnight, Katharine.'

They were so exhausted by the ceremonies and their attendant fears that soon they slept; and in the morning the virgin bride and groom were ready to continue with their wedding celebrations.

CHAPTER III

THE TRAGEDY AT LUDLOW CASTLE

All London was eager to celebrate the marriage of the Prince of Wales and the Infanta; the King was wise enough to know that his people must have some gaiety in their lives, and that if he allowed them to celebrate the marriage of his son, they might for a time forget the heavy taxes with which they were burdened.

'Let them make merry,' he said to Empson. 'A fountain of wine here and there will be enough to satisfy them. Let there be plenty of pageantry. The nobles will provide that.'

Henry was even ready to contribute a little himself, for he was very anxious that his subjects should express their loyalty to the new Tudor dynasty. There was nothing the people loved so much as a royal wedding; and as this was the wedding of the boy who was destined to become their King, it was the King's wish that the celebrations should continue.

Katharine felt a little bewildered by them. Arthur was tired of them, but young Henry revelled in them. Margaret uneasily wondered when *her* marriage would be celebrated, and as for little Mary, she was delighted whenever she was allowed to witness the pageantry.

The greatest pageant of all was staged at Westminster, to which the royal family travelled by barge. After the night following the wedding day, Katharine had been sent to Baynard's Castle

63

where she had been placed under the strict surveillance of Doña Elvira. The King had made it clear to the duenna that the marriage was not yet to be consummated; and as Elvira considered her Infanta as yet too young for the consummation she was determined that the King's wishes should be respected.

So, by barge, came the Infanta with her duenna and lovely maids of honour.

Katharine sometimes wished that her maids of honour were not so beautiful. It was true that she was always dazzlingly attired, and her gowns were more magnificent than those of the girls, but beauty such as that possessed by some of these girls did not need fine clothes to show it off.

The people lined the river banks to cheer her on her way to Westminster and as she smiled and acknowledged their cheers she temporarily forgot her longing for home.

Alighting from her barge she saw that before Westminster Hall a tiltyard had been prepared. On the south side of this a stage had been erected; this was luxuriously hung with cloth of gold; and about the open space other stages, far less magnificent had been set up for the spectators.

This, Katharine discovered, was the joust, the Englishman's idea of the perfect entertainment. Here the nobility of England would gather to tilt against each other.

On this, the occasion of the most important wedding in England, the great houses were determined to outshine each other, and this they endeavoured to do with such extravagance that, as the champions entered the arena, there were continual gasps of wonder and wild applause.

Katharine was led on to the stage amid the cheers of the people; and there she seated herself on cushions of cloth of gold. With her were the King, the Queen and all the royal family. But she herself occupied the place of honour.

She thought how pleased her parents would be if they could see her now.

Beside her sat Arthur, looking pale and tired; but perhaps that was because Henry was also there, radiant and full of health. He had seated himself on a stool at the bride's feet and sat clasping his hands about his knees in a manner which was both childish and dignified.

Margaret, of whom Katharine felt a little in awe, was seated with her mother, but Katharine noticed how she kept her eyes on young Henry. Little Mary could not resist bouncing up and down in her seat now and then with excitement. No one restrained her, for her childish ways found such favour with the people.

The King was pleased. At such moments he felt at ease. Here he sat in royal panoply, his family all about him—two Princes and two Princesses to remind any nobles, who might have disloyal thoughts concerning his right to the throne, that he was building the foundations of his house with firmness.

'Look,' said Henry. 'There's my uncle Dorset coming in.'

Katharine looked and saw the Queen's half-brother entering the arena beneath a pavilion of cloth of gold which was held over him by four riders as he came. He looked magnificent in his shining armour.

'And,' cried Henry, 'there's my uncle Courtenay.

Why, what is that he is riding on? I do declare it is a dragon!'

He gazed up at Katharine, eager to see what effect such wondrous sights were having upon her. Her serenity irritated him mildly. 'I'll warrant you do not see such sights in Spain,' he challenged.

'In Spain,' said Arthur, 'there is the great ceremony of La Corrida.'

'I'll warrant,' boasted Henry, 'that there are no ceremonies in Spain to compare with those in England.'

'It is well,' Arthur replied, 'that Katharine does not understand you or she would not admire your manners.'

Henry said: 'I wish she would learn English more quickly. There is much I would say to her.'

Katharine smiled at the boy, whose attention was now turned back to the arena, where Lord William Courtenay, who had married Queen Elizabeth's sister, came lumbering in astride his dragon.

Katharine was being introduced to English pageantry; she thought it a little vulgar, a little simple, but she could not help but marvel at the care which had gone into the making of these symbols; and the delight which they inspired was infectious.

Now came the Earl of Essex whose pavilion was in the form of a mountain of green on which were rocks, trees, flowers and herbs; and on top of the mountain sat a beautiful young girl with her long hair loose about her.

The spectators applauded wildly, but many of the nobles present whispered that Essex was a fool thus to display his wealth before the King's avaricious eyes. His 'mountain' was clearly very costly indeed and the days when nobles flaunted their wealth so blatantly were no longer with them.

So Katharine sat back in her place of honour and watched the jousting. She listened to the cheers of the people as their favourites rode into the arena; and she found her attention fixed not so much on those whose skill with the lance gave such pleasure to the company, but on the two brothers—her husband and Henry.

Henry's eyes were narrow with concentration; his cheeks were flushed. It was clear that he longed to be down there in the arena and emerge as the champion. As for Arthur, he seemed to shrink into his golden seat, closing his eyes now and then when disaster threatened one of the combatants. He knew that death could easily result from these jousts and he had never been able to accept such accidents with equanimity.

That day there were no serious casualties and he was glad that it was November so that the dusk fell early and it was necessary to leave the tiltyard for the hall of the Palace, where the banquet and further entertainments were awaiting them.

At the centre of the table on an elevated dais the King took his place, and on his left were seated Katharine, the Queen and the King's revered mother, the Countess of Richmond. On the King's right hand sat Arthur. Margaret and Mary were next to their grandmother on the Queen's side, and on the King's side next to Arthur, in order of precedence, were the nobility of England.

The monumental pies with their golden pastry, the great joints, the dishes of flesh and fowl, were brought in with ceremony; the minstrels played and the feasting and drinking began.

But there must be pageantry, and in the space made ready before the banqueting table the dancing and spectacle began.

Katharine looked on at the ship, the castle and the mountain, which in their turn were wheeled into the hall to the cries of admiration of the guests. The ship, which came first, was manned by men dressed as sailors who called to each other in nautical terms as their brilliantly painted vehicle trundled round and round the hall. On the deck were two figures which were intended to represent Hope and Desire, and suddenly there appeared beside them a beautiful girl dressed in Spanish costume.

Henry called to Katharine from his place at table: 'You see, this is all in your honour. You are the hope and desire of England.'

It was very flattering and Katharine, guessing what her young brother-in-law implied, graciously acknowledged the compliment with smiles which she hoped expressed her great pleasure and appreciation.

The mountain came next, and here again were allegorical figures all intended to pay homage to the new bride.

The most splendid of all the pageants was the castle which was drawn into the hall by lions of gold and silver; there was much whispering and laughter at the sight of these animals, for it was well known that inside each of the lion's skins were two men; one being the front part, the other the hindquarters. The spectators had seen these animals perform before, as they were a feature of most pageants; but they slyly watched Katharine to see her astonishment, for it was believed that she must be wondering what strange animals these were.

Seated on top of the castle was another beautiful girl in Spanish costume, and she, like the other, was being courted by Hope and Desire.

And when the ship, the mountain and the castle were all in the hall, the minstrels began to play; then beautiful girls and handsome men stepped from them, and as there was an equal number of both sexes they were most conveniently partnered for a dance, which they performed in the space before the banqueting table.

When this dance was over the performers bowed low and, to great applause, slipped out of the hall.

Now the company must join in, but first the royal bride and groom must dance followed by other members of the royal family.

Katharine and Arthur did not dance together. Many present thought this meant that the marriage was not yet to be consummated. So Katharine chose her maid of honour Maria de Rojas, and together they danced a *bass* dance, which was stately and more suitable, she thought, to the occasion than one of those dances known as *la volta* and which involved a good deal of high stepping and capering,

Katharine was at her best in the dance, for she moved with grace and she was an attractive figure in spite of the superior beauty of Maria de Rojas.

Two gentlemen at the table watched Maria as she danced. One was the grandson of the Earl of Derby, who thought her the most beautiful girl he had ever seen; but there was another watching Maria. This was Iñigo Manrique, the son of Doña

Elvira Manuel, who had accompanied the party to England in the role of one of Katharine's pages.

Maria was conscious of these looks as she danced, and deliberately she gave her smile to the young Englishman.

But although Maria's beauty attracted attention there were many who closely watched the young Infanta. The King and Queen were delighted with her; she was healthy and whether or not she was beautiful was of no great moment. She was fresh and young enough not to be repellent to a young man. They were both thinking that when the time came she would be fertile.

Arthur watched her and found pleasure in watching her; now that he knew he need not fear the consummation of their marriage he was very eager to win the friendship of his wife.

Henry could not take his eyes from Katharine. The more he saw of her the more his resentment rose. The precocious youth enjoyed occasions such as this, but he was never completely happy unless he was the centre of attraction. If only he had been the bridegroom! he was thinking. If only he were the future King of England!

The dance was over, the applause rang out while Katharine and Maria returned to their places. Arthur then led out his aunt, the Princess Cecily, and the dance they chose was a grave and stately one. Henry, watching them through sullen eyes, was thinking that so must Arthur dance, because the high dances made him breathless. But that was not the English way of dancing. When the English danced they threw themselves wholeheartedly into the affair. They should caper and leap and show that they enjoyed it. He would show them when his turn came. He was impatient to do so. When it came he and his sister Margaret stepped into the centre of the hall; there was immediate applause, and all sullenness left Henry's face as he bowed to the spectators and began to dance. He called to the minstrels to play more quickly; he wanted a gayer air. Then he took Margaret's hand and the colour came into their faces as they danced and capered about the hall, leaping into the air, twirling on their toes; and when Margaret showed signs of slackening Henry would goad her to greater efforts.

The company was laughing and applauding, and Henry, the sweat running down his face, threw off his surcoat and leaping and cavorting in his small garments continued to divert the company.

Even the King and Queen were laughing with pleasure, and when the music eventually stopped and the energetic young Prince with his sister returned to the table, congratulations were showered on them from every corner of the hall.

Henry acknowledged the cheers on behalf of himself and Margaret, but his small eyes rested on Katharine. He knew that his father was wishing his first-born were more like his other son.

Henry realised then that he was hoping Katharine was making a similar comparison of himself and Arthur.

*   *   *

Doña Elvira Manuel, that most domineering of duennas, was delighted with the state of affairs in England, for while Katharine had her separate household she remained in charge of it, and she

71

knew well that once Katharine became in truth the wife of Arthur she would cease to maintain the power which was now hers.

As duenna to a virgin bride she was supreme, for Katharine herself, on the instructions of Queen Isabella, must bow to her wishes.

Doña Elvira had never been chary of expressing her opinions, and it was inevitable that other ambitious people in the Spanish entourage should find her intolerable and seek to undermine her power.

There was one who held great influence with Katharine. This was Father Alessandro Geraldini who had been her tutor for many years and who now was her chief chaplain and confessor.

Since he had been in England Geraldini had become increasingly aware of the important role which was his and what a different matter it was to be adviser and confidant of the Princess of Wales after being merely tutor to the Infanta of Spain.

Not only was Katharine the most important lady in England next to the Queen, but she was also more important to her parents' political schemes than she had ever been before. And he, Geraldini, was her confessor. Was he going to allow a sharp-tongued woman to dominate him!

He sought for means of destroying her power. He asked permission to speak to Don Pedro de Ayala confidentially.

The ambassador shut the door of the ante-room in which the interview took place and begged Geraldini to state his business.

Geraldini came straight to the point. 'Doña Elvira Manuel has become insufferable. One would think she was the Princess of Wales.'

'In what way has she offended you, my friend?'

'She behaves as though she has charge of the Infanta's very soul. And that happens to be my duty.'

Ayala nodded. He was secretly amused; he liked to contemplate strife between the domineering duenna and the ambitious priest.

'The sooner our Infanta is free of such supervision the better, I say,' continued Geraldini. 'And the sooner this marriage becomes a real marriage the better pleased will be our Sovereigns.'

'I see that you are in their Highnesses' confidence,' said Ayala with a smile.

'I think I know my duty,' answered Geraldini sharply. 'Could not their Highnesses be persuaded that it is dangerous to Spanish policy if the marriage remains unconsummated?'

'Tell me how you see such danger in our Infanta's virginity.'

The priest grew pink. 'It is . . . not as it should be.'

'I will pass on your comments to the Sovereigns,' Ayala told him.

Geraldini was not satisfied. He went to Puebla. Like most of the Infanta's household he had come to despise Puebla, who was often disparagingly referred to as the *marrano.* Christianised Jews were people of whom the Inquisition had taught Spaniards to be wary.

As for the English, they had found Puebla parsimonious and, although this was a trait they had to accept in their King, they did not like it in others. Therefore Geraldini was less careful of offending Puebla than of offending Ayala.

'The marriage should be consummated,' he said at once. 'It is our duty as servants of their Catholic Highnesses to see that this unsatisfactory state of affairs is ended.'

Puebla eyed the priest speculatively. He knew of Geraldini's influence with Katharine.

'It is the wish of the Infanta?' he asked.

Geraldini made an impatient movement. 'The Infanta is innocent. She expresses no opinion. How could she, knowing little of such matters? Yet she holds herself willing to obey the command of her parents.'

Puebla was thoughtful, wondering how best he could ingratiate himself with the English King. He believed that England was to be his home for a long time, and that pleasing the King of England was as important a matter—if not more so—as pleasing the Spanish Sovereigns. Yet the consummation of the Infanta's marriage seemed to him of small importance compared with the matter of her dowry.

Even as he listened to Geraldini he was wondering what he could do to please the King of England in this matter without displeasing the Spanish Sovereigns. The dowry had been agreed on as two hundred thousand crowns, one hundred thousand of which had been paid on the wedding day. Fifty thousand more were due in six months' time and another fifty thousand within the year. The plate and jewels, which Katharine had brought with her from Spain and which were to form part of the payment, were valued at thirty-five thousand crowns. This was important to Henry because the plate and jewels were actually in England. For the remainder of the dowry he had only the word of

Isabella and Ferdinand to rely on. Why should not Henry take the plate and jewels *now*? They were in England, so protests from Spain would be fruitless. Henry had already shown when he had seen the Infanta before her wedding that in England he was determined to have his way.

So Puebla was of the opinion that the consummation of the marriage was of far less importance than the Infanta's dowry.

'It is always the King of England who will decide,' he said.

'Then I think we should let it be known that the Sovereigns of Spain *expect* consummation without delay.'

Puebla lifted his shoulders and Geraldini could see that, like Ayala, he was indifferent.

But the fact that Geraldini had approached both ambassadors in the matter was brought to the notice of Doña Elvira, and she immediately realised that the officiousness of the priest was directed against her own authority.

Doña Elvira was never a woman to consider whether or not she offended others.

She asked Geraldini to come to her apartments and, when he arrived, she went straight into the attack.

'It appears, Father Geraldini, that you choose to forget that *I* am in charge of the Infanta's household!'

'I did not forget.'

'Did you not? Then it seems strange that you should go about explaining that it is the wish of their Catholic Highnesses that the marriage should be consummated.'

'Strange, Doña Elvira? It is common sense.'

'You are in the Sovereigns' confidence?'

'I . . . I am the Infanta's confessor, and as such . . .'

Doña Elvira's eyes narrowed. And as such, she thought, you enjoy too much of her confidence. I shall remedy that.

She interrupted coldly: 'Queen Isabella put me in charge of her daughter's household, and until she removes me from that position, there I shall remain. It is for the good of all that as yet the marriage shall remain unconsummated. Our Infanta is as yet too young and her husband even younger. I will thank you, Father, not to meddle in affairs which are no concern of yours.'

Geraldini bowed to hide the hatred in his eyes, but Doña Elvira made no attempt to hide that in hers.

There was war between them, and Doña Elvira would not be satisfied until she had arranged for the insolent priest's recall to Spain.

*　　　*　　　*

Henry came running into his brother's apartments, his eyes blazing with excitement.

Arthur was stretched out on a couch looking very pale.

'Are you sick, Arthur?' asked Henry, but he did not wait for an answer. 'I have just seen a strange thing, brother. Our father has done to death his best falcon, and for no other reason than that it was not afraid to match itself with an eagle.'

'Is that so?' said Arthur wearily.

'Indeed it is so. Our father ordered the falconers to pluck off its head, and this was done.'

76

'I understand why,' said Arthur, 'because I remember how he hanged the mastiffs.'

'Yes,' said Henry. 'I remembered too. Our father said: "It is not meet for any subject to attack his superior."'

'Ah,' mused Arthur, 'our father is fond of these little parables, is he not?'

'But his best falcon! And all because the bird was game enough to show no fear of the mighty eagle. I should have treasured that falcon. I should have been proud of him. I should have used him continually. *I* should not have plucked off his head for bravery.'

'You are not King.'

'No—that is not for me.' Arthur noticed the sullen lines about the little mouth.

'It is unfortunate. You would have made a much better King than I, Henry.'

Henry did not deny this. 'But you are the elder. It is the Church for me. And you already have a wife.'

Arthur flushed. He was a little ashamed of being a husband and yet no husband. It was embarrassing to know that there was a great deal of talk about whether or not the marriage should be consummated. It made him feel foolish.

Henry was thinking of that now. His face was as usual expressive, and Arthur could always guess at his thoughts.

Henry strutted about the apartment, imagining himself as the husband. There would be no question of the consummation then.

'You find her comely?' he asked slyly.

'She is very comely,' answered Arthur.

'And she brings you much enjoyment?'

Arthur flushed. 'Indeed yes.'

Henry rocked on his heels and looked knowledgeable. 'I have heard that the Spaniards are a passionate people, for all their solemn dignity.'

'Oh, it is true . . . it is true . . .' said Arthur.

Henry smiled. 'It is said that you and she are not husband and wife in truth. I'll warrant those who say that do not know the real truth.'

Arthur began to cough to hide his embarrassment; but he did not deny Henry's suggestion.

Henry began to laugh; then suddenly he remembered the falcon. 'If I were King,' he said, 'I do not think I should have to hang my bravest dogs and destroy my most gallant falcon to warn my subjects that they must obey me.'

Henry was looking into the future, and once more Arthur guessed his thoughts. Do I look so ill then? he wondered. And he knew that he did, and that the chances were that he would not live, nor beget children, to keep Henry from the throne.

*   *   *

It was time that Arthur returned to the Principality of Wales and the question had arisen as to whether Katharine should accompany him.

The King was undecided. Each day it seemed to him that Arthur looked weaker.

Puebla had been to him and, in an endeavour to assure Henry that he, Puebla, in reality served the King of England even though he was supposed to be the servant of the Spanish Sovereigns, he suggested that Henry should immediately take possession of Katharine's plate and jewels.

'They will, of course, be Your Grace's at the end of the year, but why should you not take them now?'

Henry considered the value of the plate and jewels—some thirty-five thousand crowns, according to the valuation made by the London goldsmiths—and when he contemplated such wealth his fingers itched to take possession of it. A year was a long time to wait. Anything could happen in a year, particularly as Arthur was not strong. But once the plate and jewels were in his possession there they should remain.

He sent therefore to Katharine's treasurer, Don Juan de Cuero, and asked that the plate and jewels be handed to him.

This Don Juan de Cuero refused to do.

'Nay,' he told Henry's messenger, 'I am in charge of the Infanta's revenues, and it was the express command of the Sovereigns of Spain that the plate and jewellery should remain the property of their daughter until the time was ripe for the payment of the second half of the dowry.'

Henry was irritated when he received this reply, but he had no intention of upsetting the Spanish Sovereigns at this stage and was ready to abandon the idea of laying his hands on the plate and jewels until the appointed time.

Puebla came to him with a suggestion. Puebla had made up his mind that it would be to Spain's advantage if the marriage were consummated, and he was determined to do everything in his power to bring this about.

He had Henry's confidence. More than once he had shown the King of England that he worked with an eye to England's advantages, and now he had a suggestion to make.

'If the Infanta could be induced to wear her jewellery and use her plate it could then be called second-hand and you could decline to accept it as part payment of the dowry. Ferdinand and Isabella would then be bound to pay you thirty-five thousand crowns instead of the plate and jewels— which would remain in England so that you could always take them if you wished.'

This seemed a good idea to Henry's crafty mind. But he pointed out: 'Her treasurer keeps a firm hand on the plate and jewels which he knows are to come as part payment of the dowry. He would never consent to her using them.'

Puebla appeared to be thoughtful. He knew Isabella and Ferdinand well and he was convinced that the fact that the plate and jewels had been used by their daughter would have no effect whatsoever on the bargain they had made. They needed money too desperately to consider lightly parting with it. But Puebla's desire was not to work against Spain for the sake of Henry but only to give Henry the impression that he was doing so.

Then Puebla said: 'If the Infanta accompanied the Prince to Wales, they could set up a small court there, and the Infanta's plate could be used by them both. She would want to wear her jewels in her own little court.'

The King nodded.

'The Princess of Wales shall accompany her husband to Ludlow,' he said.

*   *   *

80

The journey westwards was pleasant enough. Arthur seemed happy to escape from his father's notice. He rode at the head of the cavalcade and Katharine was close to him, riding on a pillion behind her master of horse; and when this mode of travel tired her she took to her litter which was borne between two horses.

The people came out in the villages to welcome her and Arthur, and she was delighted that Arthur always considered the pleasure of the people and would stop and speak to them, always gentle, always with a smile, no matter how tired he was— and he was so often tired.

She was glad that his father had sent a council of men with him, headed by Sir Richard Pole, which meant that Arthur had no decisions to make which would have caused him anxiety; he travelled as the representative of the King, and could always call in his councillors if action was necessary, and should it not be carried out in accordance with the King's pleasure, it would be Sir Richard and the council who would be blamed, not Arthur.

With Katharine rode her own household headed by Doña Elvira, whose son, Don Iñigo Manrique, was among Katharine's pages. Don Iñigo strove to ride beside Maria de Rojas, who did her best to keep close to Katharine. Alessandro Geraldini was also a member of the party, and the strife between him and Doña Elvira increased as the days passed.

Many of Katharine's entourage who had accompanied her from Spain had now been sent back to their own country; and as Katharine rode towards Wales she felt a sudden desolation because she had said goodbye to the Archbishop of Santiago and many others. She envied them their return to Spain and she let herself wonder what was happening in the Madrid Alcazar or the great Alhambra. How happy she would have been if she could have burst into her mother's apartments and thrown herself into those loving arms!

I shall never cease to long for her, she thought sadly as she lay back in her litter.

They rested for a night in the royal Manor at Bewdley in Worcestershire, and it was here that Arthur showed her the chapel in which their marriage had been performed by proxy.

'Puebla stood as your proxy,' said Arthur, wrinkling his nose with disgust.

Katharine laughed. 'At least you prefer me to him!' she slowly answered in English which he was teaching her and at which she was making good progress.

'I like him not,' answered Arthur. 'And you I like so much.'

As they went back to the Manor and their separate apartments there, Katharine thought that she was fortunate indeed to have a husband as kind and gentle as Arthur.

'You are smiling,' said Arthur, 'and you look happier than I have seen you look before.'

'I was thinking,' she answered, 'that if my mother were here with us I should be completely happy.'

'When I am in truth King,' Arthur told her, 'we will visit your mother and she shall visit us. You love her so dearly, do you not? Your voice is different when you mention her.'

'She is the kindest mother anyone ever had. She is the greatest of Queens and yet . . . and yet . . .'

'I understand,' said Arthur, touching her arm

gently.

'Others did not understand her always,' went on Katharine. 'They thought her cold and stern. But to us, her children, she was always gentle. Yet none of us, not even my sister Juana, would have dared disobey her. Sometimes I wish she had not been perfect; then it would have been easier to have said goodbye to her.'

They were silent, but during that stay at Bewdley she realised that she could easily love Arthur. As for Arthur, he was happy with his bride.

He was thinking: In a year or so I shall be her husband in very truth. Then we shall have children, and she will be such a mother to them as Queen Isabella was to her.

Arthur could look forward to the future with a serenity and pleasure he had rarely known before.

And so they came to Ludlow.

*   *   *

The castle rose from the point of a headland, and its bold grey towers appeared to be impregnable.

'There are no better views in all England than those to be seen from the castle,' Arthur told Katharine. 'From the north side there is Corve Dale, and from the east you can see Titterstone Clee Hill. And stretched out beyond is the valley of the Teme with the Stretton Hills forming a background. I have a great affection for Ludlow. It is on the very borders of the Welsh country which I have always felt was my country.'

Katharine nodded. 'The people here love you,' she said.

'Am I not the Prince of Wales? And do not

83

forget that you are the Princess. They will love you too.'

'I fervently hope so,' answered Katharine.

Katharine never forgot her first nights in Ludlow Castle. There in the large hall fires had been lighted; cressets shone their light from the walls, and as she sat beside Arthur while the chieftains of Wales came to the castle to pay homage to their Prince, she felt that she was farther from the halls of the Alhambra than she had ever been.

Never had she seen such fierce men as those who came in from the Welsh mountains. She could not understand their melodious speech; some looked like mountain brigands, others appeared in odd finery, but all spoke like poets and entertained her with such sweet singing that she was astonished.

The first of the chieftains of Wales, Rhys ap Thomas, came to pay his homage and to swear to Arthur that he accepted him as his Prince and would fight for him whenever and wherever it should be necessary.

Arthur was a little in awe of the fierce chieftain who he knew hoped for much, now that there was a Tudor king on the throne. Perhaps he was a little disappointed. Perhaps the Tudor was more English than Welsh. But at least he sent his son to forge friendships with the people of Wales, and in the mountains they continued to hope that one day the Tudors would remember Wales.

With Rhys ap Thomas came his son, Griffith ap Rhys, a beautiful young boy who, said his father, sought service in the household of the Prince and Princess of Wales; and when the boy was brought forward to kneel and kiss the hands of Arthur and Katharine, he assured Arthur in the Welsh tongue of his loyalty and will to serve.

'Now speak the other tongues you know, boy,' said his father proudly; and Griffith ap Rhys began to speak in a language which Katharine recognised as French.

This delighted Katharine, because here was someone with whom she might be able to converse. She answered Griffith in French, and to her pleasure he was able to understand; and although their accents and intonations were so different they could chat together.

'I wish to make Griffith my gentleman usher,' she told Arthur, and there was nothing she could have said which would have given the boy's father more delight.

There was no doubt in the minds of any that Wales was pleased with its Princess.

*　　　*　　　*

A few weeks passed, weeks which afterwards seemed to Katharine like a dream. She was happier than she had been since she left Spain. She, Arthur and Griffith ap Rhys rode together; she found great pleasure in talking in French to Griffith, and Arthur liked to listen to them. They were like two brothers and a sister—constantly discovering interests in common. In the long evenings by the blazing fires and the lights of the torches there would be singing and dancing in the great hall; and those who watched said: 'Before long this marriage will be consummated. The Prince and the Princess are falling in love.'

They would sit side by side, and Griffith would be seated on a stool at their feet, strumming on his harp and singing songs, the favourite of which was one about a great King Arthur who had once reigned in Britain.

One day, it was said, there would be another great King Arthur to rule over England and Wales; he would be this Arthur who now sat in the hall of Ludlow Castle. He was young yet; he was a little pale and seemed weak; but he was leaving boyhood behind him, he was becoming a man, and he had the fair young Princess from Spain beside him.

*   *   *

March had set in and the snow gave place to rain. For days the mist hung about the draughty rooms of the castle; the damp seeped into the bones of all and even the great fires which blazed on the hearths could not drive the mist from Ludlow Castle.

Katharine longed for the cold, frosty weather; then she and Arthur could have gone riding together. She dared not suggest that they go out in the driving rain, for Arthur had begun to cough more persistently since they had come to Ludlow.

One day Griffith ap Rhys burst somewhat unceremoniously into their presence.

They were sitting by the fire in one of the smaller apartments of the castle and a few of their suite were with them.

Doña Elvira looked sternly at the young Welshman and was preparing to reproach him for forgetting the respect he owed to the Prince and Princess of Wales, when Griffith burst out: 'I have ill news. The sweating sickness has come to Ludlow.'

A horrified silence fell on the company. The sweating sickness was considered to be one of the greatest calamities which could befall a community. It spread rapidly from one to another and invariably ended in death, although if the patient could survive the first twenty-four hours of the disease, it was said that he usually recovered.

Questions were fired at Griffith, who said that several of the townsfolk were stricken and that he had himself seen people in the streets sinking to the ground because the fever had overcome them before they could reach their homes.

When this was explained to Elvira she began giving rapid orders. The castle was to be closed to all visitors; they were to consider themselves in a state of siege. At all costs the sweating sickness must not be allowed to enter Ludlow Castle while the Infanta of Spain was there.

The news had cast a gloom on the company, but Katharine was eager to know more about the dreaded disease, and Griffith sat beside her and told her and Arthur how it began with a fever and that many died before the sweating stage began. Then they sweated profusely and, if they could cling to life long enough, they stood a chance of recovery; for in sweating they cast off the evil humours of the body and thus recovered.

Arthur was disturbed; he told Katharine: 'The disease broke out soon after my father won the throne. I think some looked upon it as an evil omen. It is strange that it should have broken out here in Ludlow now we are come. It would seem that there is a blight on our House.'

'No,' replied Katharine fiercely, 'this sickness could happen anywhere.'

'It started in the army which landed at Milford Haven with my father.'

Katharine endeavoured to disperse his gloom, but it was not easy; and that night the singing ceased in Ludlow Castle.

*   *   *

Katharine awoke in the night. She was conscious of a curious burning sensation in her limbs; she tried to call out but her mouth was parched.

She lay still, thinking: So it has come to Ludlow Castle and I am its victim. Yet if I am to die, then I shall be with my sister Isabella and my brother Juan, and I think I should be happy.

There was another thought which came to her and which she would not voice. It was that her mother might not be long for this world, and if she too were going to pass from the Earth to be with Isabella and Juan, then Katharine would long to join them.

She felt lightheaded; she had forgotten she was in grim Ludlow Castle; she thought she was back behind the rose-tinted walls of the Alhambra; she thought that she lingered in one of the *patios,* trailing her hot fingers in the cool fountains; but the fountains were not cool; they were hot as fire and she believed she had put her fingers in the fires in which the heretics were burned, mistaking them for fountains.

She was tossing from side to side in her bed when Maria de Rojas came to bid her good morning.

Maria took one look at her mistress and was terrified. She ran screaming to Doña Elvira.

* * *

So Katharine lay a victim of the dreaded sickness. All through the day and night which followed Elvira was in the sick-room. Angrily she ordered possets and herbal drinks to be prepared in case they might be of some use to her Infanta. She cursed those who had dared bring infection into the castle. She had no thought of anything but the health of her mistress.

Katharine had passed into the sweating period. Elvira hovered anxiously about her bed. If she sweated profusely the evil humours would be thrown off; and she *was* sweating.

'The Sovereigns will never forgive me,' cried Elvira, 'for letting their daughter face such infection. She *must* recover. It is unthinkable that she should die . . . her dowry not even paid, her virginity intact.'

The energy of Doña Elvira affected all who came in contact with the sick-room.

News was brought for Katharine, but Elvira would not admit the messenger.

So the Prince was sick? Well, was not the Prince always ailing? The Infanta, who was never ill, was now laid low with their miserable sweating sickness!

It was twenty-four hours since Katharine had been taken ill. She lay limp and exhausted on her bed; but she still lived.

Doña Elvira busied herself with making a brew of aromatic herbs, laurel and juniper berries which the physicians had recommended; and when Katharine had drunk it she opened her eyes and said: 'Doña Elvira, bring my mother to me.'

'You are in your bed in Ludlow Castle, Highness. You have been very ill but I have nursed you back to health.'

Katharine nodded her head slightly. 'I remember now,' she said; and there were tears in her eyes which would never have appeared but for her bodily weakness. She wanted her mother now, even more than ever. She knew that, if only she could feel that cool hand on her brow, see those serene eyes looking into hers, commanding her to bear whatever ill fortune God had seen fit to send to her, she could have wept for joy; as it was she could not prevent herself from weeping in sorrow.

'The worst is over,' said Elvira. 'You will get well now. I have nursed you with my own hands, and shall do so until you are completely recovered.'

'Thank you, Doña Elvira.'

Elvira took Katharine's hand in hers and kissed it. 'Always I am at your service, my dearest Infanta,' she said. 'Do you not understand that?'

'I understand,' said Katharine; and she closed her eyes. But try as she might she could not prevent the tears seeping through.

If I could see her but once . . . she thought. She turned her head that Doña Elvira might not see the tears.

'Does my mother know of my illness?' she asked.

'She will hear of it and of your recovery in the same message.'

'I am glad of that. Now she will not be grieved. If I had died that would have been her greatest sorrow. She loves me dearly.'

Now the tears were flowing more freely, and it was no use trying to restrain them. These were the tears which had been demanding to be shed for so long, and which in her strength she had withheld. Now she was too weak to fight them and she wept shamelessly.

'For she loves me so,' she whispered, 'and we are parted. There will never be another to love me as my mother loved me. All my life there will never be love for me such as she gave me.'

'What nonsense is this?' said Elvira. 'You must keep well covered. It may be that you have not sweated enough. There may be more humours to be released. Come, what would your mother say if she saw those foolish tears?'

'She would understand,' cried Katharine. 'Did she not always understand?'

Elvira covered her up sharply. The Infanta's tears shocked her.

She is very weak, she thought. But the worst is over. I have nursed her through this. She is right when she says the Queen dotes on her. I shall have Isabella's undying gratitude for nursing her daughter through this illness.

*　　　*　　　*

There was a muffled silence throughout the castle. People were speaking in whispers. Griffith ap Rhys sat with his harp at his knees, but the harp was silent.

There was death in the Castle of Ludlow. Disease had struck where it could not be defeated.

In the chamber of the Prince of Wales the

91

candles were lighted by the bed and the watchers kept their vigil. Sir Richard Pole's courier was on his way to Greenwich, to break the news to the King and Queen.

In the whole of Ludlow Castle Katharine, lying on her sick bed, was the only one who did not know that this day she had become a widow.

CHAPTER IV

INTRIGUE AT DURHAM HOUSE

As soon as Queen Elizabeth received the message that she was to go with all haste to the King's chamber, as soon as she looked into the face of the messenger, she knew that some dire tragedy had befallen her House. And when she learned that the couriers had come from Ludlow she guessed that what she had been dreading so long had at last taken place.

She steeled herself for the ordeal.

Henry was standing in the centre of the chamber; his usually pale face was grey and his eyes looked stricken. He did not speak for a moment, and the Queen's glance went from her husband to the Friar Observant who was the King's confessor.

'My son?' whispered the Queen.

The Friar bowed his head.

'He is . . . ill?'

'He has departed to God, Your Grace.'

The Queen did not speak. For so many years she had waited for this news, dreading it. The fear of it had come to her in the days when she had held Arthur in her arms, a weak baby who did not cry but lay placid in his cradle, not because he was contented, but because he was too weak for aught else. It had come at last.

The King said: 'Pray leave the Queen and myself. We will share this painful sorrow alone.'

The Friar left them and even when the door

shut on them they did not move towards each other; and for some seconds there was silence between them.

It was the King who broke it. 'This is a bitter blow.'

She nodded. 'He was never strong. I always feared it. Now it has befallen us.'

She lifted her eyes to her husband's face and she was suddenly aware of a deep pity for him. She looked at the lean face, the lines etched by the sides of his mouth; the eyes which were too alert. She read the thoughts behind that lean and clever face. The heir to the throne was dead, and there was only one male child left to him. There was also a nobility which he would never trust and which was constantly on the alert to shout that the Tudors had no legitimate claim to the throne. All her life Elizabeth had lived close to the struggle to win and keep a crown. It was painful to her now that her husband should not think of Arthur as their dear son, but as the heir.

He would never know what it was to love, to feel acute sorrow such as she was feeling now. Should she feel envious of him because he did not suffer as she did through the loss of their son? No, even in this bitter moment she felt sorry for him because he would never know the joy of loving.

'Why does God do this to us?' demanded Henry harshly. 'The Friar has just said that if we receive good at the hands of God, we must patiently sustain the ill He sends us.'

'It is true,' said Elizabeth. She went to the window and looked out on the river as it flowed peacefully past this Palace of Greenwich. 'We have much for which to thank God,' she added.

94

'But this was my eldest son . . . my heir!'

'You must not grieve. You must remember that you have your duty to do. You have other children.'

'Yet the plague could carry off our children in a few hours.'

'Arthur was not strong enough to withstand the attack. The others are stronger. Why, Henry, your mother had but you, and look to what you have come. You have one healthy Prince and two Princesses.'

'Henry is my heir now,' mused the King.

Elizabeth had left the window and was walking towards him. She had to comfort him.

'Henry,' she said, 'we are not old. Perhaps we shall have more children. More sons.'

The King seemed somewhat pacified. He put his arm about her and said with more feeling than he usually displayed: 'You have been a good wife to me. But of course we shall get ourselves more sons.'

She closed her eyes and tried to smile. She was thinking of the nights ahead which must be dedicated to the begetting of children. She longed for peace at night. She was growing more and more aware of her need for rest. She thought of the weary months of pregnancy, which must precede a birth.

But it was the duty of Queens to turn their backs on sorrow, to stop grieving for the children who were lost to them, and to think of those as yet unborn.

Henry took her hand and raised it to his cold lips.

He said as he released it: 'I see trouble ahead with regard to Katharine's dowry. If only Arthur had lived another year it should all have been paid over, and perhaps by that time Arthur would have got her with child.'

The Queen did not answer; she fancied that her husband was reproving their delicate son for dying at a time most inconvenient to his father's schemes.

Poor Henry! she mused. He knows nothing of love. He knows little of anything but statecraft and the best methods of filling the coffers of his treasury.

Why should she say Poor Henry! when he was quite unaware of any lack in his life? Perhaps she should say Poor Katharine, who at this time lay sick at Ludlow, her dowry half paid, her position most insecure. What would happen to Katharine of Aragon now? The Queen of England would do all in her power to help the poor child, but what power had the Queen of England?

*   *   *

Before the burnished mirror in his apartment young Henry stood.

He had received the news with mingled feelings. Arthur . . . dead! He had known it must happen, but it was nevertheless a shock when the news came.

Never to see Arthur again! Never to show off his superior prowess, never to strut before the delicate brother. It made him feel a little sad.

But what great avenues were opening out before him. To be Prince of Wales when one had been Duke of York! This was no trifling title, for one who had been destined to become Archbishop of

Canterbury would one day be King of England.

King of England! The little eyes were alight with pleasure; the smooth cheeks flushed pink. Now the homage he received would be doubled, the cries of the people in the streets intensified.

No longer Prince Henry—but Henry, Prince of Wales, heir to the throne of England.

'Henry VIII of England!' There were no sweeter words in the English language.

When he contemplated them and all they meant he could cease to grieve for the death of his delicate brother Arthur.

*   *   *

In a litter, covered with black velvet and black cloth, Katharine travelled from Ludlow to Richmond. How different was this journey from that other which she had taken such a short time before with Arthur!

The weather had changed, but Katharine was unaware of all the beauty of an English spring. She could think only of the husband whom she had lost, the husband who had been no husband.

And then there came a sudden blinding flash of hope as she remembered the fate of her sister Isabella, which was so like her own. Isabella had gone into Portugal to marry the heir to the throne, and shortly after their marriage he had died in a hunting accident. The result was that Isabella had returned to Spain.

Now, thought Katharine, they will send me home. I shall see my mother again.

So how could she be completely unhappy at that prospect? She believed that this time next year her

97

stay in England would be like a distant dream. She would wander through the flagged corridors of the Alhambra; she would look through her windows on to the Courtyard of Lions; she would stray into the Court of Myrtles, and her mother would be beside her. The pomegranate would no longer merely be a device; it would be all about her—growing in the gardens, pictured on the shields and the walls of her parents' palace. Happiest of all, her mother would be beside her. 'You did your duty,' she would say. 'You went uncomplaining to England. Now, my Catalina, you shall stay with me for ever.'

Katharine of Aragon would again become Catalina, Infanta, beloved daughter of the Queen.

So, as she went on her way to Richmond, she thought tenderly of Arthur who had been so kind to her in life, and who in death would, she believed, bring her relief from bondage.

*   *   *

Queen Elizabeth was waiting to receive the young widow.

Poor child! she thought. She will be desolate. How will she feel, alone in a strange land? Does she realise how her position has changed? She, who was Princess of Wales, is now merely a Spanish Princess, who has been married in name only. If there had been an heir on the way the circumstances would have changed considerably. But now . . . what is her position? How sad that girls should be used thus by ambitious men.

The King came to her apartment. He gave her that cool appraising look which she knew meant that he was looking for some sign of pregnancy.

She said: 'The Infanta should arrive at Richmond tomorrow, I believe.'

A wary look replaced the speculative one in the King's eyes.

'I will keep her with me for a while,' went on the Queen. 'This is a terrible shock for her.'

'It would not be wise for her to remain at Richmond,' said the King quickly.

The Queen did not answer, but waited for his commands.

'She should be installed with her household outside the Court,' went on the King.

'I thought that, so soon after her bereavement . . .'

The King looked surprised. It was rarely that the Queen sought to question his orders.

'This is a most unsatisfactory state of affairs,' he said. 'Our son dead within a few months of his marriage, and that marriage never consummated— or at least so we believe.'

'You have reason to suspect that it was consummated?' asked the Queen sharply.

The King shrugged his shoulders. 'I ordered that it should not be, but they went to Wales together— two young people, not displeased with each other. It would not have been impossible for them to be together . . . alone.'

'If this happened,' said the Queen excitedly, 'if Katharine should be with child . . .'

'Then she would be carrying the heir to the throne. Our son Henry would not be pleased, I'll swear.'

'Henry! He is so like my father sometimes that I do not know whether to rejoice or tremble.'

'I thank God we have our son Henry, but I am not an old man myself, and I should have some years left to me . . . enough that Henry may be of age before his turn comes to take the throne. But, as you say, what if Katharine should be carrying a child? It *is* possible, although I doubt Arthur would have gone against my expressed wish. If only he had lived a few months longer. You may be sure there will be difficulty with those Spaniards.'

'They will be more inclined to meet your demands if we treat their daughter well.'

'I shall treat her as her dignity warrants. She shall stay with you at Richmond for a day or so, until she has had time to overcome her grief. Then she shall take up residence in the house opposite Twickenham Church. She shall live there with her own suite. Remember, she has no claim on us now and it would be as well that she shall not be at Court until we have negotiated with her parents as to what is to become of her.'

The Queen bowed her head. It was no use pleading with her husband. She would not be able to comfort the young girl, to treat her as she would a sorrowing daughter. The King would have the Sovereigns of Spain know that the death of the Prince of Wales had put their daughter in a precarious position.

*   *   *

Katharine was sorry that she could not stay with the Court at Richmond, but she believed this to be only a waiting period, for she was certain that, as soon as her parents heard the news, they would give orders that she return to Spain. But it would take a little time for the message to reach Spain and for the Sovereigns' orders to be sent to

England.

It would have been pleasant to have had the company of Henry and Margaret. Margaret herself was in need of comfort, for she was soon to depart to Scotland as a bride.

But this could not be and, after a brief stay at Richmond, Katharine and her household were removed to a turreted house with the church opposite, and Doña Elvira took charge of all household arrangements.

It was soon decided that the palace of the Bishop of Durham, which was situated on the Strand, would be a more suitable dwelling for the Infanta; and so to Durham House she went.

Elvira was delighted with this seclusion because it meant that, removed from the Court as they were, she was in charge of the entire household. Her husband, Don Pedro Manrique, and her son, Don Iñigo, held high posts in Katharine's household and Elvira was ambitious for them. She had determined that Maria de Rojas should be betrothed to Iñigo; she believed that Maria's dowry would be a large one.

Elvira often thought of her brother, Don Juan Manuel, whose service to the Sovereigns should not go unrewarded. Isabella, she knew, thought highly of him and he should have had more honours than he had so far received. Elvira guessed that it was Ferdinand who barred his way to success, for Ferdinand was constantly seeking favours for his illegitimate children and, although the Queen insisted on having her way, Ferdinand was full of cunning and often scored in spite of his wife.

If there were no King Ferdinand, Elvira often

101

thought, Juan would receive his dues.

She wished sometimes that she were in Spain; she felt sure that she would have been able to expedite Juan's rise to favour in the same efficient way in which she was able to look after Iñigo's in London.

But for the moment she was contented. The Infanta had reverted to her care, and as she was now a widow in a difficult situation, she relied on Elvira. Isabella would soon be sending instructions, and those instructions would come to Elvira.

So life in Durham House took on the pattern of that of a Spanish Alcazar. The English tongue was rarely heard; the English nobles who had held places in the entourage of the Prince and Princess of Wales disappeared, and their places were taken by Spaniards. Don Pedro Manrique was once more the first Chamberlain; Don Juan de Cuero was treasurer; Alessandro Geraldini remained the Infanta's confessor; and Don Iñigo was at the head of her pages. Elvira ruled the household; but that did not mean that the animosity, which she had engendered in the heart and mind of Geraldini, was abated. Rather it had intensified.

Puebla remembered insults which the duenna did not cease to heap upon him.

Ayala watched mischievously, fearing that soon he might be recalled to Spain and so miss the fun which, he felt sure, must be lurking in such a delicate situation.

*   *   *

As the party rode towards Richmond, people

stopped to stare at it.

'Spaniards!' they whispered. They knew, for they had seen Spaniards in plenty since the Infanta had come to England.

Something was afoot. Perhaps the gentleman who rode at the head of that party of foreigners had come to take the widowed Infanta back to Spain.

The party was riding towards the Palace where the King was in residence.

Hernan Duque de Estrada was thoughtful; he did not notice the attention he and his party attracted. He had a difficult task before him, which he did not relish; and it was going to be made doubly difficult because of his imperfect knowledge of the English language.

Beside him rode Dr de Puebla—a man whom he could not like. How was it possible for an Asturian nobleman to have a fondness for a *marrano*! The fellow might be clever—it was clear that the Sovereigns thought so—but his appearance and his manners were enough to make a Spanish nobleman shudder.

Ayala was of a different kind. A nobleman to his fingertips, but light-minded. Hernan Duque was not very happy with his two colleagues.

'There lies the Palace of Richmond,' said Ayala, and Hernan Duque saw the line of buildings, the projecting towers, the far from symmetrical turrets. He, who had come hot-foot from the Alhambra, was not impressed by the architecture of the country, and he forgot momentarily that the beautiful building with which he was comparing this Palace was a masterpiece of Arabic, not Spanish, architecture.

'The King is often at Richmond,' Ayala explained. 'He has a feeling for the place. It may well be that he likes to be near the river, for Greenwich is another favourite residence.'

Puebla put in: 'And so we are to obey you without question.'

'The express orders of the Sovereigns,' Hernan Duque replied.

'It seems strange,' grumbled Puebla. 'We, who have been here so long, understand the situation so much better than anyone in Spain possibly could.'

'I have their Highnesses' instructions. It would go ill with you if you did not do all in your power to help me carry them out.'

Puebla tossed his head. 'I do not envy you your task. You will find the Tudor is not an easy man with whom to drive a bargain.'

'It is so unfortunate that the death of the Prince occurred at this time.'

'What is your first move?' Ayala asked.

Hernan Duque looked over his shoulder.

'Let us ride on ahead,' said Ayala. 'It is better to be absolutely sure. Although it is doubtless safe enough to talk. The English cannot learn the languages of others. Their secret belief is that all who do not speak English are barbarians and that foreigners deserve the name in any case.'

'An insular people,' murmured Duque. 'I pity our Infanta.'

'Why should you? Do you not carry orders from their Highnesses that she is to return to Spain?'

'I brought three documents with me. You have seen the first . . . that which commanded you to obey me in all matters concerning this affair. The second and third are for the eyes of the King. But he will not see the third until he has digested the second. Nor shall he know at this stage that it exists.'

'And the second?' asked Puebla.

'It demands the return of the hundred thousand crowns, the first half of the dowry, which has already been paid.'

'Do you wish to break the heart of the King of England?' demanded Ayala.

'He will not relish this, I know.'

'Relish it!' screamed Ayala. 'The King loves those hundred thousand crowns more than he loved his son. You cannot deal him another blow— one so close on the other.'

'I shall do more. I shall demand those revenues which the Prince of Wales promised to his wife on the day of their marriage.'

'The King will never consent to that.'

'I shall then ask for the return of the Infanta to Spain.'

'With the spoils,' put in Ayala, laughing. 'Not so bad—the dowry, one third of the revenues of Wales, Chester and Cornwall, and our Infanta, virginity intact. A pleasant little adventure for the Infanta, and a remunerative one for the Sovereigns. Ah, do you think the King of England will agree?'

'He will not like this, I know,' said Duque. 'He will refuse, for I doubt not that he will never be induced to part with the money. Yet what alternative has he—except to incur the displeasure of the Sovereigns of Spain? That is why the second document is of such great importance.'

'And this second document?' Puebla asked

eagerly.

Duque looked once more over his shoulder. 'The King has a second son,' he said quietly.

'Ah!' whispered Ayala.

'Dangerous!' Puebla put in. 'He is her brother by marriage. Are we not told in Leviticus that a man is forbidden to marry his brother's widow?'

'The Pope would give the dispensation. He gave it to Emanuel of Portugal when he married the Infanta Maria on the death of her sister Isabella.'

'That was the dead wife's sister.'

'The situation is similar. There will be no difficulty if the Pope will give the necessary dispensation. And as it is said that the marriage was never consummated, that should simplify matters.'

'I should like to make sure on that point,' said Puebla. 'It is important.'

Ayala looked scornfully at the Jew. 'Your lawyer's mind boggles at unimportant details. Rest assured that if the Sovereigns want the dispensation they will get it. Spain is great enough to make sure of that.'

'At first I shall say nothing of this suggested marriage. I wish to alarm the King by demanding the return of the dowry and the transfer of the goods which the Infanta has inherited by her marriage. That will put him into a mood to agree to this second marriage—and it is the wish of the Sovereigns that it should take place.'

'I thought,' said Ayala, 'that the Queen would have wished to have her daughter back.'

'She wishes it most fervently, but duty comes before her own personal desires as always. There is another matter. Her health has declined rapidly

106

during the last months. You, who have not seen her for so long, would scarcely know her. I do not think Isabella of Castile is long for this world. She knows it, and she wishes to see her youngest daughter happily settled, with a crown in view, before she departs this life.'

'She need have no fear. Henry will agree to this marriage,' smiled Ayala. 'It is the way out for him. He would never allow anyone to take one hundred thousand crowns from him.'

They had reached the gates of the Palace.

With Puebla on one side and Ayala on the other, Hernan Duque rode in; and shortly afterwards Puebla and Ayala presented him to the King, who was very ready to conduct him to a small chamber where they might discuss this matter of the Infanta's future in private.

*   *   *

In the seclusion of Durham House, Katharine had no idea that her parents' envoy had arrived in England with such important documents affecting her future.

She felt at peace, for she was certain that very soon now she would be preparing to make the journey back to Spain. In her apartments, the windows of which overlooked the Thames, she could almost believe she *was* back in Spain. Here she sat with three of her maids of honour, all of whom were dear to her, and they stitched at their embroidery as they would in their own country.

She could almost believe that at any moment there would be a summons for her to go to her mother's apartment in this very palace, and that if she looked from the window she would not see the lively London river with its barges, its ferries, its watermen all shouting to each other in the English tongue, but the distant Sierras of Guadarrama or the crystal-clear waters of the Darro.

In the meantime she could live in Durham House as though she were in a Spanish Alcazar and wait for the summons to return home.

Maria de Rojas had grown even prettier in recent weeks. Maria was in love with an Englishman. Francesca de Carceres was only pretending to sew, because she hated to sit quietly and was not fond of the needle; she found life at Durham House irksome, longed for gaiety, and it was only the thought that soon they would be returning to Spain that made it possible for her to endure it. Maria de Salinas worked quietly. She too was happy because she believed they would soon be leaving for Spain.

Francesca, who could never contain her thoughts for long, suddenly burst out: 'Maria de Rojas wishes to talk to Your Highness.'

Maria de Rojas flushed slightly, and Maria de Salinas said in her quiet way: 'You should not hesitate. Her Highness will help you, I am sure.'

'What is this?' asked Katharine. 'Come along, Maria, tell me.'

'She is in love,' cried Francesca.

'With Don Iñigo?' Katharine asked.

Maria de Rojas flushed hotly. 'Indeed no.'

'Ah, then it is with the Englishman,' said Katharine. 'He returns your affection?'

'He does indeed, Highness.'

'And you wish to marry him?'

'I do, Highness; and his grandfather is willing

that we should marry.'

'The consent of the King of England would be necessary,' said Katharine, 'and of my parents.'

'Maria is thinking,' Maria de Salinas said, 'that if Your Highness wrote to the King and Queen of Spain, telling them that the Earl of Derby is a great English nobleman and his grandson worthy of our Maria, they would readily give their consent.'

'And her dowry also,' put in Katharine. 'You may depend upon it, Maria, that I shall write immediately to my parents and ask them to do what is necessary in the matter.'

'Your Highness is good to me,' murmured Maria gratefully. 'But it will then be necessary to have the consent of the King of England as well.'

'That will easily be obtained,' answered Francesca, 'if the Countess of Richmond is approached first. Her opinion carries more weight with the King of England than anyone else's.'

'You must ask your lover to arrange the English side of the project,' said Katharine. 'As for myself, I will write to my parents without delay.'

Maria de Rojas sank to her knees and taking Katharine's hand kissed it dramatically.

Francesca laughed and Maria de Salinas smiled.

'What a wonderful thing it is to be in love,' cried Francesca. 'How I wish it would happen to me! But there is one thing I should welcome more.'

'And that?' asked Katharine, although she already knew the answer.

'To return home, Highness. To leave this country and go home to Spain.'

'Ah yes,' sighed Katharine. 'Which of us does not feel the same—except Maria, who has a very good reason for wishing to stay here. Prepare my writing table. I will write at once to my parents and ask for their consent.'

Maria de Rojas obeyed with alacrity, and the three maids of honour stood about Katharine's table as she wrote.

'There!' said Katharine. 'It is ready. As soon as the messenger leaves for Spain he shall take this with him among other important documents.'

'None is as important as this, Highness,' cried Maria de Rojas, taking the letter and kissing it.

'So when we leave for Spain we shall leave you behind,' said Katharine. 'We shall miss you, Maria.'

'Your Highness will be so happy to return home—and so will the others—that you will all forget Maria de Rojas.'

'And what will she care?' demanded Francesca. 'She will be happy with her English lord whom she loves well enough to say goodbye to Spain and adopt this country as her own for ever more.'

'That,' answered Katharine soberly, 'is love.'

*   *   *

Dr de Puebla called at Durham House. The Infanta had no wish to see him. She found him quite distasteful, and although she was always pleased to see Ayala the little *marrano* irritated her, and because she knew that he was ridiculed throughout the English Court she felt ashamed of him.

Puebla was well aware of this, but he was not unduly put out; he was accustomed to being scorned and he had an idea that he would remain at his post longer than Don Pedro de Ayala, for the simple reasons that he was more useful to the

Sovereigns and that the King of England believed he was as good a friend as any foreign ambassador could be.

His lawyer's outlook demanded that he know the truth concerning the Infanta's marriage. Whether or not the marriage had been consummated seemed of enormous importance to him because, if it had not been, it would be a far simpler matter to get the dispensation from the Pope. He was determined to find out.

And who would be more likely to know the truth than Katharine's confessor? So when Puebla arrived at Durham House it was not to see Katharine that he came, nor yet Doña Elvira, but Katharine's confessor—Father Alessandro Geraldini.

Geraldini was delighted to be sought out by Puebla. He pretended, with everyone else, to despise the man, but he knew the power of Puebla and he felt, when the ambassador came to see him, that he was becoming of great importance. Had not Torquemada begun as confessor to a Queen? And look what power he had held! Ximenes de Cisneros was another example of a humble Friar who became a great man. Ximenes was reckoned to be the most powerful man in Spain at this time—next to the Sovereigns, of course.

So Geraldini was proud to receive Puebla.

The cunning Puebla was well aware of the feelings of the Friar, and decided to exploit them.

'I would ask your opinion on a very delicate matter,' Puebla began.

'I shall be delighted to give it.'

'It is this matter of the Infanta's marriage. It seems a very strange thing that two young people should be married and not consummate.'

Geraldini nodded.

'As the King forbade consummation it is almost certain that the Infanta would have mentioned in her confessions to her priest if she and her husband had defied the King's wish.'

Geraldini looked wise.

'A confessor is the one confidant to whom it is possible to tell that which one keeps secret from the world. Is that not so?'

'It is indeed so.'

'Therefore if anyone knows what happened on the Infanta's wedding night, that person is most likely to be yourself.' The little priest could not hide the pride which showed in his eyes. 'In the name of the Sovereigns, I ask you to tell me what happened.'

Geraldini hesitated. He knew that if he told the truth and said he did not know, he would cease to be of any importance to Puebla; that was something he could not endure. He wanted to see himself as the Infanta's confidant, as a man destined to play a part in Spanish politics.

'You see,' went on Puebla, noticing the hesitancy, 'if the marriage *was* consummated and this fact was kept hidden the bull of dispensation from the Pope might not be valid. It is necessary to lay all the facts before his Holiness. We must have the truth, and you are the man who can give it. You know the answer. Your peculiar position enables you to have it. I pray you give it to me now.'

As it was more than Geraldini could bear to admit ignorance, why should he not make a guess? The young couple had spent the wedding night together according to custom. Surely they must have consummated their marriage. It was but natural that they should.

Geraldini paused only one second longer, then he leaped.

'The marriage has been consummated,' he said. 'It is likely that it will prove fruitful.'

Puebla left Durham House with all speed. He first despatched a letter to the Sovereigns and then sought out members of the King's Council.

This was what he had hoped. He liked clean-cut facts. If the Infanta carried the heir of England in her womb then there could be no more doubt of her position in Henry's realm.

The belief that the marriage had not been consummated was highly dangerous. It was a matter about which there would continue to be conjecture.

Puebla was therefore very happy to let it be known that Arthur and Katharine had cohabited and that there might be a hope that their relationship would be a fruitful one.

*   *   *

Doña Elvira was holding in her hand a letter which she had taken from a drawer of her table, where a short while before she had hastily placed it.

The courier had left and was now well on his way to the coast with the letters he was carrying from England to Spain.

'And this,' said Elvira to herself, 'will not be one of them.'

She was going to burn it in the flame of a candle as soon as she had shown it to Iñigo, and made him aware that he would have to move faster. He was evidently slow in his courtship if he had allowed Maria de Rojas to prefer this Englishman to himself.

How had the Englishman been in a position to pay court to Maria de Rojas, she would like to know! Clearly there were traitors in the household. She, Doña Elvira Manuel, and she alone, should rule; and if her rule had been absolute, Maria de Rojas would never have exchanged anything but glances with her Englishman.

She suspected three people of seeking to wean Katharine from her. The first was that pernicious little priest, who recently had given himself airs; the second was Don Pedro Ayala whose cynicism and riotous living had earned her disapproval; and of course, like everyone else of noble blood, she disliked Puebla.

She would send for Iñigo. She would show him the letter in Katharine's handwriting, asking for a dowry for Maria de Rojas; and she would have him know that a son of hers must not allow others to get ahead of him.

She called to one of the pages, but even as she did so the door was flung open and her husband Don Pedro Manrique came into the room. He was clearly distraught, and temporarily Doña Elvira forgot Maria de Rojas and her love affair.

'Well,' she demanded, 'what ails you?'

'It is clear that you have not heard this rumour.'

'Rumour! What is this?'

'It concerns the Infanta.'

'Tell me at once,' demanded Doña Elvira, for she expected immediate obedience from her husband as she did from the rest of the household.

'Puebla has told members of the Council that

the marriage was consummated and that there is every hope that the Infanta may be with child.'

'What!' cried Elvira, her face growing purple with rage. 'This is a lie. The Infanta is as virgin as she was the day she was born.'

'So I had believed. But Puebla has told members of the Council that this is not the case. Moreover he has written to the Sovereigns to tell them what, he says, is the true state of affairs.'

'I must see Puebla at once. But first . . . let the courier be stopped. It is a lie he is carrying to the Sovereigns.'

'I will despatch a rider to follow him immediately, but I fear we are too late. Nevertheless I will see what can be done.'

'Hurry then!' Doña Elvira commanded. 'And have Puebla brought to me immediately. I must stop the spread of this lie.'

Her husband retreated in haste, leaving Doña Elvira to pace up and down the apartment.

She was certain that Katharine was still a virgin. She would have known if it had been otherwise. There had been only the wedding night when they had been together, and they were both too young, too inexperienced . . . Besides, the King had made his wishes known.

If what that miserable Puebla was saying was true, if Katharine carried a child within her, then she would no longer be exiled to Durham House; she would be at Court, and that would be the end of the rule of Doña Elvira.

'She *is* a virgin,' she cried aloud. 'Of course she is. I would swear to it. And if necessary there could be an examination.'

Dr Puebla stood before Doña Elvira and her husband. He was a little disturbed by the fury of the woman. She was formidable, and moreover he knew that Queen Isabella regarded her highly.

'I want to know,' she shouted, 'why you have dared to tell this lie to members of the Council here, and write it to the Sovereigns.'

'What lie is this?'

'You have declared that the marriage was consummated. Where were you on the wedding night, Dr de Puebla? Peering through the bed curtains?'

'I have it on good authority that the marriage was consummated, Doña Elvira.'

'On whose authority?'

'On that of the Infanta's confessor.'

'Geraldini!' Elvira spat out the word. 'That upstart!'

'He assured me that the marriage had been consummated and that there was hope of issue.'

'How had he come into possession of such knowledge?'

'Presumably the Infanta had confessed this to him.'

'He lies. One moment.' Elvira turned to her husband. 'Send for Geraldini,' she commanded.

In a few minutes the priest joined them. He was a little pale; like everyone in the household he dreaded the fury of Doña Elvira.

'So,' cried Elvira, 'you have informed Dr de Puebla that the marriage between our Infanta and the Prince of Wales was consummated, and that England may shortly expect an heir.'

Geraldini was silent, his eyes downcast.

'Answer me!' shouted Elvira.

'I . . . I did verily believe . . .'

'You verily believed indeed! You verily guessed. You fool! Do you dare then dabble in matters which are so far above you! You should be in your monastery, babbling your prayers in your lonely cell. Such as you have no place in Court circles. Confess that the Infanta never told you that the marriage was consummated!'

'She . . . she did not tell me, Doña Elvira.'

'Yet you dared tell Dr de Puebla that you knew this to be so!'

'I thought . . .'

'I know! You verily believed. You knew nothing. Get out of my sight before I order you to be whipped. Begone . . . quickly. Idiot! Knave!'

Geraldini was relieved to escape.

As soon as he had gone Elvira turned to Puebla. 'You see what this meddling has done. If you wish to know anything concerning the Infanta, you must come to me. There is only one thing to be done. You agree now that this man Geraldini has led you completely astray?'

'I do,' said Puebla.

'Then you should write to the Sovereigns immediately, telling them that there is no truth in the news contained in your previous document. If you are quick, you may prevent that first letter from reaching their Highnesses. Let us pray that the tides are not favourable for a few hours. Go at once and set right this matter.'

Although Puebla resented her high-handed manner, he could not but agree that he must do as she said; and he was indeed eager to write to the

117

Sovereigns, rectifying his mistake.

He bowed himself out and set about the task immediately.

When she was alone with her husband Doña Elvira sat at her table and began to write. She addressed her letter to Her Highness Queen Isabella, and she told of the mischief Father Alessandro Geraldini had wrought against the Infanta. She added that she believed Don Pedro de Ayala's presence in England to be no longer necessary to the welfare of Spain. She hesitated, considering Puebla. He had been docile enough and ready to admit his mistake. She decided that she might be served worse by any other ambassador the Sovereigns saw fit to send. Too many complaints could give the impression that she was hard to please. If because of this matter she could rid the household of Geraldini she would be satisfied.

As she sealed the letter, she remembered that other letter which had angered her before she heard of Geraldini's gossip.

She took it up and thrust it into her husband's hands.

'Read that,' she said.

He read it. 'But you had decided . . .' he began.

She cut him short. 'I wish Iñigo to see this. Have him brought here immediately, but first have this letter despatched to the Sovereigns. I should like it to reach them if possible before they receive Puebla's.'

Don Pedro Manrique obeyed her as, during their married life, he had grown accustomed to; and in a short time he returned to her with their son.

'Ah, Iñigo,' she said, 'did I not tell you that I had decided a match with Maria de Rojas would be advantageous to you?'

'You did, Mother.'

'Well then, perhaps you would be interested to read this letter which the Infanta has written to her parents. It is a plea that they should give their consent to the marriage of Maria de Rojas with an Englishman and provide her with a dowry.'

'But, Mother, you . . .'

'Read it,' she snapped.

Young Iñigo frowned as he read. He felt himself flushing. It was not that he was so eager for marriage with Maria, but that he feared his mother's wrath, and it seemed as though she were ready to blame him—though he could not quite understand why.

'You have finished it?' She took it from him. 'We must not allow others to step ahead of us and snatch our prizes from under our noses, must we?'

'No, Mother. But she wishes to marry the Englishman, and the Infanta supports her.'

'It would appear so.' Elvira was thoughtful. 'We shall do nothing yet.'

'But in the meantime the Sovereigns may provide the dowry and the consent.'

'Why should they,' said Elvira, 'if they do not know it has been asked for?'

'But it is asked for in the Infanta's letter,' her husband pointed out.

Elvira laughed and held the letter in the flame of the candle.

119

CHAPTER V

THE PASSING OF ELIZABETH OF YORK

The long days of spring and summer passed uneventfully for Katharine. Always she was awaiting the summons to return home.

This did not come, although others had been summoned back to Spain. One was Father Alessandro Geraldini; another was Don Pedro de Ayala.

Doña Elvira had explained their departure to Katharine. Don Pedro de Ayala, she said, was unworthy to represent Spain in England. He led too carnal a life for an ambassador, and a bishop at that. As for Geraldini, he had whispered slander against the Infanta herself, and for such she had demanded his recall.

'Her Highness your mother declares that he is indeed unworthy to remain a member of your household. I thank the saints that I was shown his perfidy in time.'

'What did he say of me?' Katharine wanted to know.

'That you were with child.'

Katharine flushed scarlet at the suggestion, and Elvira felt very confident that, if it should ever come to the point when there must be an examination, her pronouncement would be vindicated.

'I had hoped my mother would send for me,' said Katharine mournfully.

Elvira shook her head. 'My dear Highness, it is

almost certain that there will be another marriage for you in England. Had you forgotten that the King has another son?'

'Henry!' she whispered; and she thought of the bold boy who had led her to the altar where Arthur had been waiting for her.

'And why not?'

'He is but a boy.'

'A little younger than yourself. When he is a little older that will be of small account.'

Henry! Katharine was startled and a little afraid. She wanted to escape from Elvira, to think about this project.

That night she could not sleep. Henry haunted her thoughts and she was not sure whether she was pleased or afraid.

She waited for more news of this, but none came.

It was so difficult to know what was happening at home. There were only fragments of news she heard now and then. The war for Naples, in which her parents were engaged against the King of France, was not going well for them. That, she believed, was why the King of England was hesitating over her betrothal to his son. If the Sovereigns were in difficulties he could make a harsher bargain with them. He did not forget that only half her dowry had been paid.

So the months went by without much news. She found that she had very little money—not even enough to pay her servants. She was worried about Maria's dowry, for there was no news from Spain about this.

The King of England said that she had no right to a third of the property of her late husband, because the second half of her dowry had not been paid. She needed new dresses, but there was no money to buy any. There was her plate and jewels, which represented thirty-five thousand crowns; could she pawn these? She dared not do so because she knew that they had been sent from home as part of her dowry; but if she had no money, what could she do?

There were times when she felt deserted, for she was not allowed to go to Court.

'She is a widow,' said the King of England. 'It is well that she should live in seclusion for a while.'

Henry had his eyes on the Continent. It might be that, as the French seemed likely to score a victory over the Spaniards, a marriage for his son with France or with the House of Maximilian might be more advantageous than one with Spain.

Meanwhile, living in England was the daughter of Isabella and Ferdinand—a Princess, but penniless, a wife but no wife, virtually a hostage for her parents' good behaviour.

It was no concern of his that she suffered poverty, said the King. He could not be expected to pay an allowance to the woman whose dowry had not been paid.

Puebla came to see her, shaking his head sadly. He also had received no money from Spain. It was fortunate that he had other means of making a living in England.

'They are using every *maravedi* for the wars, Highness,' he said. 'We must perforce be patient.'

Katharine sometimes cried herself to sleep when her maids of honour had left her.

'Oh, Mother,' she sobbed, 'what is happening at home? Why do you not send for me? Why do you not bring me out of this . . . prison?'

*   *   *

It was almost Christmas. A whole year, thought Katharine, since she had come to England, and during that time she had married and become a widow; yet it seemed that she had been a prisoner in Durham House for a very long time.

She was not to join the Court at Richmond for the Christmas celebrations: She was a widow, in mourning. Moreover the King of England wished the Spanish Sovereigns to know that he was not showering honours on their daughter, since half her dowry was still owing to him and he was not very eager to make a further alliance with their House.

Maria de Rojas was fretful. 'No news from home?' she was continually demanding. 'How strange that the Queen does not answer your request about my marriage.' Maria was anxious, for shut up in Durham House she had no opportunity of seeing her lover. She wondered what was happening to him and whether he was still eager for the marriage.

Francesca declared that she would go mad if they had to remain in England much longer; even gentle Maria de Salinas was restive.

But the days passed, all so like each other that Katharine almost lost count of time except that she knew that with each passing week she owed the members of her household more and more, and that Christmas was coming and they would have no money for celebrations, for gifts or even to provide a little Christmas cheer for their table.

123

It was in November that Queen Elizabeth came to Durham House to call on Katharine.

Katharine was shocked when she saw Elizabeth, because she had changed a great deal since they had last met. The Queen was far advanced in pregnancy and she did not look healthy.

The Queen wished to be alone with Katharine, and as they sat together near the fire, Elizabeth said: 'It distresses me to see you thus. I have come to tell you how sorry I am, and have brought food for your table. I know how you have been placed.'

'How kind you are!' said Katharine.

The Queen laid her hand over the Infanta's. 'Do not forget you are my daughter.'

'I fear the King does not think of me as such. I am sorry the dowry has not been paid. I am sure my parents would have paid it, if they were not engaged in war at this time.'

'I know, my dear. Wars . . . there seem always to be wars. We are fortunate in England. Here we have a King who likes not war, and I am glad of that. I have seen too much war in my life. But let us talk of more pleasant things. I could wish you were joining the Court for Christmas.'

'We shall do well enough here.'

'I envy you the quiet of Durham House,' said the Queen.

'Tell me when your child is expected.'

'In February.' The Queen shivered. 'The coldest month.'

Katharine looked into the face of the older woman and saw there a resigned look; she wondered what it meant.

'I trust you will have a Prince,' Katharine murmured.

'Pray that I may have a healthy child. I have lost two at an early age. It is so sad when they live a little and then die. So much suffering . . . that one may endure more suffering.'

'You have three healthy children left to you. I have never seen such sparkling health as Henry's.'

'Henry, Margaret and Mary . . . they all enjoy good health, do they not. My life has taught me not to hope for too much. But I did not come to talk of myself, but of you.'

'Of me!'

'Yes, of you. I guessed how you would be feeling. Here you live almost a prisoner, one might say, in a strange country, while plans are made for your future. I understand, for I have not had an easy life. There has been so much strife. I can remember being taken into the Sanctuary of Westminster by my mother. My little brothers were with us then. You have heard that they were lost to us . . . murdered, I dare swear. You see, I have come to tell you that I feel sympathy for you because I myself have suffered.'

'I shall never forget how kind you are.'

'Remember this: suffering does not last for ever. One day you will come out of this prison. You will be happy again. Do not despair. That is what I have come to say to you.'

'And you came through the cold to tell me that?'

'It may be my last opportunity.'

'I hope that I may come and see you when the child is born.'

The Queen smiled faintly and looked a little sad.

'Do not look like that,' Katharine cried out in sudden panic. She was thinking of her sister

Isabella, who had come back to Spain to have her child, the little Miguel who had died before he was two years old. Isabella had had some premonition of death.

She expected some reproof from the Queen for her outburst, but Elizabeth of York, who knew what had happened to the young Isabella, understood full well the trend of her thoughts.

She stood up and kissed Katharine's brow. That kiss was like a last farewell.

*   *   *

It was Candlemas-day and the cold February winds buffeted the walls of the Palace of the Tower of London, although the Queen was unaware of them.

She lay on her bed, racked by pain, telling herself: It will soon be over. And after this, should I live through it, there cannot be many more. If this could be a son . . . if only this could be a son!

Then briefly she wondered how many Queens had lain in these royal apartments and prayed: Let this be a son.

It must be a son, she told herself, for this will be the last.

She was trying to shake off this premonition which had been with her since she knew she was to have another child. If her confinement could have taken place anywhere but in this Tower of London she would have felt happier. She hated the place. Sometimes when she was alone at night she fancied she could hear the voices of her brothers calling her. She wondered then if they called her from some nearby grave.

This was a sign of her weakness. Edward and Richard were dead. Of that she was certain. The manner of their dying could be of little importance to them now. Would they come back to this troublous Earth even if they could? For what purpose? To denounce their uncle as a murderer? To engage in battle against their sister's husband for the crown?

'Edward! Richard!' she whispered. 'Is it true that somewhere within the grey walls of these towers your little bodies lie buried?'

A child was coming into the world. Its mother should not think of the other children—even though they were her own brothers—who had been driven out of it before their time.

Think of pleasant things, she commanded herself: Of rowing down the river with her ladies, with good Lewis Walter, her bargeman, and his merry watermen; think of the Christmas festivities at Richmond. The minstrels and the reciters had been more engaging than usual. She smiled, thinking of her chief minstrel who was always called Marquis Lorydon. What genius! What power to please! And the others—Janyn Marcourse and Richard Denouse—had almost as much talent as Lorydon. Her fool, Patch, had been in great form last Christmas; she had laughed lightheartedly at his antics with Goose, young Henry's fool.

How pleased Henry had been because Goose had shone so brilliantly. It had pleased the boy because his fool was as amusing as those of the King and Queen.

Henry must always be to the fore, she mused. 'Ah well, it is a quality one looks for in a King.'

There had been a pleasant dance too by a Spanish girl from Durham House. Elizabeth had rewarded her with four shillings and fourpence for her performance. The girl had been indeed grateful. Poor child, there were few luxuries at Durham House.

The Queen's face creased into anxiety. Where will it all end? she asked herself. She thought of her son Henry, his eyes glistening with pride because his fool, Goose, could rival the fools of his parents. She thought of the lonely Infanta at Durham House.

The fate of Princes is often a sad one, she was thinking; and then there was no time for further reflection.

The child was about to be born, and there was nothing left for the Queen but her immediate agony.

*   *   *

The ordeal was over, and the child lay in the cradle—a sickly child, but still a child that lived.

The King came to his wife's bedside, and tried not to show his disappointment that she had borne a girl.

'Now we have one son and three bonny girls,' he said. 'And we are young yet.'

The Queen caught her breath in fear. Not again, she thought. I could not endure all that again.

'Yes, we are young,' went on the King. 'You are but thirty-seven, and I am not yet forty-six. We still have time left to us.'

The Queen did not answer that. She merely said: 'Henry, let us call her Katharine.'

128

The King frowned, and she added: 'After my sister.'

'So shall it be,' answered the King. It was well enough to name the child after Elizabeth's sister Katharine, Lady Courtenay, who was after all the daughter of a King. He would not have wished the child to be named Katharine after the Infanta. Ferdinand and Isabella would have thought he was showing more favour to their daughter, and that would not have been advisable.

The bargaining had to go on with regard to their daughter; and he wanted them to know that it was they who must sue for favours now. He was still mourning for that half of the dowry which had not been paid.

He noticed that the Queen looked exhausted and, taking her hand, he kissed it. 'Rest now,' he commanded. 'You must take great care of yourself, you know.'

Indeed I must, she thought meekly. I have suffered months of discomfort and I have produced but a girl. I have to give him sons . . . or die in the attempt.

*   *   *

It was a week after the birth of the child when the Queen became very ill. When her women went into her chamber and found her in a fever they sent a messenger at once to the King's apartments.

Henry in shocked surprise came hurrying to his wife's bedside, for she had seemed to recover from the birth and he had already begun to assure himself that by this time next year she might be brought to bed of a fine boy.

129

When he looked at her he was horrified, and he sent at once for Dr Hallyswurth, his best physician, who most unfortunately was at this time absent from the Court in his residence beyond Gravesend.

All through the day the King waited for the arrival of Dr Hallyswurth, believing that, although other physicians might tell him that the Queen was suffering from a fever highly dangerous after childbirth, Dr Hallyswurth would have the remedy which would save her life.

As soon as the doctor was found and the King's message delivered he set out for the Court, but dusk had fallen when he came, lighted by torches into the precincts of the Tower.

He was taken at once to the Queen's bedchamber, but, even as he took her hand and looked into her face, Elizabeth had begun to fight for her breath and the doctor could only sadly shake his head. A few minutes later Elizabeth sank back on her pillows. The daughter of Edward IV was dead.

Henry stared at her in sorrow. She had been a good wife to him. Where could he have found a better? She was but thirty-seven years of age. This dolorous day, February 11th of the year 1503, was the anniversary of her birth.

'Your Grace,' murmured Dr Hallyswurth, 'there was nothing that could have been done to save her. Her death is due to the virulent fever which often follows childbirth. She was not strong enough to fight it.'

The King nodded. Then he said: 'Leave me now. I would be alone with my grief.'

*   *   *

The bells of St Paul's began to toll; and soon others joined in the dismal honour to the dead, so that all over London the bells proclaimed the death of the Queen.

In the Tower chapel she lay in state. Her body had been wrapped in sixty ells of holland cloth and treated with gums, balms, spices, wax and sweet wine. She had been enclosed by lead and put into a wooden coffin over which had been laid a black velvet pall with a white damask cross on it.

She had been carried into the lying-in-state chamber by four noblemen. Her sister Katharine, the Earl of Surrey and the Lady Elizabeth Stafford led the procession which followed the coffin; and when mass had been said, the coffin remained in the lighted chamber while certain ladies and men-at-arms kept vigil over it.

All through the long night they waited. They thought of her life and her death. How could they help it if they remembered those little boys, her brothers, who had been held in captivity in this very Tower and had been seen no more?

Where did their bodies lie now? Could it be that near this very spot, where their sister lay in state, those two little boys were hidden under some stone, under some stair?

*　　　*　　　*

A week after the death of Queen Elizabeth, the little girl, whose existence had cost the Queen her life, also died.

Here was another blow for the King, but he was not a man to mourn for long. His thoughts were busy on that day when his wife was carried to her tomb.

It was the twelfth day after her death and, after mass had been said, the coffin was placed on a carriage which was covered with black velvet. On the coffin a chair had been set up containing an image of the Queen, exact in size and detail; this figure had been dressed in robes of state and there was a crown on its flowing hair. About the chair knelt her ladies, their heads bowed in grief. Here they remained while the carriage was drawn by six horses from the Tower to Westminster.

The people had lined the streets to see the cortège pass and there were many to speak of the good deeds and graciousness of the dead Queen.

The banners which were carried in the procession were of the Virgin Mary, of the Assumption, of the Salutation and the Nativity, to indicate that the Queen had died in childbirth. The Lord Mayor and the chief citizens, all wearing the deepest mourning, took their places in the procession; and in Fenchurch Street and Cheapside young girls waited to greet the funeral carriage. There were thirty-seven of them—one for each year of the Queen's life; they were dressed in white to indicate their virginity and they all carried lighted tapers.

When the cortège reached Westminster the coffin was taken into the Abbey, ready for the burial which would take place the next morning.

The King asked to be left alone in his apartments. He was genuinely distressed, because he did not believe that he could ever find a consort to compare with the one he had lost. She had had everything to give him—royal lineage, a right to

132

the crown of England, beauty, docility and to some extent fertility.

Yet, there was little time in the life of kings for mourning. He was no longer a young romantic. That was for youth, and should never be for men who were destined for kingship.

He could not prevent his thoughts from going back to the past. He remembered now how, when Edward IV's troops had stormed Pembroke Castle, he had been discovered there, a little boy five years old, with no one to care for him but his old tutor, Philip ap Hoell. He could recall his fear at that moment when he heard the rough tread of soldiers mounting the stairs and knew that his uncle, Jasper Tudor, Earl of Pembroke, had already fled leaving him, his little nephew, to the mercy of his enemies.

Sir William Herbert had been in charge of those operations, and it was well that he had brought his lady with him; for when she saw the friendless little boy she had scolded the men for daring to treat him as a prisoner, and had taken him in her arms and purred over him as though he were a kitten. That had been the strangest experience he had ever known until that time. Philip ap Hoell would have died for him, but their relationship had never been a tender one.

He recalled his life in the Herbert household. Sir William had become the Earl of Pembroke, for the title was taken from Uncle Jasper Tudor and bestowed on Sir William for services rendered to his King.

It had been strange to live in a large family; there were three sons and six daughters in the Herbert home, and one of these was Maud. There had been fighting during his childhood—the

133

continual strife between York and Lancaster; and, when Lancastrian victory brought back the earldom and castle of Pembroke to Jasper Tudor, Henry was taken from the Herberts to live with his uncle once more.

He remembered the day when he had heard that Maud had been married to the Earl of Northumberland. That was a sad day; yet he did not despair; he had never been one to despair; he considered his relationship with Maud, and he was able to tell himself that, although he had loved her dearly, he loved all the Herberts; and if marriage with Maud was denied him he could still be a member of that beloved family by marrying Maud's sister, Katharine.

And then fortune had changed. A more glorious marriage had been hinted at. Why should not the Tudor (hope of the Lancastrian House) marry the daughter of the King, for thus the red and white roses could flower side by side in amity?

He had then begun to know himself. He was no romantic boy—had never been a romantic boy. Had he wished to marry Maud that he might become a member of a family which had always seemed to him the ideal one, because from loneliness he had been taken into it by Lady Herbert and found youthful happiness there? Perhaps, since it had seemed that Katharine would do instead of Maud.

But the match with Elizabeth of York had been too glorious to ignore and he was ready to give up all thoughts of becoming a member of his ideal family, for the sake of a crown.

Life had never been smooth. There had been so many alarms, so many moments when it had seemed that his goal would never be reached. And while he had waited for Elizabeth he had found Katherine Lee, the daughter of one of his attendants—sweet gentle Katherine, who had loved him so truly that she had been ready to give him up when, by doing so, he could be free to marry the daughter of a King.

He was a cold man. He had been faithful to Elizabeth even though Katherine Lee had been one of her maids of honour. He saw her often, yet he had never given a sign that she was any more to him than any other woman of the Palace.

Now Elizabeth was dead, and she left him three children. Only three! He must beget more children. It was imperative.

Forty-six! That is not old. A man can still beget children at forty-six.

But there was little time to lose. He must find a wife quickly. He thought of all the weary negotiations. Time . . . precious time would be lost.

Then an idea struck him. There was a Princess here in England—she was young, personable and healthy enough to bear children.

What time would be saved! Time often meant money, so it was almost as necessary to save the former as the latter.

Why not? She would be agreeable. So would her parents. This half-hearted betrothal to a Prince of eleven—what was that, compared with marriage with a crowned King?

His mind was made up; his next bride would be Katharine of Aragon. The marriage should be arranged as quickly as possible; and then—more sons for England.

The next day Queen Elizabeth was laid in her

135

grave; but the King's thoughts were not with the wife whom he had lost but with the Infanta in Durham House who should take the place of the dead woman.

CHAPTER VI

BAD NEWS FROM SPAIN

Katharine was horrified.

She sat with her maids of honour, staring at the embroidery in her hands, trying in vain to appear calm.

They tried to comfort her.

'He will not live very long,' said the incorrigible Francesca. 'He is old.'

'He could live for twenty years more,' put in Maria de Rojas.

'Not he! Have you not noticed how pale he is ... and has become more so? He is in pain when he walks.'

'That,' Maria de Salinas said, 'is rheumatism, a disease which many suffer from in England.'

'He is such a cold man,' said Francesca.

'Hush,' Maria de Salinas reproved her, 'do you not see that you distress the Infanta? Doubtless he would make a kind husband. At least he was a faithful one to the late Queen.'

Francesca shivered. 'Ugh! I would rather such a man were unfaithful than show me too much attention.'

'I cannot believe that my mother will agree to this match,' Katharine exclaimed anxiously, 'and unless she does, it will never take place.'

Maria de Salinas looked sadly at her mistress. There was no doubt that Queen Isabella loved her daughter and would be happy if she returned to Spain, but she would certainly give her blessing to the marriage if she considered it advantageous to Spain. Poor Infanta! A virgin widow preserved for an ageing man, whose rheumatism often made him irritable; a cold, dour man, who wanted her only because he wanted to keep a firm hand on her dowry and believed that she could give him sons.

* * *

There was no news from Spain. Each day, tense and eager, Katharine waited.

She knew that the affairs of her parents must be in dire disorder for them so to neglect their daughter. If only they would send for her. If she could sail back to Spain the treacherous seas would have no menace for her. She would be completely happy.

Never, she believed, had anyone longed for home as she did now.

Maria de Rojas was restive. Why did she never hear from the Sovereigns about their consent to her marriage? Why was there no reply regarding her dowry? Katharine had written again because she feared her first letter might not have reached her mother; but still there was no reply to the questions.

Francesca gave loud voice to her grievances; Maria was filled with melancholy. Only Maria de Salinas and Inez de Veñegas alternately soothed and scolded them. *They* were unhappy, but what of the Infanta? How much harder was her lot. Imagine, it might well be that she would have to submit to the will of the old King of England.

* * *

At last came the news from Spain. Katharine saw the messengers arrive with the despatches and had them brought to her immediately.

Her mother wrote as affectionately as ever, and the very sight of that beloved handwriting made the longing for home more intense.

Isabella did not wish her daughter to marry the King of England. She was eager for a match between Katharine and the young Prince of Wales. She was writing to the King of England suggesting that he look elsewhere for a bride.

Katharine felt limp with relief, as though she had been reprieved from a terrible fate.

Unless some satisfactory arrangement could be made for Katharine's future in England, Isabella wrote, she would demand that her daughter be returned to Spain.

This made Katharine almost dizzy with happiness and, when her maids of honour came to her, they found her sitting at her table smiling dazedly at the letter before her.

'I am not to marry him,' she announced.

Then they all forgot the dignity due to an Infanta and fell upon her, hugging and kissing her.

At last Maria de Rojas said: 'Does she give her consent to *my* marriage?'

'Alas,' Katharine told her, 'there is no mention of it.'

*   *   *

Henry sat for a long time listening to Puebla's account of his instructions from Spain. So the Sovereigns did not want him for a son-in-law. He

139

read between the lines. They would be delighted if their daughter became the Queen of England, but he was old and she was young; they believed that he could not live for a great number of years and, when he died, she would be merely the Dowager Queen, who would play no part in state affairs. Moreover even as Queen, she would have no power, for Henry was not the man to allow a young wife to share in his counsels.

Isabella was emphatic in her refusal of this match.

'Her Highness,' Puebla told the King, 'suggests that it might be well if the Infanta returned to Spain.'

This was high-handed indeed. Henry had no wish to send the Infanta back to Spain. With their daughter living in semi-retirement in England he had some hold over the Sovereigns. He wanted the rest of her dowry, and he was determined to get it.

'These are matters not to be resolved in an hour,' replied Henry evasively.

'Her Highness suggests that, since you are looking for a wife, the Queen of Naples, now widowed, might very well suit you.'

'The Queen of Naples!' Henry's eyes were momentarily narrowed. It was not a suggestion to be ignored. Such a marriage should give him a stake in Europe; so if the widow were young and handsome and likely to bear children, she would be a good match; and Henry, ever conscious of his age, was eager to marry soon.

He therefore decided to send an embassy to Naples immediately.

It was rather soon after his wife's death and he did not wish to appear over-eager.

Puebla was whispering: 'The Infanta might write a letter to the Queen of Naples, to be delivered into her hands and hers alone. This would give some messenger on whom you could rely the opportunity of looking closely at the Queen.'

Henry looked with friendship on the Spaniard who had ever seemed a good friend to him.

It was an excellent idea.

'Tell her to write this letter at once,' he said. 'You will find me a messenger on whom I can rely. I wish to know whether she be plump or lean, whether her teeth be white or black and her breath sweet or sour.'

'If Your Grace will leave this matter with me I will see that you have a description of the lady which shall not prove false. And, Your Grace, you will remember that it is the hope of the Sovereigns that there should be a betrothal between their daughter and the Prince of Wales.'

'The Prince of Wales is one of the most eligible bachelors in the world.'

'And therefore, Your Grace, well matched to the Infanta of Spain.'

Henry looked grave. 'The wars in Europe would seem to be going more favourably for the French than the Spaniards. It might be well if the Infanta did return to Spain.'

Puebla shook his head. 'If she returned, the Sovereigns would expect you to return with her the hundred thousand crowns which constituted half of her dowry.'

'I see no reason why I should do that.'

'If you did not, Your Grace, you would have a very powerful enemy in the Sovereigns. Where are your friends in Europe? Do you trust the French?

And who in Europe trusts Maximilian?'

Henry was silent for a few moments. But he saw the wisdom of Puebla's advice.

He said: 'I will consider this matter.'

Puebla was jubilant. He knew that he had won his point. He would soon be writing to the Sovereigns to tell them that he had arranged for the betrothal of their daughter with the Prince of Wales.

*   *   *

Prince Henry came in, hot from the tennis court. With him were his attendants, boys of his own age and older men, all admiring, all ready to tell him that they had never seen tennis played as he played it.

He could never have enough of their praises and, although he knew they were flattery, he did not care. Such flattery was sweet, for it meant they understood his power.

Each day when he awoke—and he awoke with the dawn—he would remember that he was now his father's only son and that one day there would be a crown on his head.

It was right and fitting that he should wear that crown. Was he not a good head taller than most of his friends? It was his secret boast that, if anyone had not known that he was the King's heir, they would have selected him from any group as a natural leader.

It could not be long before he was King. His father was not a young man. And how he had aged since the death of the Queen! He was in continual pain from his rheumatism and was sometimes bent double with it. He was growing more and more irritable and Henry knew that many were longing for the day when there would be a new King on the throne—young, merry, extravagant, all that the old King was not.

Henry had no sympathy for his father, because he who had never felt a pain in his life could not understand pain. The physical disabilities of others interested him only because they called attention to his own superb physique and health.

Life was good. It always had been. But during Arthur's life-time there had been that gnawing resentment because he was not the firstborn.

He made his way now from the tennis court to the apartments of his sister Margaret. He found her there and her eyes were red from weeping. Poor Margaret! She was not the domineering elder sister today. He did feel a little sorry. He would miss her sorely.

'So tomorrow you leave us,' he said. 'It will be strange not to have you here.'

Margaret's answer was to put her arms about him and hug him tightly.

'Scotland!' she whimpered. 'It is so cold there, I hear. The castles are so draughty.'

'They are draughty here,' Henry reminded her.

'There they are doubly so. And how shall I like my husband, and how will he like me?'

'You will rule him, I doubt not.'

'I hear he leads a most irregular life and has many mistresses.'

Henry laughed. 'He is a King, if it is only King of Scotland. He should have mistresses if he wishes.'

'He shall not have them when he has a wife,' cried Margaret fiercely.

'You will make sure of that, I'll swear. So there will only be one sister left to me now. And Mary is little more than a baby.'

'Always look after her, Henry. She is wayward and will need your care.'

'She will be my subject and I shall look after all my subjects.'

'You are not yet King, Henry.'

'No,' he murmured reflectively, 'not yet.'

'I wish that the Infanta might be with us. It is sad to think of her in Durham House, cut off from us all. I should have liked to have had a sister of my own age to talk to. There would have been so much for us to discuss together.'

'She could tell you little of the married state,' said Henry. 'Unless rumour lies, our brother never knew his wife. What a strange marriage that was!'

'Poor Katharine! I suffer for her. She felt as I feel now. To leave one's home . . . to go to a strange country . . .'

'I doubt your James will be as mild as our brother Arthur.'

'No, it may be that he will be more like my brother Henry.'

Henry looked at his sister through narrowed eyes.

'They say,' went on Margaret, 'that Katharine is to be *your* bride.'

'I have heard it.'

He was smiling. Margaret thought: He must have everything. Others marry, so he must marry. Already he seems to be contemplating his enjoyment of his bride.

'Well, what are you thinking?' Henry asked.

'If you are like this at twelve, what will you be at

144

eighteen?'

Henry laughed aloud. 'Much taller. I shall be the tallest English King. I shall stand over six feet. I shall outride all my subjects. I shall be recognised wherever I go as the King of England.'

'You do it as much as ever,' she said.

'What is that?'

'Begin every sentence with *I*.'

'And why should I not? Am I not to be the King?'

He was half laughing, but half in earnest. Margaret felt a new rush of sadness. She wished that she need not go to Scotland, that she could stay here in London and see this brother of hers mount the throne.

*　　　*　　　*

Puebla brought the news to Katharine. The little man was delighted. It seemed to him that what he had continued to work for during many difficult months was at last achieved. In his opinion there was only one way out of the Infanta's predicament: marriage with the heir of England.

'Your Highness, I have at last prevailed upon the King to agree to your betrothal to the Prince of Wales.'

There had been many occasions when Katharine had considered this possibility, but now she was face to face with it and she realised how deeply it disturbed her.

She had at once to abandon all hope of returning home to Spain. She remembered too that she had been the wife of young Henry's brother, and she felt therefore that the relationship

145

between herself and Henry was too close. Moreover she was eighteen years old, Henry was twelve. Was not the disparity in their ages a little too great?

Yet were these the real reasons? Was she a little afraid of that arrogant, flamboyant Prince?

'When is this to take place?' she asked.

'The formal betrothal will be celebrated in the house of the Bishop of Salisbury in the near future.'

Katharine said quickly: 'But I have been his brother's wife. The affinity between us is too close.'

'The Pope will not withhold the Bull of Dispensation.'

There was no way out, Katharine realised, as she dismissed Puebla and went to her own apartment. She wanted to think of this alone, and not share it even with her maids of honour as yet.

She had escaped the father to fall to the son. She was certain that the King filled her with repugnance, but her feelings for young Henry were more difficult to analyse. The boy fascinated her as he seemed to fascinate everyone. But he was too bold, too arrogant.

He is only a boy, she told herself; and I am already a woman.

There came to her then an intense desire to escape, and impulsively she went to her table and sat down to write. This time she would write to her father, for she was sure of her mother's support, and if she could move his heart, if she could bring him to ask her mother that she might return, Isabella would give way immediately.

How difficult it was to express these vague fears.

She had never been able to express her emotions. Perhaps it was because she had always been taught to suppress them.

The words on the paper looked cold, without any great feeling.

'I have no inclination for a second marriage in England . . .'

She sat for some time staring at the words. Of what importance were her inclinations? She could almost hear her mother's voice, gentle yet firm: 'Have you forgotten, my dearest, that it is the duty of the daughters of Spain to subdue their own desires for the good of their country?'

What was the use? There was nothing to be done. She must steel herself, become resigned. She must serenely accept the fate which was thrust upon her.

She continued the letter:

'But I beg you do not consider my tastes or convenience, but in all things act as you think best.'

Then firmly she sealed the letter and, when her maids of honour came to her, she was still sitting with it in her hands.

She turned to them and spoke as though she were awakening from a dream. 'I shall never again see my home, never again see my mother.'

*　　　*　　　*

The hot June sun beat down on the walls of the Bishop's house in Fleet Street.

Inside that house Katharine of Aragon stood beside Henry, Prince of Wales, and was formally betrothed to him.

Katharine was thinking: It is irrevocable. When

147

this boy is fifteen years old, I shall be past twenty. Can such a marriage be a happy one?

Henry studied his fiancée and was aware that she was not overjoyed at the prospect of their marriage. He was astounded, and this astonishment quickly turned to anger. How dared she not be overjoyed at the prospect! Here he was, the most handsome, the most popular and talented of Princes. Surely any woman should be overjoyed to contemplate marriage with him.

He thought of some of the girls he had seen about the Court. They were a constant provocation; they were very eager to please him and delighted when he noticed them. John Skelton was amused at such adventures, implying that they were worthy of a virile Prince. And this woman, who was not outstandingly beautiful, who had been his brother's wife, dared to appear doubtful.

Henry looked at her coldly; when he took her hand he gave it no warm pressure; his small eyes were like pieces of flint; they had lost something of their deep blueness and were the colour of the sea when a storm is brewing.

He was annoyed that he must go through with the betrothal. He wanted to snatch his hand away and say: 'You do not care to marry me, Madam. Well, rest assured that affects me little. There are many Princesses in the world who would count you fortunate, but since you are blind to the advantage which is yours, let us have no betrothal.'

But there was his father, stern, pale, with the lines of pain etched on his face, and while he lived Prince Henry was only Prince of Wales, not King of England. It was doubly humiliating to realise that he dared not flout his father's orders.

As for the King, he watched the betrothal with satisfaction. He was to keep the hundred thousand crowns which he had already received as the first payment of Katharine's dowry and another hundred thousand crowns would be paid on her marriage. Meanwhile she would receive nothing of that third of the revenues of Wales, Chester and Cornwall, which was her right on her marriage to Arthur; although when she married Henry she would receive a sum equal to that.

This was very satisfactory, mused the King. Katharine would remain in England; he would keep the first half of the dowry; she would not receive the revenues due to her; and the betrothal was merely a promise that she should marry the heir to England; so that if the King should change his mind about that before the Prince reached his fifteenth birthday—well, it would not be the first time that a Prince and Princess had undergone a betrothal ceremony which was not followed by a wedding.

Yes, very satisfactory. Thus he could keep what he had, maintain a truce with the Sovereigns of Spain, and shelve the marriage for a few years.

Now he was only waiting to hear from Naples. His own marriage was of more urgency than that of his son.

Out into the June sunshine of Fleet Street came a satisfied King, a sullen Prince and an apprehensive Princess.

*　　　*　　　*

Now that Katharine was formally betrothed to the Prince of Wales, she could not be allowed to live in

149

seclusion at Durham House, and life became more interesting for her.

The maids of honour were delighted by the turn of events because it meant that now they could go occasionally to Court. There was activity in their apartments as they hastily reviewed their wardrobes and bewailed the fact that their gowns were shabby and not of the latest fashion.

Katharine was upset. Badly she needed money. Her parents had written that they could send her nothing, because they needed everything they could lay their hands on to prosecute the war, and military events were not going well for Spain. Katharine must rely on the bounty of her father-in-law.

It had been uncomfortable having to rely on the bounty of a miser. And it was the fact that she was unable to pay her servants that had upset Katharine most.

But now that she was betrothed to his son, the King could no longer allow her to live in penury, and grudgingly he made her an allowance. This was a relief, but as it was necessary to maintain a large household, and debts had been steadily mounting, the allowance was quickly swallowed up, and although the situation was relieved considerably, comparative poverty still prevailed at Durham House.

Doña Elvira was the only one who resented the change. She was jealous of her power and was becoming anxious to settle the matter of Maria de Rojas and Iñigo.

It was all very well to prevent letters, concerning Maria's hoped-for marriage to the grandson of the Earl of Derby, from reaching the Sovereigns, but this was not arranging a match between Maria and Iñigo.

She had given Iñigo full power over the pages and he was continually seeking the company of the maids of honour—Maria de Rojas in particular. He was not popular however and Hernan Duque complained of his insolent manner.

This infuriated Elvira, who promptly wrote off to Isabella declaring that, if she were to be responsible for the Infanta's household, she could not have interference from their Highnesses' ambassadors and envoys.

Isabella, who put complete trust in Elvira as her daughter's guardian, wrote reprovingly to Hernan Duque; and this so delighted Elvira that she became more domineering than ever.

Katharine was growing weary of Elvira's rule. She was no longer a child and she felt that it was time that she herself took charge of her own household. She began by commanding Juan de Cuero to hand over some of her plate and jewels, which she pawned in order to pay her servants' wages.

When Elvira heard of this she protested, but Katharine was determined to have her way in this matter.

'These are my jewels and plate,' she said. 'I shall do with them as I will.'

'But they are part of the dowry which you will bring to your husband.'

'I will use them instead of the revenues I was to have received from my late husband,' answered Katharine. 'The jewels and plate will not be needed until I am married to the Prince of Wales. Then I shall receive an amount similar to that which I have had to renounce. I shall redeem the jewels with that.'

Doña Elvira could not believe that her hold on Katharine was slackening, nor that it was possible for her to be defeated in any way.

So she continued, as determined as ever to govern the household, not realising that Katharine was growing up.

*　　　*　　　*

Katharine found Maria de Rojas in a state of despondency.

'What ails you, Maria?'

Maria blurted out that she had met her lover at the Court and that he was less ardent.

'What could one expect?' demanded Maria. 'All this time we have waited, and your mother ignores your requests on my behalf.'

'It seems so very strange to me,' said Katharine. 'It is unlike her to ignore such a matter, for she would clearly see it as her duty to look to the welfare of my attendants.'

Katharine pondering the matter remembered that Iñigo was hoping for Maria, and that Doña Elvira approved of his choice. That was certain, for he would never have dared show it if that had not been so.

Katharine said slowly: 'I will write to my mother again, and this time I will send the letter by a secret messenger—not through the usual channels. It has occurred to me, Maria, that something—or someone—may have prevented my mother from receiving those letters.'

Maria lifted her head and stared at her mistress.

Understanding dawned in Maria's eyes.

*   *   *

The letter was written; the secret messenger was found. A few days after he had left—far too soon to hope for a reply to that letter—Katharine, seated at her window, saw a courier arrive and knew that he brought despatches from Spain.

It was six months since her betrothal to Henry in the Bishop of Salisbury's house in Fleet Street, and now that she had become accustomed to the idea that she must marry young Henry she had come to terms with life. The slight relief which the new turn of affairs had brought to her living standards was welcome, and life was far more tolerable.

She found that she could speak English fairly fluently now, and as she grew accustomed to her country of adoption she was even growing fond of it.

News from Spain always made her heart leap with hope and fear; and this message was obviously an important one. There was an urgency about the courier as he leaped from his saddle and, not even glancing at the groom who took his horse, hurried into the house.

She did not wait for him to be brought to her, but went down to meet him. She was determined now that letters should come direct to her, and that they should not first pass through the hands of Doña Elvira.

She came into the hall and saw the courier standing there. Doña Elvira was already there. The courier looked stricken, and when she saw that Doña Elvira had begun to weep, a terrible anxiety

153

came to Katharine.

'What has happened?' she demanded.

The courier opened his mouth as though he were trying to speak but could not find the words. Doña Elvira was holding a kerchief to her eyes.

'Tell me . . . quickly!' cried Katharine.

It was Doña Elvira who spoke. She lowered her kerchief and Katharine saw that her face was blotched with tears, and that this was no assumed grief.

'Your Highness,' she began. 'Oh . . . my dearest Highness . . . this is the most terrible calamity which could befall us. How can I tell you . . . knowing what she meant to you? How can I be the one?'

Katharine heard her own voice speaking; she whispered: 'Not . . . my mother!'

There was no answer, so she knew it was so. This was indeed the greatest calamity.

'She is sick? She is ill? She has been sick for so long. If she had not been sick . . . life would have been different here. She would never have allowed . . .'

She was talking . . . talking to hold off the news she feared to hear.

Doña Elvira had recovered herself. She said: 'Highness, come to your apartment. I will look after you there.'

'My mother . . .' said Katharine. 'She is . . .'

'God rest her soul!' murmured Elvira. 'She was a saint. There will be rejoicing in Heaven.'

'It is so then?' said Katharine piteously. She was like a child pleading: Tell me it is not so. Tell me that she is ill . . . that she will recover. What can I do if *she* is not there? She has always been there

154

. . . even though we were parted. How can I live with the knowledge that she is gone . . . that she is dead?

'She has passed peacefully to her rest,' said Doña Elvira. 'Her care for you was evident right at the end. The last thing she did was to have the Bull of Dispensation brought to her. She knew before she died that an affinity with Arthur could not stand in the way of your marriage with Henry. She satisfied herself that your future was assured and then . . . she made her will and lay down to die.'

Katharine turned away, but Elvira was beside her.

'Leave me,' said Katharine. 'I wish to be alone.'

Elvira did not insist and Katharine went to her room. She lay on her bed and drew the curtains so that she felt shut in with her grief.

'She has gone,' she said to herself. 'I have lost the dearest friend I ever had. No one will ever take her place. Oh God, how can I endure to stay in a world where she is not?'

Then she seemed to hear that voice reproving her—stern yet kind, so serene, so understanding always. 'When your time comes, my daughter, you will be taken to your rest. Until that time you must bear the tribulations which God sees fit to lay upon you. Bear them nobly, Catalina, my dear one, because that is what I would have you do.'

'I will do all that you wish me to,' said Katharine.

Then she closed her eyes and began to pray, pray for courage to bear whatever life had to offer her, courage to live in a world which no longer contained Isabella of Castile.

Chapter VII

MARIA DE ROJAS

The King of England was furious.

His envoy had returned from Naples with reports that the Queen of Naples was plump and comely; she had remarkably beautiful eyes and her breath was sweet.

Henry cared nothing for this, since he had discovered that the Queen of Naples had no claim whatsoever on the crown of Naples and was nothing more than a pensioner of Ferdinand.

He had been deceived. The Sovereigns had tried to trick him into marriage. Much valuable time had been lost and he was no nearer to getting himself sons than he had been at the time of his wife's death.

One could not trust Ferdinand. There was not a more crafty statesman in the whole of Europe.

Moreover what was Ferdinand's position since the death of Isabella? All knew that the senior in the partnership had been the Queen of Castile. What was Aragon compared with Castile? And although the marriage of the Sovereigns had united Spain the Castilians were not prepared to accept Ferdinand as their King now that Isabella was dead.

Isabella's daughter Juana had been declared heiress of Castile, which meant that her husband Philip was the King. He was in a similar position to that which Ferdinand had occupied with Isabella. And Ferdinand? He was merely relegated to be

King of Aragon . . . a very different rank from King of Spain.

Ferdinand was sly; he was unreliable. He would feel little anxiety concerning his daughter in England. All that had come from Isabella.

There was another matter which had upset the King of England. He had made a treaty with the Spanish Sovereigns to the effect that English sailors should have the freedom of Spanish ports and that they should be able to do business there on the same terms as Spaniards. He had just received news from certain merchants and sailors that this agreement had not been respected, and that they who had gone to Seville in good faith had found the old restrictions of trading brought against them, so that, unprepared as they were, they had suffered great losses.

'So this,' Henry had said, 'is the way Ferdinand of Aragon keeps his promises.'

He sent for Puebla, and demanded an explanation.

Puebla had none. He was bewildered. He would write with all speed to Ferdinand, he had said, and there should be just restitution for the Englishmen.

This he had done, but Ferdinand was in no position to refund what had been lost. His authority in Castile was wavering and he was deeply concerned about the accession of his daughter Juana, for he feared the duplicity of her husband.

'And here am I,' raged the King, 'giving an allowance to Ferdinand's daughter. It shall be immediately stopped.'

His eyes were speculative. Was the daughter of the King of Aragon such a prize? Was she worthy to mate with one of the most desirable *partis* in Europe?

Maximilian might be unreliable, but then so was Ferdinand; and as events were turning out it seemed that very soon the Hapsburgs would be the most influential family in Europe. Young Charles, the son of Juana and Philip, would be heir not only to Isabella and Ferdinand but to his paternal grandfather's dominions. Surely the greatest catch in Europe was little Charles.

His aunt Margaret, Maximilian's daughter, had married the heir of Ferdinand and Isabella—Juan, who had died a few months after the marriage, and had again become a widow on the decease of the Duke of Savoy.

Henry began to consider an alliance with the Hapsburgs. Margaret for himself; she was both comely and rich. Young Charles for his daughter Mary; and Eleanor, daughter of Juana and Philip, for Henry Prince of Wales. His betrothal to Katharine of Aragon? What of that? Isabella of Castile was dead, and what did he care for Ferdinand, now merely King of Aragon, who was almost certain to find trouble with his son-in-law Philip and his daughter Juana when they came to claim the crown of Castile!

Henry had made up his mind. He sent for a certain Dr Savage, a man in whose ability he believed.

He said to him: 'I want you to prepare to leave for the Court of Brussels. Don Pedro de Ayala is the Spanish ambassador at that Court and I believe him to be well disposed towards me, for we became friends during his term in England. I wish you to make it known to the Archduke Philip that I seek his friendship. As for his Archduchess, now Queen Juana of Castile, you need only to win her husband's friendship to make sure of hers. Ayala will help you, I am sure.'

Henry then began to lay before Dr Savage his plans for an alliance between his family and the Hapsburgs.

'Proceed,' he said, 'with all speed, for although my son and daughter can wait for their partners, there is not a great deal of time left to me. Do your work well and I doubt not that before long the Duchess Margaret will be on her way to England.'

Dr Savage declared his desire to serve his King in all ways.

He would prepare to leave for Brussels at once.

*   *   *

How different had life at Durham House become!

Katharine's presence was no longer required at Court; there was no money coming in; poverty and boredom had returned.

The maids of honour grumbled together and despaired of ever returning to Spain. They used their jewelled brooches to pin their torn gowns together; their food consisted of stale fish and what little could be bought at the lowest prices in the street markets. It was small consolation that such food was served on plates of gold and silver.

Katharine rarely saw the Prince to whom she was supposed to be affianced; she heard gossip that he was going to marry her little niece, Eleanor. Life was even worse than it had been in previous times of neglect, because then she could always write to her mother.

In desperation she wrote to Ferdinand.

'I pray you remember that I am your daughter. For the love of our Lord help me in my need. I have no money to buy chemises of which I am in great need. I have had to sell some of my jewels to buy myself a gown. I have had but two dresses since I left Spain, for I have been wearing those which I brought with me. But I have very few left and I do not know what will become of me and my servants unless someone helps me.'

Ferdinand ignored such pleas. He had too many troubles of his own to think about his daughter's chemises.

So the weeks passed.

Dr Savage made little progress in Brussels; this was largely because of circumstances which were unknown to Henry. Since Isabella's death there had arisen certain factions which were determined to oust Ferdinand from Castile; and at the Court of Brussels there were two rival factions from Spain, one working for Ferdinand, one for Philip, his son-in-law. The head of Philip's faction was Juan Manuel, brother of Doña Elvira, who had worked for the Sovereigns when Isabella was alive because of his admiration for the Queen. He had never admired Ferdinand; and now that the Queen was dead he was determined to force him out of Castile by supporting his son-in-law, Philip. Ferdinand's supporters were his ambassador to Brussels, Don Gutierre Gomez de Fuensalida, and Don Pedro de Ayala. Ayala, to whom Dr Savage presented himself, was certainly not going to bring Philip and the doctor together, because an alliance between Philip and England would be to Ferdinand's detriment.

Thus, although Ayala received Dr Savage with a show of friendship, he was secretly working all the time to avoid bringing the doctor to Philip's notice. Negotiations hung fire, and this was very irritating to the English King, who knew little of the intricacies of politics at the Brussels Court.

The delays did not endear his daughter-in-law to him, and as his rheumatism was growing gradually more painful he became more irascible than ever and quite indifferent to the hardship which Katharine was suffering.

Katharine began to pawn more and more of her jewels, and she knew that when the time came for them to be valued and handed over to the King, as part of her dowry, they would be very much depleted. But what could she do? Her household had to eat even if they had received no payment for many months.

The entire household was becoming fretful, and one day Katharine came upon Maria de Rojas sobbing in distress, so deep that it was some time before Katharine could understand what had happened.

At length the sad little story was wrung from Maria.

'I have had news that he has married someone else.'

'My poor Maria!' Katharine sought to comfort the forlorn maid of honour. 'But since he could not remain faithful, surely he would have made a bad husband.'

'It was all the waiting,' cried Maria. 'His family insisted. They believed we should never have the consent of the Sovereigns and that there would be no dowry. Why, only half of your own was paid,

161

and consider the poverty in which your father allows you to live!'

Katharine sighed.

'Sometimes,' she said, 'I wonder what will become of us all.'

Maria continued to weep.

*   *   *

It was a few days later when Doña Elvira called Maria de Rojas to her.

Maria, who had been listless since she had heard the news of her lover's marriage, was not apprehensive as she would ordinarily have been by a summons from Doña Elvira. She simply did not care. Whatever Doña Elvira did to her, she said to Maria de Salinas, whatever punishment she sought to inflict, she would not care. Nothing could hurt her now.

With Doña Elvira was her son, Iñigo, who looked sheepishly at Maria as she entered.

Maria ignored him.

'Ah, Maria,' said Doña Elvira smiling, 'I have some good news for you.'

Maria lifted her leaden eyes to Elvira's face, but she did not ask what the good news was.

'You poor girl!' went on Elvira. 'If the Prince of Wales had not died, good matches would have been found for all of you. You must have suffered great anxiety as to your future.'

Maria was still silent.

'You however are going to be very fortunate. My son here wishes to marry you. His father and I are agreeable to this match. I see no reason to delay.'

Maria spoke then, recklessly, for the first time in

her life not caring what Doña Elvira could do to her: 'I do not wish to marry your son, Doña Elvira,' she said.

'What!' screeched the duenna. 'Do you realise what you are saying?'

'I am perfectly aware of what I am saying. I mean it. I wished to marry but was prevented from doing so. Now I do not wish to marry.'

'You wished to marry!' cried Elvira. 'You persuaded the Infanta to plead with the Sovereigns for their consent and a dowry. And what happened, eh? Did you get that consent? I have seen no dowry.'

Elvira was smiling so malevolently that Maria suddenly understood. Did not Elvira see all the letters which were despatched to the Sovereigns? Katharine must have realised this, because that last letter she wrote—and she must have written it at the very time when Isabella lay dying—was to have been delivered by a secret messenger, which meant, of course, that it should not pass through Elvira's hands.

Maria knew then that this woman had wrecked her hopes of happiness; she hated her, and made no attempt to control her emotion.

'So it was you,' she cried. 'You have done this. They would have given what I asked. I should have married by now, but you . . . you . . .'

'I fear,' said Doña Elvira quietly, 'that this cannot be Maria de Rojas, maid of honour to the Infanta. It must be some gipsy hoyden who looks like her.'

Iñigo was looking at Maria with big pleading eyes; his look was tender and he was imploring her: Maria be calm. Have you forgotten that this is my mother, whom everyone has to obey?

Maria gave him a scornful look and cried out in anguish: 'How could you do this, you wicked woman? I hate you. I tell you I hate you and will never marry your stupid son.'

Doña Elvira, genuinely shocked, gripped Maria by the shoulders and forced her on to her knees. She took her long dark hair and, pulling it, jerked the girl's head backwards.

'You insolent little fool,' she hissed. 'I will show you what happens to those who defy me.' She turned to Iñigo. 'Do not stand there staring. Go and get help. Call my servants. Tell them to come here at once.'

She shook Maria, whose sobs were now choking her and, when her servants came, Doña Elvira cried: 'Take this girl into the ante-room. Lock the door on her. I will decide what is to be done with her.'

They carried the sobbing Maria away, and Elvira, her mouth firm, her eyes glittering, said to her son: 'Have no fear. The girl shall be your wife. I know how to make her obedient.'

Iñigo was shaken. It had hurt him to see Maria so ill treated. He was certain that she would be his wife, because his mother had said she would, and whatever Doña Elvira decreed came to pass.

*   *   *

Katharine was deeply disturbed by what had happened to Maria de Rojas. Doña Elvira had kept her locked away from the other maids of honour, and they all knew that Doña Elvira was determined that Maria should be forced to accept

164

Iñigo as her betrothed.

Katharine considered this matter and asked herself why she allowed her household to be dominated by Doña Elvira. Was she herself not its head?

She remembered her parting from her mother. She could almost hear that firm voice warning her: 'Obey Doña Elvira in all things, my dearest. She is a strong woman and a wise one. Sometimes she may seem harsh, but all that she does will be for your good. Always remember that I trust her and I chose her to be your duenna.'

Because of that Katharine had always sought to obey Doña Elvira, and whenever she had felt tempted to do otherwise she remembered her mother's words. But what duplicity Elvira had used in not allowing Katharine's requests on Maria's behalf to reach Isabella!

Katharine asked Elvira to come to her apartment and, as soon as the duenna entered, saw that her mouth was set and determined and that she was going to do fierce battle in this matter of Maria's marriage.

'You have removed my maid of honour from my service,' Katharine began.

'Because, Highness, she has behaved in a most undignified manner, a manner of which your dear mother would heartily disapprove.'

That was true. If Maria had sobbed and wept and declared her hatred of Elvira, as Katharine had heard she had, Isabella would certainly have disapproved.

'Doña Elvira, I wrote some letters to my mother and I believe she never received them.'

'Storms at sea,' murmured Elvira. 'It invariably

happens that some letters do not reach their destination. If I wish to send important news I send two couriers, and not together. Did you take this precaution?'

Katharine looked boldly into the face of her duenna. 'I believe these letters never left this house.'

'That is an accusation, Highness.'

'I meant it to be.'

'Your mother put me in charge of your household, Highness. I never forget that. If I believe that I should sometimes act boldly on any matter, I do so.'

'Even to destroying letters which were meant for my mother?'

'Even to that, Highness.'

'So you were determined that Maria should marry Iñigo, and not the man of her choice.'

'Indeed that is so, Highness. She wished to marry an Englishman. There are many matters which are hidden from Your Highness. It is only seemly that it should be so. Your mother instructed me that I must be careful of those who would spy against you. I must not too readily trust the English. What an excellent opportunity for spying an Englishman would have if he were married to one of your own maids of honour!'

'But this was not a case of spying. They loved . . .'

'So dearly did he love her that he married someone else . . . not so long after plighting his troth to her.'

'They were kept apart.'

'And this great love could not endure against a little absence? Nay, Highness, trust your duenna, as your mother did. Always remember that it was

166

our dearest Queen who put me in this position of trust. She will be looking down from her place in Heaven now—for who can doubt that such a saint is now in Heaven?—and she is imploring me—can you not sense her? I can—she is imploring me to stand firm, and you to understand that all I do is for your good.'

Any mention of her mother unnerved Katharine. Merely to say or hear her name brought back so clearly an image of that dear presence that she could feel nothing but her bitter loss.

Doña Elvira saw the tears in Katharine's eyes; she seized her opportunity: 'Come, Highness, let me take you back to your apartments. You should lie down. You have not recovered from the terrible shock of her death. Who of us have? Do not distress yourself about the love affairs of a lighthearted maid of honour. Trust me . . . as *she* always wished you to.'

Katharine allowed herself to be led to her apartments, and there she lay on her bed continuing to think of her mother.

But when her grief abated a little she thought with increasing distrust of Doña Elvira, and although there was nothing she could do now to bring Maria's love back to her she determined from that moment that in future she was going to take a firmer hand in the management of her own household.

*   *   *

Iñigo scratched at the door. Maria heard him but she took no notice.

'Maria,' he whispered.

'Go away,' she answered.

'I will when I have spoken to you.'

'I do not wish to see you.'

'But you can hear me as I speak to you through the keyhole.'

She did not answer.

'I know you can,' he went on. 'I have come to say that I am sorry.'

Still she was silent.

'My mother is determined that we shall marry. She always has been. It is no use fighting against my mother, Maria. Maria, do you hate me so much?'

'Go away,' she repeated.

'I shall always be kind to you. I will make you love me. Then you will forget what my mother has done.'

'I shall never forget what she has done.'

'Do you wish to remain locked up here?'

'I do not care what becomes of me.'

'You do, Maria. When you marry me I will take you back to Spain. Just answer one question: Do you want to go back to Spain, Maria?'

'To Spain!' the words escaped her. She thought of her home, of being young again. If she were ever going to forget her faithless lover she might do so at home.

'Ah,' he said, 'you cannot deceive me. It is what you long for. If you marry me, Maria, I will take you home as soon as it can be arranged.'

She was silent.

'Can you hear me, Maria? I want to please you. I will do anything you ask.'

'Go away. That is what I ask. That is the way to please me.'

He went away, but he returned a little later. He came again and again; and after a few days she began to look for his coming.

He was always gentle, always eager to please her.

She found that she was able to laugh as she said: 'You are not overmuch like your mother, Don Iñigo Manrique.'

He laughed with her; and from that moment their relationship changed.

It was a few days later when she rejoined the maids of honour.

She was subdued and sullen.

'I have agreed to become betrothed to Don Iñigo Manrique,' she told them.

CHAPTER VIII

THE PROTEST OF THE PRINCE
OF WALES

The Prince of Wales was approaching his fourteenth birthday, and he was determined that it should be celebrated with all the pomp due to his rank.

He would have masques and pageants such as had never been seen during his father's reign. Fourteen was an age when one left childhood behind and became a man.

He was already taller than most men and had the strength of two. People often said that he was going to be a golden giant. He liked to hear that.

He refused to do lessons and commanded John Skelton to plan a masque.

'The kind I like best,' declared the Prince, 'are those in which masked men appear at the joust and beg leave to be able to take part. One of them, taller than the rest and clearly noble, in spite of his disguise, challenges the champion.'

'And beats him,' whispered Skelton.

'Yes, and beats him; and then there is a cry of 'This is a god, for no man on Earth could beat the champion'. Then the ladies come forward and there is a dance . . .'

'And the masked hero will allow only the most beautiful lady to remove his mask,' added Skelton.

'That is so, and when the mask is removed . . .'

'The god is revealed to be His Grace the Prince of Wales!' cried Skelton. 'Fanfares.'

170

'Why, but that is exactly what I had planned,' cried Henry in surprise.

'Does it not show that our minds are in unison, Your Grace?'

'It would seem so.'

'But then we have had these pageants before, and methinks the unmasked hero has already made his debut. But, there is no reason I can see why he should not appear again . . . and again and again.'

Henry was never quite sure whether or not Skelton was laughing at him, but because he admired the man and believed he had much to learn from him, he preferred to think he was not, and invariably laughed with him.

'Fourteen,' he mused. 'In another year I shall be betrothed.'

'A year will pass like a day, in the full life of Your Royal Highness.'

'It is indeed so, my good John. And have you heard that I am now to marry Marguerite d'Angoulême? They say she is very beautiful.'

'All high-born ladies are said to be beautiful,' answered John.

'It is not true, though their jewels and clothes often make them seem so.'

'I did not speak of what they are but what they are said to be.'

The Prince was thoughtful. Then he said: 'They say that Marguerite adores her brother Francis. They say he is handsome and excels at all sports; that there is none like him in the whole of France and, if ever he comes to the throne, he will make a great King.'

'So there are two such paragons—one in

England, one in France.'

The Prince drew himself up to his full height. 'I believe him not to be as tall as I, and he is dark.'

'A minor paragon,' murmured Skelton.

'And,' went on the Prince, 'there is no doubt that I shall one day be King. But Francis will only ascend the throne if old Louis dies childless. He must be beside himself with terror.'

'Why, my Prince, it is not easy for old men to beget children.'

'But for his future to hang on such a thread! His mother and sister call him Caesar. I hope Marguerite is soon brought to England.'

'Your Grace will have much to teach her, and not least of the lessons she will learn will be that there is a Prince more handsome, more excellent, more god-like than her brother.'

The Prince did not answer. His eyes were narrowed in the characteristic way; his small mouth was set. What a King he will make! thought Skelton. His ministers will have to learn to pander to his wishes, or it will go hard with them. Our golden god will be a despot, and heads will doubtless fly like tennis balls.

Henry was thinking of Marguerite. Surely she must come soon. He was going to insist on marrying this girl. Many had been offered to him, and then the offers had been withdrawn. He wanted Marguerite. She was beautiful, he had heard, and it was all very well for Skelton to say that all high-born ladies were beautiful; he did not believe it. Look at Katharine of Aragon in her faded gown, and her face pale and stricken with mourning. He rejoiced that it was Marguerite who had been chosen for him and not Katharine.

While he sat with Skelton a messenger from the King arrived and told the Prince that his father wished to see him without delay.

Skelton watched the Prince as he immediately obeyed the summons. There is one person alone who can deflate our great Prince, mused Skelton—his Royal Father. When he is no longer there, what an inflated King we shall have.

As soon as Henry came into his father's presence the King waved his hand to those attendants who were with him, indicating that he wished to be alone with his son.

He looked at Henry sternly. The boy's glowing health could not but give him the utmost satisfaction, yet he was afraid that young Henry had extravagant tastes. He must have a serious talk with him in the very near future; he must make him realise how carefully his father had built up a firm exchequer. It would be terrible if the wealth of the country and the Tudors were frittered away in useless pageants.

But he had not summoned the boy to talk of extravagance. That could wait. There was a matter which he considered more urgent.

'My son,' said the King, 'one day you will be married, and that day is not far distant.'

'I hear, Sire, that a new bride is being suggested now. I like what I hear of Marguerite.'

'Yes, Marguerite,' said his father. 'Do you remember that when you were thirteen you were betrothed to another in the house of the Bishop of Salisbury?'

'I remember it well—a hot day. The people cheered me as I came into Fleet Street!'

'Yes.' Henry's tone was curt. 'We know full well

173

that the people cheer you wherever you go. Katharine of Aragon is not the match today that she was at that time. Circumstances change. Now that her mother is dead, her father's position is not what it was. I do not trust her father. I feel sure that were a marriage to take place there would still be difficulty about getting the remainder of the dowry. In other words, I do not favour the marriage with Katharine.'

'No, Sire. I . . .'

The King lifted his hand. 'We will not discuss your wishes because they are at this time of no moment.'

The blood flamed into young Henry's face. A protest rose to his lips; then he remembered that this was his father; this was the King. One did not argue with Kings. He tried to suppress his anger. His mouth was tight and his eyes a blazing blue.

'According to what was arranged in the Bishop of Salisbury's house a year ago, when you are fifteen you would marry Katharine. That is in a year's time. I now desire you to make a formal protest. You are to meet Archbishop Warham here in the Palace. He is waiting now. You will solemnly protest that you have no wish for this marriage with Katharine of Aragon.'

'But . . .' began Henry.

'You will do as you are told, my son. The Archbishop is waiting to see you now.'

All the egoism in the Prince's nature was rising in protest—not against marriage with Katharine but against his father's management of what he considered to be his personal affair. Young Henry knew that royal marriages were usually arranged, but he was no ordinary Prince. He was old enough

174

to have a say in his own affairs.

If he, of his own free will, decided against marrying Katharine, all well and good. But to be told to make such a protest offended his *amour propre,* which was extremely sensitive.

His father said testily: 'This is what you will say: "The betrothal was contracted in my minority. I myself was not consulted in the matter. I shall not ratify it when the time comes, and it is therefore null and void."'

'I should like time to consider this matter,' said Henry boldly.

'That is enough,' his father retorted; 'you do as you are told. Come . . . say those words after me.'

For a few seconds Henry's blazing eyes looked into his father's. But he knew he must obey. He was only a boy not yet fourteen, and this man, whose face was lined with suffering, was the King. He murmured the words he had been told to repeat.

'Again,' said his father.

It was humiliating. Why should I? he asked of himself. Then a cunning thought came into his mind. It would not always be as it was now. One day he would be King, and the man who was now commanding him would be nothing but a mouldering corpse. What did words matter? When young Prince Henry was King Henry, then he would have his way and, if he wished to marry Katharine of Aragon, there would be none to deny him his wish.

He repeated the words sullenly.

'Come,' said the King. 'I dare swear Warham has arrived already.'

So, in the ground floor apartment in Richmond

175

Palace, young Henry repeated the words which were his formal protest against a marriage with Katharine of Aragon.

Words, thought Henry as he went back to his own apartments. He would never allow a few words to stand between himself and what he wanted.

After that he thought of Katharine of Aragon more frequently. He remembered her as she had been when he had led her to the Palace after her wedding ceremony.

His father had made up his mind that he should never have Katharine, yet his father himself had wanted to marry her. Katharine was now out of reach. She represented a challenge. She had suddenly become quite attractive—more so than Marguerite, who was so enamoured of her own brother that she thought him the handsomest boy in the world.

CHAPTER IX

THE TREACHERY OF ELVIRA

Doña Elvira was in very secret conference with her husband, Don Pedro Manrique. She spoke quickly and quietly, for she was very eager that what she was saying should reach no other ears but those of her husband.

'Juan is certain of it,' she was saying. 'If this meeting can be arranged, it will teach Ferdinand the lesson he needs.'

Don Pedro was alarmed. It was true that his wife was a woman who always had her way; but the domestic politics of the Infanta's household were a very different matter from those of Europe. She had become more confident than ever, since she had successfully arranged the betrothal of Iñigo and Maria de Rojas. But Don Pedro wished she would leave intrigue to her brother.

Elvira's great aim was to bring power to the Manrique and Manuel families. Therefore she was going to stand firmly behind her brother, Don Juan Manuel, who at the Court of Brussels represented the Castilian faction, the aim of which was to oust Ferdinand from power and support Philip.

'He is asking your help in this matter?' asked Don Pedro.

Elvira nodded proudly. 'Why not? I hold an important position here in England. There is a great deal I could do.'

'What do you propose? Are you going to consult Puebla?'

'That little fool! Indeed I am not. This is a matter which I shall trust to no one.'

'But how do you propose to bring about a meeting between Henry and Philip? And what would Ferdinand's reaction be if this were done?'

'I do not think we should concern ourselves with Ferdinand's reactions. Ferdinand is growing old. He is like a lion whose teeth have been drawn. He understands now that he owed much to Isabella. He is going to realise that it was more than he suspects, even now. Ferdinand's days as a power in Europe are numbered. Once I have arranged this meeting . . .'

'Elvira, have a care.'

'Oh you are a fool, Pedro. You are too timid. If it had been left to you, Iñigo would still be looking for a bride.'

'All I ask is that you should go warily.'

'Can you not trust me to do that?'

'You are clever, Elvira; you are shrewd. But this is dangerous politics. Tell me what you propose to do.'

She looked at him with a scornful smile, made as though to speak and then paused. 'No,' she said, 'I think I will tell you afterwards. You are too timid, my dear Pedro. But have no fear. I know exactly how to handle this matter.'

*　　　*　　　*

Katharine's maids of honour were helping her to dress when Elvira came to them.

'Is that the best gown you can find for Her Highness?' she demanded, staring at the stiff brocade skirt which had been mended in several places.

'It is the least shabby of Her Highness's gowns,' said Inez de Veñegas.

Elvira clicked her tongue and murmured as though to herself: 'A pretty pass . . . a pretty pass . . .'

She watched while the maids dressed Katharine's hair, then she waved her hands in a gesture they knew well, shooing them away as though they were chicken.

When they had gone Elvira said: 'It distresses me, Highness. I often wonder what your mother would have said if she could see what has befallen you in England.'

'She knew how I was placed, even before she died, yet there was nothing she could do. Had it been possible she would have done it.'

'An Infanta of Spain to be so shabby! I feel it should not be allowed to continue.'

'It has gone on so long that one grows accustomed to it.'

'There is a new Queen of Spain now. I wonder what she would say if she could see her sister.'

'Ah . . . Juana!' murmured Katharine, and thought of that wild sister who laughed and cried too easily. 'It is strange to think of her as Queen in our mother's place.'

'How would you like to see her again?'

Katharine did not speak. To see Juana! It would be the next best thing to seeing her mother.

'I do not see,' whispered Elvira, watching her closely, 'why it should not be arranged.'

Katharine turned to her swiftly. 'But how?'

'Suppose you wrote to her, telling her of your desire to see her. Do not forget, she is the Queen

179

now. Suppose you told her of your homesickness, your longing to see a member of your family; I feel sure she would be as eager to see you as you are to see her.'

'You mean that I should leave England . . . ?'

'Why not? They could come to the coast to meet you. The King might accompany you; it would be an opportunity for him to meet the new Queen and her husband.'

'Doña Elvira, do you really think . . . ?'

How young she is, thought Elvira. How innocent. How easily she is deluded!

Elvira turned away as though to hide an emotion of which she was ashamed because it showed a weakness.

'I think it is worth trying. Why should you not write a note to your sister, suggesting such a meeting. What harm could that do?'

'I can see no harm in it. I should so rejoice to hear from Juana.'

'Then write the note and we will send it by special courier to Brussels. He shall wait there and bring back your sister's answer to you.'

Katharine rose and went to her table. Her fingers were trembling with excitement as she took up her pen.

*   *   *

Katharine looked at the note. It brought back memories of Juana.

How wonderful for them to be together, to exchange experiences, to give themselves up to the joy of 'Do you remember?' It would be almost like living those days of childhood again.

180

We *should* be together, thought Katharine; there are so few of us left now.

Juana had written that she would be delighted to see her sister, that there was nothing she wanted more. Why should not the two parties meet half way?

If King Henry and Katharine would cross to Calais and travel to Saint-Omer, which was but eight leagues away, there Juana and her husband, Philip, would be waiting to meet them.

Katharine showed the letter to Doña Elvira, who was overjoyed. Juan had been clever to get the unbalanced Juana to write the letter exactly as he wished, so the strategy had succeeded even beyond her hopes.

There was now of course the difficulty of persuading the King to enter into the plan, but Elvira did not think that would be difficult, since Henry desperately needed a bride and was desirous of linking up with the Hapsburgs. He was feeling his age, it was true, and a sea journey would not be very comfortable, but he was ever a man to put diplomacy before comfort. Elvira had little doubt that he would accept the invitation.

She was jubilant. She would have achieved for her brother that which he had been working hard to bring about: A meeting between Henry and Philip which could only work out to the detriment of Ferdinand and the Aragonese faction.

'You should write to the King at once,' said Elvira, 'showing him this invitation from your sister. If you will do it now, I myself will give the order for your chamberlain to prepare to take it to Richmond with all speed.'

'I will write at once. Tell Alonso de Esquivel to

make ready. He rides faster than any, and I can scarcely wait for the King's answer. I will take it down to him myself when I have written it, with special instructions that it is to be put into no hands other than those of the King.'

Elvira nodded, well pleased, and went off at once to tell the chamberlain to make ready.

Katharine carefully wrote her letter to the King, sealed it and was making her way down to the courtyard when she came face to face with Dr de Puebla.

She felt so happy that she could not resist confiding in the ambassador, and said almost childishly: 'I have had an invitation from my sister. She has invited me . . . and the King . . . to see her. I am asking the King to agree to this.'

Puebla put his hand out to the wall to steady himself. He knew at once what this meant. Katharine would not go alone. There would be a royal party and the King would most certainly be at the head of it. The enemies of Ferdinand had been working long and secretly to bring about such a meeting. This was direct treachery towards Katharine's father.

He took the letter from her and she, unthinking, let it go.

Katharine said sharply: 'Give me back that letter.'

The little ambassador continued to clutch it tightly.

'Highness,' he began, 'this could be a matter of policy . . .'

Katharine's habitual calm deserted her. She thought of the months of loneliness, boredom, poverty and humiliation. She did not trust Puebla, whom she had never liked, and Elvira had lost no opportunity of poisoning her mind against him. She snatched the letter from the ambassador and went past him.

His ambassadorial duties had accustomed Puebla to quick thinking. He guessed that Elvira was behind these arrangements, for he was well aware that her brother, Juan Manuel, was working in Brussels for the Castilian party against the Aragonese.

It was useless to follow Katharine. Glancing hastily through a window he saw the chamberlain, ready for his journey, standing by while his horse was being saddled. There were a few moments left to him in which to act. He sped along to Elvira's apartment and on his way there met her returning from the courtyard.

'This is treachery,' he cried, 'treachery against our Sovereign master.'

Elvira was too much taken off her guard to feign surprise. 'If the Infanta wishes to see her sister, why should she be prevented?'

'This meeting has been arranged at the instigation of your brother, who is a traitor to Ferdinand. We are Ferdinand's servants. Your brother is a traitor, and you know that full well. If that letter of invitation is sent to the King I shall have no alternative but to acquaint Ferdinand with *your* treachery. It is one thing for your brother to work against the King of Aragon in Brussels, but quite another for you to do so here in the household of Ferdinand's daughter. He could recall you to Spain, and he will do so. I do not think your fate would be a very happy one if that should happen.'

'I do not understand . . .' began Elvira, but for once she was trembling. The success of her venture depended entirely on its seeming innocence. The meeting for which she had planned must appear to have been brought about through Katharine and Juana. She understood her danger if Ferdinand were informed that she had played a part in it.

'There is little time to lose,' said Puebla. 'In less than five minutes Esquivel will be on his way to Richmond.'

Doña Elvira made a quick decision. 'I will go down at once and tell him that he must not take the letter to the King.'

Puebla, who was sweating with the excitement and dismay of those moments, now relaxed.

She understood the danger to herself and her family. She had not only her own but her family's future to think of. She would not want it known that Juan Manuel had played his part in this; and although Ferdinand had been weakened by the death of Isabella, he was still a power in Spain, and it might be that he would act as Regent for Juana and Philip, who must necessarily spend a certain time in their other dominions.

Elvira knew very well that she was playing a dangerous game.

She went down to the courtyard, while Puebla watched from a window. Katharine had given the chamberlain her letter with instructions to ride to Richmond with all speed, and had returned to the house.

That made Elvira's task more easy. Puebla watched her take the letter from the chamberlain; he saw the look of surprise on the man's face as the horse was led back to the stables.

184

The ambassador sighed with relief. A chance meeting with the Infanta had diverted a catastrophe. He felt exhausted. He would return immediately to his lodgings in the Strand and there rest awhile.

I am too old for such alarms, he told himself.

As he came out of Durham House his servant, who had been waiting for him, came hurriedly to his side, surprised to see his master so weary.

Puebla was about to start on his way when he stopped abruptly. 'Wait here,' he said. 'If you should see Don Alonso de Esquivel ride off in some haste towards Richmond lose no time in coming straight to me.'

He then made his way to his lodging. He did not trust Elvira. He had always known that the woman sent adverse reports of him to Isabella, and was doubtless doing so to Ferdinand. He had an inkling that she might attempt to thwart him even now that he was aware of her duplicity.

He was right.

He had not been in his lodgings very long when his servant came panting into his presence, to tell him that the chamberlain had, very soon after the departure of Dr de Puebla from Durham House, set off in the direction of Richmond, riding at great speed.

Puebla was horrified. He should have foreseen this.

The mischief was done. The King was being offered what was tantamount to an invitation to meet Philip and Juana; if he accepted, months of diplomacy were ruined.

He could not prevent Katharine's letter from reaching the King, but he could at least warn

Katharine of the part she had been inveigled into playing. Then perhaps he could warn the King of the unreliable character of the Archduke Philip.

He had no time to form elaborate plans. He must act with speed. Of one thing he could be certain: The Infanta was completely loyal to her own family; if she knew that she had been used in a plot against her father, she would be horrified.

He lost no time in returning to Durham House, and there burst unceremoniously into the presence of the Infanta.

Katharine was with some of her maids of honour and, when he stammered out the plea that he speak to her alone, she was so shocked by his distress that she immediately agreed that he should do so.

As soon as they were alone he said: 'Highness, you are the victim of a plot against your father.' He then explained how for months the Castilian faction in Brussels had been working to bring about a meeting between Henry of England and her brother-in-law, Philip.

'You must understand, Highness, that your brother-in-law is no friend of your father. He seeks to take from him all the power he has in Castile and relegate him solely to the affairs of Aragon. You know how distressed your mother would be if she could know what is happening now. In her will she asks that in the absence or incapacity of your sister Juana, your father should be sole regent of Castile until the majority of her grandson Charles. Philip is determined to increase the discord and distrust between your father and the King of England. He will seek to make a pact with him against your father. Doña Elvira's brother, Don

Juan Manuel, is the leader in this plot. It is for this reason that she has urged you to help bring about this meeting.'

Katharine was staring at the ambassador in horror. She was remembering how Doña Elvira had commiserated with her, how she had urged her to write to Juana. So she and Juana were being used by their father's enemies! Katharine thought of her mother, who had always stood firmly beside her father. How shocked and horrified she would be at the idea of her daughters' working with their father's enemies.

She was trembling as she said: 'I believe what you say. I see that I have been their dupe. What can I do now?'

Puebla shook his head sadly, for he had realised that there was nothing now to be done. The King would receive the letter from his daughter-in-law, enclosing that from Juana. It was entirely in his hands whether or not that invitation would be accepted.

'At least, Highness,' he said, 'you know your duenna for the scheming woman she is. With your leave I will retire now. I shall go with all speed to Richmond, and there I shall try to use my influence with the King to avoid this meeting.'

*   *   *

Henry was studying the letter from Katharine and that from Juana.

To cross to Saint-Omer, to meet the heir of Isabella and her husband! Perhaps to make the arrangements for those alliances which he coveted? Philip would have the backing of his

187

father, Maximilian, and if they could come to some agreement it might mean that he would have his bride in England soon. Maximilian's daughter, a beautiful young woman, though twice widowed . . . They could get children. He was very eager to have a bride for himself and those alliances for his family. Charles, the heir of the Hapsburgs and of Isabella and Ferdinand, would be the richest monarch in Europe when he came of age. Little Mary was the bride for him. And Eleanor, the daughter of Philip and Juana, would do very well for young Henry. All this could be arranged if he met Philip and Juana.

They would want something in exchange— promises of help, doubtless, against Ferdinand, because there would certainly be trouble in Castile between Ferdinand and Philip. It was easy to make promises.

A meeting was desirable, but it would be expensive; a King could not travel abroad in modesty; that gave an impression of poverty and would not be wise. He did not like travel; he was getting too old, and his limbs were often so stiff when he arose in the mornings that he could scarcely put his feet to the ground. Yet those alliances were what his family needed.

Puebla was announced, and the ambassador, when he entered and stood before the King, was clearly distraught.

'You look disturbed,' said Henry.

Puebla, feeling the situation to be too dangerous for subterfuge, explained in detail how Doña Elvira had used Katharine to suggest this meeting.

'Well, are the means so important?'

'Your Grace, the Spanish situation is fluid . . .

very fluid. There is so much treachery involved in this that it is difficult to know who is one's friend, who one's foe. There are the two rival factions in Brussels. How can you know who it is who have arranged this meeting? Is it your friends? Is it your enemies? A King is vulnerable when he leaves his own shores. Philip is as wayward as thistledown. He will sway this way and that. He does not keep his promises if the whim takes him to break them. You would be ill advised to take this suggestion of a meeting seriously.'

The King was thoughtful. There was spying and counter-spying in all countries, he knew, but the Spanish situation at this time was certainly dangerous.

He knew Philip for a pleasure-loving young man whose political ambitions waxed and waned. Ferdinand he looked upon as a rogue, but at least he and Ferdinand were of a kind.

'I will consider this matter,' he said, and Puebla's spirits rose.

He did not believe that Henry would make that journey. Clearly he was dreading it. Crossing the Channel could be hazardous, and if he suffered even a slight wetting he could be sure that his rheumatism would be the worse for it.

Henry was thinking that this meeting, plotted by women, was perhaps not the wisest course at this time. What if Philip had no wish to see him? What if it should turn out to be a reunion of Katharine and her sister merely? He shuddered to think of the expense that would be involved, the money wasted.

'I will ponder on this,' he said.

189

*   *   *

At the window of her apartments at Durham House Katharine sat for a long time looking out. Puebla had gone to Richmond and would now be with the King.

Katharine was deeply shocked. She could not free her mind of the memory of her mother's face. Isabella had been at her happiest when she had her family about her. Katharine could remember those occasions when the family sat with her, the girls at their needlework, Juan reading to them; then perhaps Ferdinand would join them, and her mother's face would take on that look of serene contentment she loved to recall.

Now they were scattered. Her brother Juan and sister Isabella were dead, Maria was the Queen of Portugal, Juana the wife of Philip and she herself in England; and here in England she had become involved in a plot against her father.

Her horror gave place to anger. She forgot that her father had never loved her in the same tender way in which her mother had; she forgot how pleased he had been to send her to England. She thought of him only as the father who had joined their family group and added to her mother's happiness. Ferdinand was her father. Her mother would always have her remember that. There had been times when Isabella deferred to Ferdinand; that was when she was reminding them all that he was their father. At such times she forgot that she was the Queen of Castile and he merely the King of Aragon. Where the family was concerned he, Ferdinand, was the head.

And Doña Elvira had tricked her into working

against her own father!

Katharine stood up. She could not see her reflection or she would have noticed that a change had come over her. She held her head higher, and her shabby gown could not hide the fact that she was a Princess in her own household. She had ceased to be the neglected widow; she was the daughter of Isabella of Castile.

She called to one of her maids and said: 'Tell Doña Elvira that I wish to see her without delay.'

Her tone was peremptory and the girl looked at her in astonishment; but Katharine was unaware of the glance. She was thinking of what she was going to say to Doña Elvira.

Elvira came in, gave the rather curt little bow which was her custom, and then, as she looked into the Infanta's face, she saw the change there.

'I sent for you,' said Katharine, 'to tell you that I understand full well why you persuaded me to write to my sister.'

'Why, Highness, I knew you wished to see your sister, and it seemed shameful that you should live here as you do . . .'

'Pray be silent,' said Katharine coldly. 'I know that your brother, Don Juan Manuel, plots against my father in Brussels and has persuaded you to help him here in Durham House.'

'Highness . . .'

'Pray do not interrupt me. You forget to whom you speak.'

Elvira gasped in amazement. Never before had Katharine spoken to her in that manner. She knew that Puebla had betrayed her to Katharine, but she had been confident that she could continue to rule Durham House.

'I do not wish,' said Katharine, 'to have here with me in England servants whom I do not trust.'

'What are you saying . . . ?' Elvira began in the old hectoring manner.

'That I am dismissing you.'

'You . . . dismissing me! Highness, your mother appointed me.'

It was a mistake. Elvira realised it as soon as she had mentioned Isabella. Katharine's face was a shade paler, but her eyes flashed in a new anger.

'Had my mother known that you would plot against my father, you would have spent these last years behind prison walls. It is where you should be. But I will be lenient. You will prepare to leave Durham House and England at once.'

'This is quite impossible.'

'It shall be possible. I will not send you back to my father with an explanation of your conduct. I will spare you that. But since you are so eager to help your brother in Brussels you may go there.'

Elvira tried to summon all the old truculence, but it had deserted her.

'You may go now,' continued Katharine. 'Make your preparations with all speed, for I will not suffer you for a day longer than I need under this roof.'

Elvira knew that protest was useless. If she attempted to assert her authority, Katharine would expose the part she had been playing in her brother's schemes.

It was hard for a proud woman to accept such defeat.

She bowed and, without another word, left the presence of the Infanta.

Katharine was shaken, but she felt exultant.

For so long she had been, not so much the prisoner of Durham House, as the prisoner of Doña Elvira. Now she was free.

CHAPTER X

JUANA IN ENGLAND

Katharine had begun to wonder whom she could trust, for when her anger against Doña Elvira had subsided she realised how shocked she had been by the duenna's duplicity.

Maria de Rojas was steeped in melancholy. Yet another marriage which had been planned for her was not to take place because Iñigo had departed with his mother.

It was true that the household was free of the tyranny of Doña Elvira, but poverty remained.

Katharine summoned Puebla to her, and he came limping into her presence. He was growing old and shocks such as that which he had sustained seemed to add years to his age in a few weeks.

In her newly found independence Katharine spoke boldly.

'This situation cannot go on. I must have some means of supporting my household. I am the daughter-in-law of the King of England and I think that you, as my father's ambassador, should bestir yourself and do something about it.'

Puebla spread his hands helplessly.

'You should go to the King,' went on Katharine, 'and speak boldly to him. Tell him that it is a disgrace to his name that he allows me to live in this way.'

'I will do my best, Highness,' answered Puebla.

He shuffled out of the apartment, not relishing his task and yet agreeing with Katharine that she

194

could not continue in such penury for much longer.

He sought audience with the King.

Henry was still brooding on the suggested meeting with Philip and Juana. Perhaps in the spring or the summer . . . he had been thinking, for the prospect of the damp seeping into his bones alarmed him. It would be disastrous if he became completely crippled. It seemed so ridiculous that he could not get himself a bride. Yet it was not easy for Kings to find suitable partners. So many qualifications were necessary in a Queen.

He frowned at Puebla as he came in, but he listened quietly while the ambassador laid before him Katharine's complaint.

Henry nodded gravely. 'It is true,' he said, 'that Durham House must be an expensive household to manage. I am sorry for the Infanta. I will help her.'

Puebla's face lighted up with pleasure.

'She shall give up Durham House,' went on Henry, 'and come to Court. I am sure, when she no longer has such a large establishment to support, she will live more comfortably.'

Puebla thanked the King, but he was dubious as he went back to Durham House, being unsure how Katharine would receive this news. He knew that with an adequate allowance and without Doña Elvira life at Durham House might be quite pleasant; and it was this allowance for which Katharine had hoped; but if she went to Court she would be under supervision as strict as that of Doña Elvira.

He was right. Katharine was far from pleased.

She looked at the shabby little man and was filled with disgust. This man . . . an ambassador from that country which she had always been taught was the greatest in the world! How could she hope to be treated with respect, how could she possibly retain her dignity when her father's representative in England was this little *marrano*!

She spoke coldly to him. 'I see that my position has changed very little for the better. Sometimes I wonder whether you work more for the King of England than for the King of Spain.'

Puebla was deeply wounded. How could she understand the intricacies of state policies? How could she realise the dangerous and difficult game he must continually play?

It seemed to be his fate in life to be misunderstood, to be scorned by those to whom he gave his services.

Katharine was thinking as he left her: Was Doña Elvira really spying for her brother, or did Puebla, with diabolical cunning, contrive the whole situation in order to have Elvira removed? Was the King of England behind the scheme? Did he wish to close Durham House, to bring her to Court where many might gloat over her poverty and the indignity of her position? Whom could one trust?

*   *   *

There was news from Spain which shocked Katharine.

Her father was proposing to marry again.

Katharine was so disturbed that she shut herself in her apartments and told her maids of honour that she must be left alone. Kings remarried speedily when they lost their Queens; she knew that. It was a continual need of Kings to get heirs. But this seemed different. There would be

196

someone to take the place of Isabella of Castile, and in Katharine's eyes this was sacrilege.

Moreover her father proposed to marry a young girl of eighteen.

She was very beautiful, rumour said; and that hurt Katharine even more. She thought of her father, showering caresses on a beautiful young girl, and she pictured her mother, looking down from Heaven in sorrow.

Nonsense! she admonished herself. It is a political marriage.

It was true that Ferdinand was anxious to make an alliance with the French King, Louis XII. The situation had changed. The French had been driven from Naples, for a too easy success had made them careless; and Ferdinand had Gonsalvo Cordova, the Great Captain, to fight for him.

In the circumstances, Louis was delighted to see the trouble between Ferdinand and his son-in-law Philip. Philip or his son Charles was going to be the most powerful man in Europe. There would be Maximilian's dominions to come to him, including Austria, Flanders and Burgundy; but that was not all; for from Juana would come the united crowns of Spain, and in addition all the overseas dependencies.

To Louis alliance with Ferdinand seemed advisable, even though Louis' daughter had been promised to young Charles.

Louis laid down his conditions. He would relinquish his claim to Naples, which he would give to the young bride as her dowry. Germaine de Foix was the daughter of Jean de Foix, Viscount of Narbonne; this viscount's mother had been Leonora, Queen of Navarre, half sister to

Ferdinand, and she had poisoned her sister
Blanche to win the Crown of Navarre. The
Viscount had married one of the sisters of Louis
XII, so Germaine was therefore not only related to
Louis but to Ferdinand.

Ferdinand also agreed to pay Louis a million
gold ducats during the course of the following ten
years to compensate Louis for what he had lost in
the Naples campaign.

This was the news which came to Katharine and
which seemed to her such an insult to her mother.
It was not merely that her father had taken a young
wife in her mother's place, but, as she realised, this
marriage could result in destroying that policy for
which Isabella had worked during the whole of her
reign: the unity of Spain. It had been Isabella's
delight that when she married Ferdinand she
united Castile and Aragon; and when together they
drove the Moors from the kingdom of Granada
they had made a united Spain. But if this new
marriage were fruitful, if Germaine bore
Ferdinand a son, that son would be the heir of
Aragon, while Juana and her heirs—and she
already had sons—would be rulers of Castile. Thus
by his selfish action—perhaps to have a beautiful
young wife, but more likely to grasp the somewhat
empty title of King of Naples—Ferdinand was
showing his indifference to the lifelong wishes of
Isabella.

This treaty between Ferdinand and Louis had
already been signed in Blois.

Katharine, no longer a child, no longer ignorant
of state politics and the overwhelming greed and
pride of ambitious men and women, wept afresh
for her mother.

*   *   *

It was bleak January and there were storms all along the coast; the wind swept up the Thames and not even the great fires which blazed in Windsor Castle could keep out the cold. Katharine sat huddled about the fire with some of her maids of honour. They were very gloomy and rarely ceased talking of their desire to return to Spain.

Francesca de Carceres, who was impulsive and never could control her tongue, blamed the various members of Katharine's household in turn. First she blamed Puebla, then Juan de Cuero. They were all in league with the King of England, she declared, and their desire was to keep them all in this island until they grew crippled with rheumatism.

Maria de Rojas was sunk in gloom. As she had mourned for her Englishman, now she mourned for Iñigo Manrique.

Katharine was dipping into her store of plate and jewels, and often wondered what would happen when the time came for the remainder of them to be valued.

There was no news from Spain. Ferdinand rarely had time to write to his daughter. He was too busy, she supposed bitterly, thinking of his new marriage which would shortly take place.

As they sat thus they heard the clatter of horses' hoofs and shouts from without, and Francesca ran to the window.

'There is some excitement below,' she said. 'It is evidently important news.'

'News from home?' asked Katharine quickly.

'No,' answered Francesca, as the others came to the window to stand beside her. 'That is no Spanish courier.'

Katharine who had risen sat down listlessly.

'There is never news from Spain . . . never news that one wishes to hear.'

The other girls turned from the window, and Maria de Salinas said: 'It must change soon. It cannot go on like this. Perhaps when there is a new King . . .'

'He will marry Her Highness,' cried Francesca.

Katharine shook her head. 'No, he is promised to Marguerite of Angoulême.'

'Oh, he has been promised to so many,' Francesca said.

'That happens to most of us,' put in Maria de Rojas bitterly.

Katharine was silent; she was thinking of the Prince of Wales, whom she saw occasionally. It was a strange position; she did not know whether she was still affianced to him or not. It was true there had been a formal betrothal in the Bishop of Salisbury's house, but ever since then there had been rumours of other brides who had been chosen for him.

He was growing up quickly, for he seemed much older than his years. When they were together she would often find his eyes fixed on her broodingly. It was a little disquieting; it made her wonder what the future would hold for her when the old King died and Henry VIII was King of England.

Someone was at the door, begging to be allowed to see the Infanta, and Inez de Veñegas came bursting unceremoniously into the apartment. She was clearly excited.

'Highness,' she stammered. 'There is great excitement below. Ships broken by the storm have sought refuge here in England.'

Francesca said impatiently: 'That's to be expected in such weather.'

'But these are the ships of Her Highness the Queen of Castile.'

Katharine had risen; she grew pale and then flushed scarlet.

'Juana . . . my sister . . . in England!'

'Highness, she is here . . . seeking refuge from the storm. Her fleet of ships has met with disaster on their way from Flanders to Spain. And she and her husband and their suite . . .'

Katharine clasped her hands across her breast; her heart was leaping with excitement.

Juana here . . . in England!

This was the happiest news she had heard for years.

*   *   *

Juana, Queen of Castile, was happy at last. She was on a ship bound for Castile, and her husband was with her; and while they sailed together it was impossible for him to escape her.

She was wildly gay; she would stand on deck, her face held to the wind while it loosened her hair and set it flying about her head. Her attendants looked at her anxiously, then covertly; as for her husband, sometimes he jeered at her, sometimes he was ironically affectionate—so much depended on his mood.

Philip was a man of moods. He changed his plans from day to day, as he changed his

201

mistresses. If he had held a place less prominent in world politics this would have been of less importance; as it was he was becoming noted for his inconsequential ways, and this was dangerous in a son of Maximilian. There was no ruler in Europe who did not view him with disquiet. Yet, he was one of the most powerful men in Europe on account of his position; he knew it. It delighted him. He loved power, whether it was in politics or in his affairs with women.

He came on deck to stand beside his wife.

How mad she looks! he thought, and he was exultant. He would exact complete obedience or he would have her put away. It would be no lie to say: 'I must keep her in safe custody. Alas, my wife is a madwoman.'

Yet there were times when it was necessary to say: 'Oh no, she is not mad. A little impulsive, a little hysterical, but that is not madness.'

This was one of the latter occasions, because he was going to claim her Crown of Castile. The people of Spain would never accept the son of Maximilian as their ruler; they would only accept the husband of their Queen Isabella's daughter, Juana, who was now herself Queen of Castile.

Juana turned to look at him, and that soft, yearning look, which sometimes amused, sometimes sickened him, came into her eyes.

How beautiful he is! she thought. The wind had brought a richer colour to his cheeks, which were always rosy; his long golden hair fell to his shoulders; his features were like those of a Greek god; his blue eyes sparkled with health and the joy of living. He was not tall, nor was he short; he was slim and he moved with grace. The title of Philip the Handsome, by which he was known, had not been given out of idle flattery.

'The wind is rising,' she said, but her expression said something else, as it always did when he was near her. It implored him to stay with her every hour of the day and night, it betrayed the fact that she was only happy when he was with her.

Philip turned to her suddenly and gripped her wrist. She felt the pain of this, but he was often cruel to her and she welcomed his cruelty. She was happier when he laid his hands on her—no matter how brutally—than when he reserved his affection or anger for others.

'I anticipate trouble with that sly old fox, your father.'

She winced. She was, after all, Isabella's daughter, and Isabella had taught her children the importance of filial duty. Even in wild Juana, besotted as she was by her desire for this cruelly wayward husband, the influence of the great Isabella still persisted.

'I doubt not that he will be pleased to see us,' she began.

'Pleased? I'll tell you what, my dear wife: He's hoping we shall perish at sea. He's hoping that he can take our son Charles under his guidance and rule Castile and Aragon as the boy's Regent. That's what Ferdinand hopes. And we are in his way.'

'It cannot be so. He is my father. He loves me.'

Philip laughed. 'That's your foolish woman's reasoning. Your father never loved anything but crowns and ducats.'

'Philip, when we are in Castile, don't put me away. Let me stay with you.'

He put that handsome head on one side and smiled at her sardonically. 'That depends on you, my dear. We cannot show a madwoman to the people of Castile.'

'Philip, I am not mad . . . I am not mad . . . not when you're kind to me. If you would only be affectionate to me. If there were no other women . . .'

'Ah,' Philip mocked. 'You ask too much.' Then he began to laugh and laid an arm about her shoulder. Immediately she clung to him, her feverish fingers tearing at his doublet. He looked at her with distaste and, turning from her to stare at the heaving water, he said: 'This time, you will obey me. There shall be nothing like that Conchillos affair again, eh?'

Juana began to tremble.

'You have forgotten that little matter?' went on Philip. 'You have forgotten that, when your father sought to become Regent of Castile, you were persuaded by that traitor, Conchillos, to sign a letter approving of your father's acts?'

'I did it because you were never with me. You did not care what became of me. You spent all your time with that big Flemish woman . . .'

'So you turned traitor out of jealousy, eh? You said to yourself, I will serve my father, and if that means I am the enemy of my husband, what do I care?'

'But I did care, Philip. If you had asked me I would never have signed it. I would have done everything you asked of me.'

'Yet you knew that by signing that letter you went against my wishes. You set yourself on the side of your father against me. You thought you would take a little revenge because I preferred another woman to you. Look at yourself sometimes, my Queen. Think of yourself, and then ask yourself why I should prefer to spend my nights with someone else.'

'You are cruel, Philip. You are too cruel . . .'

He gripped her arm, and again she bore the pain. She thought fleetingly: It will be bruised tomorrow. And she would kiss those bruises because they were the marks made by his fingers. Let him be cruel, but never let him leave her.

'I ask you to remember what happened,' said Philip quietly. 'Conchillos was put into a dungeon. What became of him there I do not know. But it was just reward, was it not, my cherished one, for a man who would come between a husband and his wife. As for my little Queen, my perfidious Juana, you know what happened to her. I had her put away. I said: My poor wife is suffering from delusions. She has inherited her madness from her mad grandmother, the old lady of Arevalo. It grieves me that I must shut her away from the world for a while. Remember. You are free again. You may be a sane woman for a while. You may go to Castile and claim your crown. But take care that you do not find yourself once more shut away from the world.'

'You use me most brutally, Philip.'

'Remember it,' he murmured, 'and be warned by it.'

He turned then and left her, and she looked after him longingly. With what grace he walked! He was like a god come to Earth from some pagan heaven. She wished she could control her desire for him; but she could not; it swamped all her emotions, all her sense. She was ready to jettison pride, dignity, decency—everything that her mother had taught her was the heritage of a Princess of Spain—all these she would cast aside for a brief ecstatic hour of Philip's undivided attention.

*   *   *

There was disaster aboard. A few hours before, when they had sailed into the English Channel, there had been a strange calm on the sea and in the sky which had lasted almost an hour; then suddenly the wind rose, the sky darkened and the storm broke.

Juana left her cabin; the wind pulled at her gown and tore her hair from the headdress. She laughed; she was not afraid. There was no one on board who feared death less than she did.

'We shall die together,' she shouted. 'He cannot leave me now. I shall be by his side; I shall wrap my arms about him and we shall go to meet Death together . . . together at last.'

Two of her women came to her; they believed that a fit of madness was about to take possession of her. It seemed understandable. Everyone on board ship was terrified and fearful that they would never reach Castile.

'Highness,' they said, 'you should be at your prayers.'

She turned to them, her eyes wide and wild. 'I have prayed so much,' she said quietly, 'and my prayers have rarely been answered. I prayed for love. It was denied me. So why should I pray for life?'

The women exchanged glances. There is no doubt, said those looks, the madness is near.

One of them whispered: 'Your mother would wish you to pray if she were here.'

Juana was silent and they knew that she was thinking of Queen Isabella.

'I must do what she would wish,' she murmured as though to herself. Then she shouted: 'Come, help me dress. Find my richest gown and put it on me. Then bring me a purse of gold pieces.'

'Your richest dress, Highness,' stammered one of the women.

'That is what I said. My richest dress and gold which shall be strapped to my body. When I am washed up on some distant shore I would not have them say: "Here is a woman done to death by the sea" but "Here is a Queen!" That is what my mother would wish. I will write a note to say that the money is for my burial . . . a Queen's burial. Come, why do you stand there? There may be little time left. We can scarcely hear ourselves speak now. We can scarcely keep upright. My dress . . . the purse . . .'

She was laughing wildly as they went to obey her.

*   *   *

In her ceremonial gown, her purse strapped firmly to her waist, Juana stumbled to her husband's cabin. She scarcely recognised Philip the Handsome in the pale-faced man who shouted orders in a high voice cracked with fear, while his attendants helped him into an inflated leather jacket. Where was the swaggering heir of

Maximilian now? The fair hair was in disorder, there were smudges of fatigue under the blue eyes, and the beautiful mouth was petulant and afraid.

'Come,' screamed Philip. 'Is this thing safe? Fasten it. Do you think we have hours to waste. At any minute . . .'

Even as he spoke there was a sudden cry of 'Fire!' and an ominous flickering light rapidly lightened the darkness.

Juana, standing serene now in her rich garments, said in a voice much calmer than usual: 'The ship is on fire.'

'On fire!' shouted Philip. 'Put out the fire. Put out the fire. What will become of us!'

Don Juan Manuel, who was accompanying the royal party to Spain, said quietly: 'All that can be done is being done, Highness.'

'Where are the rest of the ships? Are they standing by?'

'Highness, we have lost the rest of the ships. The storm has scattered them.'

'Then what is to be done? We are doomed.'

No one answered, and then Philip turned and looked into the face of his wife who stood beside him. They seemed in that moment to take measure of each other. She in her rich gown with the purse tied to her waist was calmly awaiting death. Philip, in his inflated leather garment which his attendants swore would keep him afloat in a rough sea, was afraid.

She laughed in his face. 'We are together now, Philip,' she cried. 'You cannot leave me now.'

Then she flung herself at his feet and embraced his knees.

'I will cling to you,' she went on. 'I will cling so

closely that Death will not be able to separate us.'

Philip did not answer; he remained still, looking down at her; and it seemed to some who watched them that he found comfort in her arms which were about him.

She became tender and astonishingly calm, as though she realised that his fear made it necessary for her to be the strong one now.

'Why, Philip,' she said, 'whoever heard of a King's being drowned? There was never a King who was drowned.'

Philip closed his eyes as though he could not bear to contemplate the signs of impending disaster. His hand touched the leather garment on which the words 'The King, Don Philip' had been painted in huge letters. He who had been so vital had never thought of death. He was not yet thirty years of age, and life had given him so much. It was only Juana whose mind often led her into strange paths, only Juana, who had suffered deeply, who could look death in the face with a smile which was not without welcome.

He heard her voice shouting amid the tumult: 'I am hungry. Is it not time we ate? Bring me a box with something to eat.'

One of the men went off to do her bidding while she remained smiling, her arms about her trembling husband's knees.

*   *   *

The fire was now under control, thanks to the almost superhuman efforts of the crew. The ship was listing badly, and with the coming of day it was seen that land was close at hand.

209

Philip cried out in relief, shouting that they must make for dry land with all speed.

Don Juan Manuel was at his side. 'This is England,' he said. 'If we land, we put ourselves in the hands of the Tudor.'

'What else could we do?' demanded Philip. 'Is the Tudor more to be feared than a grave in the ocean bed?'

Don Juan admitted that until their ship was repaired they would have little hope of reaching Spain.

Philip spread his hands. The sight of land had restored his good spirits, because in his youthful arrogance he believed himself capable of handling the Tudor King; and it was only death that terrified him.

'We'll make for the shore with all speed,' he said.

So at last into the shallow harbour of Melcombe Regis came the battered ship carrying Juana and Philip. The people all along the coast as far as Falmouth had seen that a fleet of ships was in distress, and they were unsure as to whether these ships belonged to friends or enemies.

They gathered on the beaches, brandishing bows and arrows and their farming implements; and when Philip and Juana came into Melcombe Regis harbour they found a crowd of uncertain English men and women waiting for them.

The ship's company had gathered on the deck, and for some moments the people ashore believed that the strangers had come to attack them, for their pleas for help were unintelligible.

Then a young man, obviously of the gentry, pushed himself to the front of the crowd on the quay and shouted to the people on deck in French: 'Who are you? And why do you come here?'

The answer came: 'We are carrying The Archduke and Duchess of Austria, King and Queen of Castile, who were on their way to Spain and have been wrecked on your shores.'

That was enough. A stout, red-faced man came to stand beside the young man who had spoken in French.

'Tell them,' he said, 'that they must accept my hospitality. Let them come ashore and rest awhile in my house while I inform the King's Grace of their arrival.'

Thus Philip and Juana landed in England, and while they were given a sample of lavish English hospitality in the manor house of Sir John Trenchard in Melcombe Regis, close by Weymouth, couriers rode to Court to inform the King of the arrival of the royal pair.

*   *   *

How pleasant it was to be on dry land, and how generous was the hospitality bestowed upon the party by Sir John Trenchard and his household.

Juana and Philip were introduced to the comforts of an English manor house. Fires roared in enormous open fireplaces; great joints of meat turned on the kitchen spits and from the kitchens came the smell of baking.

Philip was happy to relax, and so delighted to be on *terra firma* that, for a few days, he was kind to Juana, who was accordingly filled with bliss.

News came that other ships of their fleet had found refuge along the coast as far west as

Falmouth. Some were not damaged beyond repair and could in a short time put to sea again.

This was comforting news, for when the storm had abated the weather was mild and the seas so calm that Don Juan Manuel was eager to continue with the journey.

Sir John Trenchard was bluffly indignant when this was suggested.

Nay, he declared. He'd not allow it. He would not be denied the honour of offering a little more entertainment to his distinguished guests. Why, his King would never forgive him if he let them go. It would seem churlish.

Don Juan Manuel understood.

'He is waiting for instructions from Henry,' he told Philip. 'I doubt that the King of England will allow you to go until there has been a meeting.'

'I see no reason why there should not be a meeting,' retorted Philip. 'Although if I wished to go, nothing would deter me.'

'The King of England might. Who knows, there might be an army approaching now to detain you.'

'Why should he do that?'

'Because you are in his country, and here he is all-powerful. It would be easier if you stayed here awhile as a guest rather than as a prisoner.'

'I should like to see my sister Catalina,' said Juana. 'How strange that a little while ago she wanted to arrange a meeting. Now the storm may have done that for us.'

Philip studied his wife. She was in one of her sane periods at this time. The ordeal at sea had calmed her while it had distressed others. None would guess now that the seed of madness lurked in her.

'Then,' said Philip, 'we must perforce enjoy English hospitality a little longer. And I have no fears of a meeting with the King of England. Indeed there is much I would like to discuss with him.'

Juan Manuel lowered his eyes. There were times when he was afraid of and for his reckless master.

Philip was aware of Juan Manuel's apprehension, and it amused him. He was going to make all his servants understand that he and he alone would make decisions as to policy. Seeing Juana quite normal now, Queen of Castile, Philip made up his mind that when he met Henry he would do so in his own right. He would meet him as the Archduke Philip, heir to Maximilian, not as the consort of the Queen of Castile, although of course it was Castile he wished to discuss with Henry. He was going to attempt to win Henry's support against Ferdinand; and as Juana, in her sudden return to sanity, might remember that Ferdinand was her father, it would be well for him to go on ahead of Juana to meet the King of England.

*   *   *

News from Henry came quickly to Melcombe Regis. He would not allow his guests to leave England until they had talked together. He was delighted to have such august visitors, and he was sending an escort to bring them to Windsor, where he and the Prince of Wales would be waiting to receive them.

Philip was delighted when he saw the

213

magnificence of the cavalcade which had been sent to take him to Windsor, but Don Juan Manuel and his more sober advisers were apprehensive. They knew that it was useless to caution their headstrong master. To do so might make him more reckless than ever.

Juana came to her husband as he stood by a window looking out on the brilliantly caparisoned horses which were waiting below.

'And they say,' cried Philip, 'that Henry is a mean man.'

'He has certainly treated my sister with great meanness,' replied Juana.

Philip looked pleased. The King of England was mean to the daughter of Ferdinand but eager to shower honours on the son of Maximilian.

Then he remembered that part of this show was for another of Ferdinand's daughters, and that this was his wife, the Queen of Castile.

'I look forward to the journey,' went on Juana. 'It will be pleasant to see this country which is now Catalina's. And what joy to see her at the end of the journey! My poor Catalina, her letters were often sad.'

'Juana,' said Philip, 'I am most solicitous for your comfort.'

A smile of happiness touched her lips and she gazed at him ardently. 'Oh Philip,' she murmured, 'you need have no fear for me. I only have to be with you to be happy.'

He gently unlaced her clinging fingers which were on his arm.

'I must travel with all speed to Windsor,' he said. 'You shall follow at a slower pace.'

'You mean . . . you will go without me!' Her

voice was shrill.

'I would not submit you to the hazards of rapid travel. You shall come slowly and with dignity.'

'Why, why?' she screamed. 'I have faced the dangers of the sea with you. What hazards would there be on the road? You shall not be rid of me. I know full well why you seek to escape me. There is that woman . . .'

'Be silent,' he said sharply. 'You weary me with your eternal jealousies.'

'Then remove the cause of my jealousy.'

'I should die of boredom, which I believe would be more tiresome than death by drowning.'

'You are so cruel,' she complained pathetically.

'You will do as I say,' he told her.

'Why should I? Am I not the Queen? But for me, Castile would never be for you.'

'So you boast once more of the titles you have brought me. Have I not paid dearly for them? Do I not have to endure you also?'

'Philip, I shall come with you.'

'You will do as I say. Do you want me to have you put away again?'

'You cannot do it.'

'Can I not? I did it before. Why should I not do it again? All know that you are mad. You make no secret of the fact. You shall say a wifely farewell to me and I will go on ahead of you. You will be calm and follow me. You will travel the same road, but some days after me. Is that such hardship?'

'It is always hardship not to be with you.'

He took her cheek between his fingers and pinched hard.

He said: 'If you do as I say, I will promise to be a loving husband to you this night.'

'Philip . . .' She could not quench the longing in her voice.

'Only if,' he went on, 'you promise to say a nice, pleasant, calm farewell to me on the morrow.'

'It is bribery,' she said. 'It is not the first time. You give me as a concession that which is mine by right, and always you demand a price for it.'

He laughed at her. He was so sure of his power over her. He would spend his last night at Melcombe Regis with her, and in the morning he would leave her behind while he rode on to Windsor to meet the King of England.

* * *

Windsor looked pleasant to Katharine that winter's day. She was pleased now that she had left Durham House and was at Court. It would be wonderful to see Juana again, to whisper confidences, to recall the old days and perhaps to explain the difficulties of her position here in England.

With her maids of honour ranged about her she was at the window, waiting for the first signs of the cavalcade.

'I wonder if I shall recognise her,' murmured Katharine. 'She will have changed since I saw her, doubtless.'

'It is long since she went to Flanders,' Maria de Salinas reminded her.

Katharine thought of that day, nearly ten years ago, when Juana had set out for Flanders. She remembered the sadness of her mother who had accompanied Juana to Laredo, and how Isabella had returned to find that her own mother—so like

Juana in her wildness—was dying in the Castle of Arevalo.

It was all so long ago. What resemblance would Juana, Queen of Castile, bear to that high-spirited, wayward girl who had gone into Flanders to marry Philip the Handsome?

She looked at her maids of honour, but their expressions were blank and she knew that they were thinking of the wild stories they had heard of her sister—how she had bound one of her husband's mistresses and cut off her long golden hair, how she had thought herself to be a prisoner at Medina del Campo and had escaped from her apartments and refused to return, spending the bitterly cold night out of doors in her night attire. Uneasy rumours of Juana's conduct continued to come from Flanders.

When I see her, thought Katharine, she will talk to me of her life; I shall be able to comfort her as she will comfort me.

So there she waited, and when the fanfares of trumpets heralded the arrival of the cavalcade, and the King and the Prince of Wales went down to the courtyard to receive the guests, Katharine saw the fair and handsome Philip, but she looked in vain for her sister.

She stood at her window watching the greetings between the royal parties. Surely Juana must be there. She was in England with Philip. Why was she not with him now?

Soon she herself would be expected to descend and greet the guests of the King; but she must wait until summoned; she must remember that there were many at the Court of greater importance than she was.

217

She gazed at her brother-in-law. He was indeed a handsome man. How haughty he looked, determined to stand as the equal of the King of England; and as he greeted him, by very comparison Henry VII of England seemed more aged and infirm than usual.

But there was the Prince of Wales—already taller than Philip himself—the golden Prince, even more arrogant than Philip, even more certain of his right to the centre of the stage.

Katharine could never look upon the Prince of Wales unmoved, and even at such a time as this she temporarily forgot Juana, because she must wonder whether or not that disturbing boy would eventually be her husband.

She heard her maids of honour whispering together.

'But how strange this is! What can have happened to the Queen of Castile?'

*   *   *

Those were uneasy days at Windsor for Philip's followers—not so for Philip; he was determined to enjoy the lavish hospitality. It was a pleasure to show his skill at hunting and hawking in the forests of Windsor; he liked to ride through the straggling street which was the town of Windsor, and to see the women at their windows, or pausing in the street, as he passed, all with those looks and smiles which he was accustomed to receive from women everywhere. He liked to sit in the great dining hall on the King's right hand and sample the various English dishes, to listen to the minstrels, to watch the baiting of bears, horses and mastiffs.

He did not know that the King of England only entertained on such a lavish scale when he hoped to profit from doing so.

Glorious days these were, and Philip was in no hurry to leave for Spain. He had met his sister-in-law, poor little Katharine, who seemed to be somewhat ill-used by this wily old Tudor. The girl was dull, he thought; too melancholy, lacking in the gaiety which he liked to find in women. She was shabby compared with the other Court ladies; he had little interest in her.

On the rare occasions when they met she persistently questioned him about Juana. Why was Juana not with him? Why did they not travel together?

'Ah,' he had replied, 'I came with all speed on the King's express desire. I did not wish to subject Juana to such a tiring journey.'

'Would she not have preferred to travel with you?'

'I have to be firm with her. I have to consider her health.'

Katharine did not trust him, and more than ever she longed to see her sister.

Meanwhile the King was making headway with Philip.

There was, sheltering in Burgundy under the protection of Maximilian, a cousin of that Earl of Warwick whom Henry had executed because of his claim to the throne; this cousin was Edmund de la Pole who called himself Duke of Suffolk; and, while such a man lived, Henry could not feel entirely secure. His great aim was to eliminate all those who laid claim to the throne and, with Edmund de la Pole skulking on the Continent, he could never be sure when the man might land in England and seek to take the Crown from him. He remembered his own days of exile and how he had lain in wait for the opportune moment to rise and snatch the throne for himself.

He was subtle in his dealing with Philip, and Philip had not learned subtlety. It was gratifying to the King of England that he had such an arrogant young man to deal with, for this made the way so much easier than if it had been necessary to bargain with Philip's wiser ministers.

He knew what Philip wanted from him: help against Ferdinand. Well, reasoned the King of England, that sly old fox Ferdinand was ever an enemy of mine.

Henry was finding Philip's visit stimulating, and he was enjoying it as much as his rheumatism would allow him to enjoy anything.

Henry was eager that there should be a commercial treaty with Flanders and this he obtained—making sure that it should be very advantageous to England.

It was not so easy to bring about the expulsion of Edmund de la Pole, but slyly and subtly Henry reminded Philip that he was held a prisoner in England—by the weather. But Philip knew that there was a veiled threat in the words; and even he did not see how they could leave England if Henry did not wish them to do so.

So de la Pole was thrown to the King, and Henry blessed that storm which had cast this incautious young man upon his shores.

'This is indeed a happy day,' he cried. 'See, we have come to two agreements already. We have a commercial treaty between our two countries, and you have agreed to give me the traitor, de la Pole. It was a happy day when you came to visit us.'

Happy for England, thought Juan Manuel; and he was already wondering how soon the fleet of ships, which were now assembling at Weymouth, could be ready to put to sea. He hoped it would be before the rash Philip had made more concessions to his wily host.

'Let us make even happier arrangements,' went on the King of England. 'It is the maxim of your House that it is better to wed than to war. If you will give me your sister Margaret I shall be a happy man.'

'There is none to whom I would rather give her,' answered Philip.

'And the Emperor?'

'My father and I are of one mind in this matter.'

'A speedy marriage would please me greatly.'

'A speedy marriage there shall be,' answered Philip. He did not mention that his sister had loudly protested against a match with the old King of England and that, since she had been twice married and twice widowed and was now Duchess of Savoy, she could not be forced against her will into a marriage which was unattractive to her.

But Philip would say nothing of this. How could he, to a man who might be his host but was also to some extent his jailer?

To discuss the marriage of the King's daughter Mary to Charles was a pleasant enough occupation. That marriage, if it ever took place, would occur far in the future when Philip would be miles away from England. The Prince of Wales' marriage to Philip's daughter Eleanor would not, if it ever came about, be so far distant. It was very

221

pleasant to discuss it, although Henry was on dangerous ground, thought Philip, when he talked of marrying to Juana's daughter a son who had already been promised to her sister.

Well, Juana had no say in these matters.

*　　　*　　　*

Katharine in her apartments in the Castle was being prepared by her ladies for the entertainment in the great hall.

They were sighing, all of them, because they had no new gowns, and even the one Katharine must wear had been mended.

'How shall we look?' wailed Francesca. 'The Archduke will be ashamed of us.'

'Perhaps he will be sorry for us,' put in Maria de Salinas.

'I do not think he would ever be sorry for anyone,' Maria de Rojas countered.

Katharine listened to their chatter. Poor Juana, she thought. How strange that you are not here with us!

She watched them putting the jewels in her hair.

'This brooch will cover the thin part of the bodice,' said Maria de Salinas.

It was incongruous to have a great ruby covering a threadbare bodice. But then, thought Katharine, my whole life has been incongruous since I came to England.

'I wonder if the Prince of Wales will dance,' said Francesca, 'and with whom.'

Katharine felt their eyes upon her and she tried not to show her embarrassment; the strangest part of all was not to know whether she was seriously

222

affianced to the Prince of Wales. He would soon be fifteen and it was on his fifteenth birthday that they were to have been married.

If that day comes and goes, and I am still a widow, Katharine pondered, I shall know that Henry is not intended for me.

The Princess Mary came into the apartment, carrying her lute, at which she had become very skilful.

'I hope,' she said, 'that I shall be able to play to the company tonight.'

How eagerly they sought the attention of the crowd, these Tudors, mused Katharine.

Mary was a beautiful girl, now about ten years old, wilful, wayward but so fascinating that even the King's face softened when he looked at her; and, when he was irritable with her, all knew that his rheumatism must be particularly painful.

'They will surely ask you to do so,' Katharine assured her.

'I hope I may play while Henry dances. I should like that.'

'Doubtless you will if you ask that you may.'

'I shall ask,' said Mary. 'Did you know that we are to return to Richmond on the eleventh?'

'Indeed no. I had not heard.'

'You are to return with me. It is my father's order.'

Katharine felt numb with disappointment. Each day she had waited for the arrival of Juana. It was now the eighth of the month, and if she left on the eleventh she had only three more days in which to wait for her sister—and even if she came now they would have only a short time together.

She said nothing. It was no use protesting. At

223

least she had learned the folly of that.

Oh, let her come soon, she prayed. Then she began to wonder why Juana was not with them and what mystery this was surrounding her sister who was Queen of Castile and yet was lacking in authority. Why, Juana had taken the place of their mother, and none would have dared dictate to Isabella what she must do—not even Ferdinand.

In the great hall that day there was feasting, and Katharine danced the Spanish dances with some of her women. The women enjoyed it; and Francesca in particular was very gay. After this, thought Katharine, they will long more than ever to return to Spain.

Mary played the lute while her father watched her fondly, and Prince Henry danced vigorously to loud applause. When he returned to his seat his eyes were on Katharine. Was she applauding as loudly as the rest?

He seemed satisfied; and Katharine noticed throughout the evening that his eyes were often fixed upon her, brooding, speculating.

She wondered what he was thinking; but she soon forgot to wonder. Her thoughts continually strayed to Juana and she was asking herself: What is this mystery in my sister's life? Is she deliberately being kept from me?

*   *   *

On the tenth of February, one day before that on which, at the King's command, Katharine was due to leave with the Princess Mary, Juana arrived at Windsor.

She was carried into the castle in her litter, and

Katharine was among those who waited to receive her.

Katharine looked in dismay at the woman her sister had become. Could that be young Juana, the gay—too gay—girl who had left Spain to marry this man who now obsessed her? Her hair was lustreless, her great eyes were melancholy; it seemed that all that vitality which had been so much a part of her had disappeared.

She was received with ceremony. First the King took her hand and kissed it; then the Prince of Wales bowed low in greeting.

'We have missed you at our revels,' said Henry.

Juana could not understand, but she smiled graciously.

Then Katharine was face to face with her sister. She knelt before her not forgetting, even at such a moment, that she was in the presence of the Queen of Castile.

Then the sisters looked into each other's faces and both were astonished at what they saw. Juana's little sister had become a tragic woman, no less than she had herself.

'Juana . . . oh, how happy I am to see you at last!' whispered Katharine.

'My sister! Why, you are no longer a child.'

'I am a widow now, Juana.'

'My poor, sweet sister!'

That was all. There were others to be greeted; there were the formalities to be considered; but even while these were in progress Katharine noticed how hungrily her sister's eyes followed the debonair figure of her husband, and she thought: What torture it must be to love a man as Juana loves him!

How brief was the time they could spend together. Had it been arranged, Katharine wondered, that her sister should arrive the day before she was to leave for Richmond, so that they might have a glimpse of each other and nothing more?

Yet at last when they were alone together Katharine was conscious of the rapid passing of time. She wanted to hold it back. There was so much to say, so many questions to ask that she, in fear of not having time to say half, was temporarily unable to think of any of them.

Juana was not helpful; she sat silent as though she were far away from the Castle at Windsor.

'Juana,' cried Katharine desperately, 'you are unhappy. Why, my sister? Your husband is in good health and you love him dearly. You are Queen of Castile. Are you unhappy, Juana, because you can only be Queen of Castile since our mother is no more?'

'He loves me,' said Juana in a low melancholy voice, 'because I am Queen of Castile.' Then she laughed, and Katharine was filled with uneasiness by the sound of that laughter. 'If I were not Queen of Castile he would throw me out into the streets to beg my bread tomorrow.'

'Oh, Juana, surely he is not such a monster.'

She smiled. 'Oh yes, he is a monster . . . the handsomest, finest monster that the world ever knew.'

'You love him dearly, Juana.'

'He is my life. Without him I should be dead. There is nothing in the world for me . . . except him.'

'Juana, our mother would not have you say such

things, or think such thoughts. You are the Queen even as she was. She would expect you to love Castile, to work for Castile, as she did. She loved us dearly; she loved our father; but Castile came first.'

'So it would be with Philip. He will love Castile.'

'He is not master in Castile. Even our father was not that. You know how our mother always ruled, never forgetting for one moment that she was the Queen.'

'It is the women,' sighed Juana. 'How I hate women. And in particular golden-haired women . . . big-breasted, big-hipped. That is the Flanders women, Catalina. How I loathe them! I could tear them all apart. I would throw them to the soldiers . . . the lowest of the soldiers . . . and say: They are the true enemies of the Queen of Castile.'

'Our father was not always faithful to our mother. It grieved her, I know. But she did not let it interfere with the affection she bore him.'

'Our mother! What did she know of love?'

'She knew much of love. Do you not remember her care for us? I verily believe that, when we left her, she suffered even more than we did.'

'Love!' cried Juana. 'What do you know of love? I mean love like this which I have for him. There is nothing like it, I tell you.' Juana had stood up; she began beating her hands against her stiffly embroidered bodice. 'You cannot understand, Catalina. You have never known it. You have never known Philip.'

'But why are you so unhappy?'

'Do you not know? I thought the whole world knew. Because of those others. They are always there. How many women have shared his bed since

227

he came to England? Do you know? Of course you do not. Even he will have forgotten.'

'Juana, you distress yourself.'

'I am in continual distress . . . except when he is with me. He says he does his duty. I am often pregnant. I am happiest when I am not, because he always remembers that I should become so.'

Katharine covered her face with her hands. 'Oh, Juana, please do not talk so.'

'How else should I talk? He went on in advance of me. Can you guess why? Because there were women with whom he wished to amuse himself. I tell you, I hate women . . . I hate . . . hate . . . hate women.'

Juana had begun to rock herself to and fro, and Katharine was afraid her shouts would be heard in those apartments of the Castle near her own.

She tried to soothe her sister; she put her arms about her, and Juana immediately clung to her, rocking Katharine with her.

'Why, Juana,' whispered Katharine, 'you are distraught. Would you like to lie on your bed? I would sit beside it and talk to you.'

Juana was silent for a while, and then she cried out: 'Yes. Let it be so.'

Katharine took her sister's arm and together they went to Juana's bedchamber. Some of her attendants were waiting there, and Katharine knew from their expression that they were prepared for anything to happen.

'The Queen wishes to rest,' said Katharine. 'You may go. I will look after her.'

The women retired, leaving the sisters together, and Katharine realised that Juana's mood had changed once more. Now she had sunk into melancholy silence.

'Come,' said Katharine, 'lie down. Your journey must have been very tiring.'

Still Juana did not answer but allowed herself to be led to the bed and covered with the embroidered coverlet.

Katharine sat by the bed and reached out for the white ringed hand. She held it, but there was no response to her tenderness from the hand which lay listlessly in hers.

'There is so much we have to say to each other,' said Katharine. 'You shall tell me your troubles and I shall tell you mine. Oh, Juana, now that I have seen you I know how wretched I have been in England. Imagine my position here. I am unwanted. When our mother was alive I longed to return to Spain. Now that she is gone I do not know what I want. I do not understand the King of England. His plans change abruptly, and a marriage is planned one day and forgotten the next. You must see how poor I have become. Look at this dress . . .'

She stood up and spread her skirt, but Juana was not even looking at her.

She went on: 'I suppose my only hope is marriage with the Prince of Wales. If that should take place, at least I should be accorded the dignity due to my rank. But will it ever take place? He is much younger than I and they say he is to marry Marguerite of Angoulême, but the King has arranged something other with your husband.'

At the mention of Philip a faint smile touched Juana's lips.

'They say he is the handsomest man in the world, and they do not lie.'

'He is indeed handsome, but it would have been better if he had been kind,' said Katharine quickly. 'While you are here, Juana, cannot you do something to alleviate my poverty? If you would speak to King Henry . . .'

The door opened and Philip himself came into the room. He was laughing and his fair face was slightly flushed.

'Where is my wife?' he cried. 'Where is my Queen?'

Katharine was surprised at the change which came over Juana. She had leaped from the bed, all melancholy gone.

'Here I am, Philip. Here I am.'

Without ceremony she flung herself into his arms. It nauseated Katharine to see her sister clinging to this man, who stood, his arms limp at his sides, while he looked over Juana's head at Katharine.

'I see,' said Philip, 'that you have an august visitor.'

'It is Catalina . . . only my little sister.'

'But I disturb you. And it is so long since you have met. I must leave you together.'

'Philip, oh Philip . . . do not go. It is so long since we have been alone together. Philip, stay now . . .'

Katharine stood up. She could bear no more.

'Pray give me leave to retire,' she said to her sister.

But Juana was not looking at her; she was breathless with desire and completely unaware of her sister's presence.

Philip smiled at her sardonically; and she saw that he was not displeased. Was he showing her how abject the Queen of Castile could become in her need for the comfort only he could give? Was he telling her that the present King of Castile would be very different from the previous one? Ferdinand had been a strong man, but his wife had been stronger. Juana would never be another Isabella of Castile.

Katharine went swiftly to her own apartments. What will become of her? she asked herself. What will become of us all?

So this was the meeting for which she had longed. There would be no time for more meetings, because she was to leave Windsor for Richmond tomorrow. There were no concessions for Katharine from the King of England, any more than there were for Juana, Queen of Castile, from her cruel careless husband, Philip the Handsome.

She did not even listen to what I was telling her, thought Katharine. She completely forgot my existence, the moment he entered the room.

*   *   *

There was little to do, with the Court at Richmond, but sit and embroider with her maids of honour and listen to their laments for Spain. The Princess Mary was with her often. She would sit at Katharine's feet playing her lute, listening to her comments and being instructed by them, for Katharine herself excelled with the lute. Sometimes they sang together the old songs of Spain, but more often the songs of England. 'For,' complained Mary, 'your songs are sad songs.'

'They sound sad,' Katharine told her, 'because I sing them in a strange land.'

Mary scarcely listened; she was too absorbed by

her own affairs; but Katharine enjoyed the company of this light-hearted, beautiful child who was the favourite of everyone at Court.

She had seen nothing of the King or the Prince since she had left Windsor; she knew that the fleet of ships which had been in difficulties in the Channel were now being refitted and made ready for the journey to Spain. With the coming of spring they would sail away again.

I shall never see Juana again, thought Katharine. And if I did, what could we have to say to each other?

In April, Philip and Juana embarked at Weymouth and on a calm sea they set out for Spain.

Katharine remembered all the hopes that had come to her when Doña Elvira had first suggested such a meeting. How different the reality had been!

She knew, as she had never known before, that she was alone, and her future lay not with her own people but the English rulers.

CHAPTER XI

PHILIP AND FERDINAND MEET

News was brought to Ferdinand that his son-in-law had landed at Corunna.

This was disquieting news. Ferdinand knew he had good reason to mistrust Philip and that his son-in-law's intention was to drive him out of Castile, become King himself and reduce Ferdinand to nothing but a petty monarch of Aragon.

This Ferdinand would fight against with all his might.

He was not an old man, he reminded himself. He felt younger than he had for many years. This was doubtless due to the fact that he had acquired a new wife, his beautiful Germaine.

Many eyebrows had been raised when Germaine had arrived at Duefias, close by Valladolid, for there, thirty-seven years before, he had come in disguise from Aragon for his marriage to Isabella.

There were many people in Castile who looked upon Isabella as a saint, and they were deeply shocked that Ferdinand should consider replacing her; and to do so by a young and beautiful girl seemed double sacrilege; moreover as any fruit of the union might result in the breaking up of Spain into two kingdoms, this was not a popular marriage.

Ferdinand was realising how much of his popularity he had owed to Isabella. Yet he had lost none of his ambition; and he was ready enough to end his six weeks' honeymoon with the entrancing Germaine in order to go forward and meet Philip, to match his son-in-law's rashness with his own experience and cunning.

There was one man in Spain whom he heartily disliked but who, he knew, was the country's most brilliant statesman. This man was Ximenes, whom, against Ferdinand's advice, Isabella had created Archbishop of Toledo and Primate of Spain. Ferdinand summoned Ximenes to his presence and Ximenes came.

There was a faint contempt in the ascetic face, which Ferdinand guessed meant that the Archbishop was despising the bridegroom. This was a marriage which would seem unholy to Ximenes, and when he received him Ferdinand was conscious of a rising indignation. But he calmed himself. Ferdinand had learned to subdue his hot temper for the sake of policy.

'You have heard the news, Archbishop?' he asked when the Archbishop had greeted him in his somewhat superior manner, which Ferdinand thought implied that he, Ximenes, was the ruler.

'I have indeed, Highness.'

'Well?'

'It will be necessary to walk carefully. There should be a meeting between you and the Archduke, and it should be a peaceful one.'

'Will he agree to this?'

'He will if he is wise.'

'He is young, Archbishop. Wisdom and youth rarely go together.'

'Wisdom and age mate almost as rarely,' replied the Archbishop.

That allusion to the marriage made the hot

234

blood rush to Ferdinand's cheeks. He had often advised Isabella to send the insolent fellow back to his hermit's cell. But he was too useful. He was too clever. And he was ready to devote that usefulness and cleverness to Spain.

'What in your opinion should be done in the matter?' asked Ferdinand shortly.

The Archbishop was silent for a while; then he said: 'As husband of the *Reina Proprietaria,* Philip has a stronger claim to the Regency than Your Highness. Yet since you are a ruler of great experience and this is a young man who has had a greater experience of light living than of serious government, it might be that the grandees of Spain would prefer to see you as Regent rather than your son-in-law.'

'And you would support my claim?'

'I would consider Your Highness the more likely to do good for Spain, and for that reason I would give you my support.'

Ferdinand was relieved. Much depended on the Archbishop. It was fortunate that Philip's reputation for licentious behaviour had travelled ahead of him; it would not serve him well with Ximenes.

'Philip is now in Galicia,' said Ferdinand. 'It will take a little time for us to meet; and in the meantime, I understand that many of the grandees are flocking to him, to welcome him to Spain.'

Ximenes nodded. 'I fear the recent marriage has not endeared Your Highness to many of the late Queen's subjects.'

'She would not have wished me to remain unmarried.'

'One of her most proud achievements was the

union of Castile and Aragon under one crown.'

Ferdinand's brows were drawn together in a frown and he needed a great deal of restraint not to send this insolent fellow about his own business. But this *was* his business. Ximenes was Primate of Spain and he was not a man to diverge from what he considered his duty, no matter whom he upset by doing it. Such a man would go cheerfully to the stake for his opinions.

One should rejoice in him, thought Ferdinand grudgingly. He seeks no honours for himself. He thinks only of Spain; and because he believes I shall make a better Regent than Philip he will support me.

'There must be a speedy meeting between Your Highness and your son-in-law.'

'Should I go cap in hand, across a country which I have ruled, to implore audience of this young man who has no right to be here except for the fact that he is married to my daughter?'

Ximenes was silent for a few seconds; then he said: 'I myself could go to him as your emissary. I could arrange this meeting.'

Ferdinand studied the gaunt figure of the Archbishop in those magnificent robes of office which he wore carelessly and under protest. It was only an order from the Pope which had made him put on such vestments, and Ferdinand knew that beneath them he would be wearing the hair shirt, and the rough Franciscan robe. Such a man would surely overawe any—even such as Philip the Handsome.

Ferdinand knew he could trust this affair in such hands. He was greatly relieved and it occurred to him in that moment that Isabella had been right when she had insisted on giving this man the high office of Archbishop of Toledo, even though Ferdinand had wanted it for his illegitimate son.

It seemed that, now she was dead, Ferdinand was continually discovering how right Isabella had so often been.

*   *   *

In the village of Sanabria, on the borders of Leon and Galicia, Ferdinand met Philip. Philip came at the head of a large force of well-armed troops, but Ferdinand brought with him only some two hundred of his courtiers riding mules. On the right hand of Philip rode Juan Manuel, but on the right hand of Ferdinand rode Ximenes.

The meeting was to take place in a church and, when Philip entered, only Juan Manuel accompanied him; and Ximenes was the sole companion of Ferdinand.

Ximenes studied the young man and found that he did not despise him as he had thought he would. Philip was not merely a philanderer and seeker after pleasure. There was ambition there also. The mind of this extraordinarily handsome young man was light, and he had never learned to concentrate on one subject for long. He had been born heir to Maximilian; and consequently all his life he had been petted and pampered. But there was material there, mused Ximenes, which could be moulded by such as himself; once this young man had realised the brief satisfaction which the indulgence of his sensuality could bring him, a ruler of significance might emerge.

As for Ferdinand, he and Ximenes had never

237

been friends. It was the Queen whom Ximenes had served from the time Isabella had brought him from his hermit's hut until her death, when he had occupied the highest position in Spain; and although Ximenes had not—so he assured himself—ever sought such honours, since they were thrust upon him he had done all in his power to deserve them. The welfare of Spain was of the utmost importance to him. He would serve Spain with his life; and now he was ranged on the side of Ferdinand, and his great desire was to prevent civil strife between these two.

He did not like Juan Manuel—a trouble-maker and a self-seeker, decided Ximenes. His presence would hamper the proceedings greatly, for it was clear to Ximenes that Philip relied on the man.

Ximenes turned to Juan Manuel and said: 'Their Highnesses wish to speak in private. You and I should leave them for a while. Come.'

He took Juan Manuel's arm and with him went from the church.

Juan Manuel was so overcome by the personality of this strange man that he obeyed without question; and when they were outside the church, Ximenes said: 'Ah, but there should be someone to guard the door. It would not be well if their Highnesses were interrupted. As a man of the Church I will undertake this task. Return to your army and I will send for you immediately your presence is required.'

Juan Manuel hesitated, but when he looked into those deep-set eyes he felt that he was in the presence of a holy man and dared not disobey. So he left Ximenes, who returned to the church, which he entered, thus joining Philip and

Ferdinand.

Ferdinand was asking Philip why his daughter had not accompanied her husband to this meeting place, for she was in truth the ruler of Castile; and Philip was explaining that his wife, alas, was not always in her right mind. There were occasions when she was lucid enough, but there were others when it was necessary to put her under restraint.

Ferdinand accepted this. It suited him, no less than Philip, that Juana should be at times sane and at others insane. Her unbalanced state was a matter which men such as her husband and father would use according to their needs.

It soon became clear that the advantages were all in Philip's hands and he was not going to relinquish them. Juana was Queen of Castile; her son Charles was heir to the crowns both of Castile and Aragon. Therefore as husband of Juana and the father of the heir he had a greater right to govern Castile as Regent.

There was nothing Ferdinand could do about that and Ximenes was aware of this. Ferdinand must sign those documents required of him; he must surrender the entire sovereignty of Castile to Philip and Juana, and all that was left to him were the grand masterships of the military orders and those revenues which Isabella had left to him in her will.

Thus Ferdinand, in the village of Sanabria, lost all that he had so longed to hold. He was merely King of Aragon; and there was a Regent of Castile. It seemed as though the provinces were once more divided and Isabella's dream of a united Spain might be in danger of destruction.

Ximenes agreed that this was the only course. In

any case to have refused to accept it would have meant civil war in Spain, and that was unthinkable. The Archbishop therefore decided that it was his duty to attach himself to Philip. He did not trust the young man and he felt a great desire to guide him. Moreover, as Archbishop of Toledo his place was with the ruler of Castile. But he knew how Isabella would have been saddened by this scene in the church; and Ximenes was determined that he would watch the interests of Isabella's husband.

As they came out of the church Ferdinand's expression was enigmatic. Yet he did not look like an ambitious man who has signed away a kingdom.

CHAPTER XII

THE MYSTERIOUS DEATH OF PHILIP

Philip was triumphant. Now he would ride into Valladolid and all should proclaim him as the ruler of Castile. As for Juana, he had determined to shut her away. He had long been wearied by her passion and possessiveness; Ferdinand had surrendered Castile. So why should he hesitate to go forward and take it; and since Juana was an encumbrance, why not rid himself of her by shutting her away as her grandmother had been shut away before her?

Philip usually acted on impulse, and he immediately called together the most influential noblemen of Castile, and when they were assembled he told them how concerned he was regarding his wife's mental state.

'I have pondered this matter deeply, as you may well imagine,' he went on, 'and it is my considered judgment that the Queen's interests could best be served if she were allowed to live in retirement. My greatest desire is to do what is best for her, and on this account I ask you all to sign a declaration agreeing to her retirement into seclusion.'

There was silence among the nobles. They could not forget that the Queen was the daughter of the great Isabella and that this young man's only claim to the crown was through his marriage with Juana and the fact that he was the father of Charles, the boy who would immediately become their King should Juana die.

Was it not possible, they asked themselves, that

cunning men might trick them? Could they be sure that Juana was mad?

The Admiral of Castile, who was Ferdinand's cousin, spoke for that faction which was in doubt.

'It would seem that, although the Queen's mind is said to be at times deranged, there are many who declare her to be sane; and we must all remember that she is the true Queen of Castile and heir of Isabella. Before agreeing to such measures I should wish to have an interview with the Queen.'

Philip was nonplussed. He had no wish for Juana to come face to face with these men. How could he be sure of what she would say to them? He might threaten Juana or bribe her with offers of his company as he had on other occasions; but Juana was growing suspicious. If she were mad she was not without cunning. She guessed that he was considering putting her away, and that was something against which she would fight with all her strength.

But he dared not refuse to allow the Admiral to see the Queen.

*　　　*　　　*

Juana lifted leaden eyes to the Admiral's face. He was regarding her with kindness; he was trying to tell her that he was her cousin; that it grieved him to see Castile ruled by one who was not related to them except by his marriage to her.

'You have recently seen my father?' asked Juana at length.

'Yes, Highness. I said farewell to him but yesterday. That was at Tudela. He is now on his way to Aragon.'

'It seems so strange. I did not see him. It is so many years since I have seen him; yet I, his daughter, did not see him.'

'That is strange, Highness, and sad.'

Her eyes were melancholy.

'So much that is strange would seem to happen to me now,' she said sadly. 'I should have been so happy to see my father, even though he has a new wife now and I cannot understand how he could have replaced my mother. But I should dearly have liked to see him again. God guard him always.'

'Highness, we of Castile wish to see you govern side by side with your husband.'

She nodded.

'That is the wish of us all. Our great Queen Isabella appointed you her heir. It was her wish that you should govern Castile with your husband beside you. But, as her daughter, *you* are our Queen.'

At the mention of her mother Juana's expression lightened a little.

'It was her wish,' she said. 'Here in Castile I recall the past so much more readily than I did in Flanders. It was her wish, was it not? And it is true that I am Queen of Castile.'

'It is true, Highness,' answered the Admiral.

When he left her he went to his friends and gave them his opinion.

'She seemed as lucid as one could wish. We must guard against ambitious men.'

*　　　*　　　*

The knowledge came to Juana one morning when she awoke after a restless night which she had

243

spent alone.

He wants to be rid of me, she thought. He is planning to put me away.

Where had he spent the night? With one of his women doubtless. He had never considered her feelings, and he wanted her out of his sight. It was not because she was in the way of his having other women, but because he wanted her crown. He did not wish to be merely her consort. He wanted to rule alone.

She would not part with her crown. It was the one possession which made her desirable to him.

The dull melancholy had left her eyes. They sparkled with purpose. She would show him now that she was ready to fight, that she was not as stupid as he thought.

He came to her apartments, all smiles.

They were to make a solemn entry into Valladolid, and he dared not go without her. The people were suspicious of him; they wanted to see their Queen. They would not accept his word for her madness, but wanted to judge for themselves.

Ah, Philip, she thought, you may be master of Castile's Queen but you are not yet master of Castile.

He took her hand and kissed it; how gracious he could be, how charming! She yearned to throw herself into his arms, but she was able to restrain herself because she kept thinking of the castle of Arevalo where her grandmother had lived out her clouded days.

Not for me! she wanted to shout. I am Queen of Castile and I will not allow you to put me away.

'Are you ready for the ceremony?' he asked.

'Ready,' she countered, 'and determined to

accompany you.'

'I am glad to hear it.'

'Are you, Philip? I thought you were hoping that you would go alone.'

'But why should you have such an idea?'

She smiled, saying nothing, and the quietness of her smile alarmed him. Could it be that he was losing his hold over her?

'I thought that in your condition . . .'

'But three months' pregnant. That is nothing, Philip.'

He could scarcely bear to look at her, he was so dismayed. Now that he wished her to show her madness she was being perfectly restrained. She did not cling to him as he had become accustomed to her doing. She seemed almost aloof. It was that Admiral of Castile who had put notions into her head. He would have to go a little warily where she was concerned.

He put his arms about her and held her against him. 'I am concerned for your health,' he said, and when he felt her body quiver a triumphant smile curved his lips. The old power was still there. She was fighting a desperate battle to resist it, but he was determined it should be a losing battle.

'Your concern is appreciated,' she said, 'the more so because it is rare.'

'Oh come, Juana, you know how fond I am of you.'

'I did not know. Perhaps because your ways of showing it are so strange.'

'You have allowed yourself to be jealous . . . unnecessarily.'

'That was foolish of me,' she said. 'Now that I am in Castile I remember so much my mother taught me. I hear that there are two banners. I should like to see them.'

'They shall be brought to you,' said Philip, hiding his chagrin. This new calmness, this undoubted sanity, was more disturbing than her madness, and he was going to strain every effort to have her put away because, if she persisted like this, he would find himself in a similar position to that endured by Ferdinand in his relationship with Isabella. That was something Philip would never endure.

But for the time he must act cautiously.

The banners were brought and Juana studied them. 'But it would seem,' she said, 'that there are two rulers of Castile. There is only one; that is the Queen.'

'Have you forgotten that I am your husband?' demanded Philip hotly.

'In the past *you* have forgotten that more readily than I have. My husband you are indeed; that is why you ride beside me as my consort. But there is only one ruler of Castile.'

What could he say? He was surrounded by strong men who would be ready to fly to her support against him. Philip had not believed this situation possible; but when they came to Valladolid, Juana rode as the Queen of Castile, and her companion was not the King but merely her consort.

Mounted on her white jennet, dressed in the sable robes of royalty, Juana delighted the people of Valladolid. They remembered that this was the daughter of their own Isabella; and their cheers were for their Queen.

Philip was dissatisfied. The Cortes had declared its allegiance to Queen Juana and had stated its willingness to accept Philip only as her consort.

Philip fumed with rage.

'The Queen is mad!' he cried. 'She is not in the least like her mother. Sometimes I wonder who is the madder—the Queen or the people who insist on making her their ruler.'

The Admiral of Castile stood firm.

'I and many others with me will not allow this iniquitous deed to be done,' he said. 'We shall never stand aside and see our Queen sent into seclusion that others may rule in her stead.'

Philip saw that it was no use expecting help from the Castilian nobles; he turned to his own supporters, the chief of whom was Juan Manuel, who saw that with Philip as ruler many rich pickings would fall into his hands. He was continually at Philip's side and he assured him that in good time they would achieve their end, and Juana would be forced into retirement leaving the field clear for Philip.

Philip was lavishly generous to those whom he considered to be his friends, and recklessly he distributed revenues to them which should have gone to the maintenance of the state. Juan Manuel, on whom he relied as on no other, was becoming richer every week; but Juan was rapacious; he had been led to Philip's side because he believed that Ferdinand had denied him the honours due to him, and he could not grasp enough.

He greatly desired the Alcazar of Segovia which

was in the charge of the Marquis and Marchioness of Moya—the latter was that Beatriz de Bobadilla who had been Isabella's greatest friend—and Philip, deciding that the Alcazar should be given to Juan Manuel as a reward for his fidelity, sent orders to the Marquis and Marchioness to leave the Alcazar immediately.

The command was delivered into the hands of the intrepid Beatriz de Bobadilla, who retorted that the Alcazar should be handed over to one person only, and that was Isabella's daughter, Queen Juana.

Philip was furious when he heard this and sent troops ahead to take the Alcazar, while he himself prepared to follow them, Juana with him.

Juana's resistance was beginning to break down. The effort of remaining calm had been too much for her. If she could have overcome her passionate need of Philip she could have continued in her calm restraint; but he was always there, always taunting her, understanding how she needed him and enjoying baiting her in this way. He was luring her to display her hysteria before the nobles of Castile who had declared her to be sane. She knew this, but she could not always fight against it. And when he mocked her, she wanted to throw herself into his arms, as she had done on so many previous occasions, and implore him to be a good and faithful husband to her.

'Philip,' she said, 'why are you so eager to take the Alcazar of Segovia?'

'Because that insolent woman has denied it to us.'

'She is a formidable woman. I remember her in my childhood. She would even advise my mother.'

248

'She will see that we will brook none of her insolence.'

'Yet she was a good friend. Should you not leave her in peace out of respect to my mother?'

'I leave no one in peace to insult me.'

His mouth tightened and the newly realised fear came back to her.

'Why do you want the Alcazar of Segovia?'

He did not answer. 'I know,' she cried. 'It is because you want to make me a prisoner there. Segovia will be for me what Arevalo was to my grandmother. You are going to shut me away . . . away from the world. You are going to make them believe I am mad.'

Still he did not answer.

She went on wildly: 'I will go no further. I will not be put away. I am not mad. I am the Queen. You wish to take my crown from me, but you shall not.'

Philip laid a hand on her jennet's bridle, but she hit him. She heard his low, devilish laugh.

Now she was really alarmed; now she was certain that her premonition was true. He was going to imprison her in Segovia and announce to the world that she was no longer capable of living among ordinary people.

She slid down from her jennet and lay on the ground.

'I will not go a step farther towards Segovia,' she announced.

The cavalcade had halted and Philip was delighted. Now there was going to be one of those scenes which surely must convince all who saw it of her madness.

'Mount your jennet,' he said quietly. 'They will

249

be waiting for you at Segovia.'

There seemed to be a grave threat behind his words which terrified her, and she lay writhing on the ground.

Philip leaped from his horse and bent over her with a show of tenderness.

'Juana,' he said audibly, 'I pray you remount. Do you want everyone to say that you are mad?'

She looked into his eyes and she was afraid of him; and yet she knew that her great fear was not that she would be shut away from the world but that she would be shut away from him.

She rose obediently and mounted her jennet; then she turned away from the party and cried: 'I shall not enter Segovia, because I know that you plan to lock me away in the Alcazar there.'

Then she galloped ahead of them across country and back again, refusing to ride towards Segovia or back the way they had come.

Dusk had fallen and night came; and Juana continued to ride back and forth over the country round Segovia, determined not to enter the town.

Philip thought: If ever anyone doubted her madness, can they do so any longer?

Nothing could have pleased him more.

Such conduct in the Queen of Castile could scarcely be called sanity.

*　　　　*　　　　*

Philip's troops had driven Beatriz de Bobadilla from Segovia, and the Alcazar was now in the possession of Juan Manuel.

There was a certain discontent throughout Castile that this foreigner should come among

250

them and take their castles with their revenues and distribute them among his friends. Soon, it was said, all the strongholds of Castile would be in the hands of Philip's followers, and the old Castilian nobility would have no power in the land.

Philip had decided against going into Segovia, as Juana showed such fear of the place, and had gone instead to Burgos where he, Juana and their party lodged at the palace of the Constable of Castile, who belonged to the Enriquez family and was related to Ferdinand.

In view of Juana's strange conduct on the way to Segovia Philip felt justified in putting guards outside her apartments, so that she was to some extent under supervision.

The Constable's wife, who was the hostess to the party, expressed her concern that the Queen should be treated so, and as a result Philip ordered her to leave the palace.

This seemed the utmost arrogance, and the whisperings against the Queen's consort intensified; but Philip cared little for this and laughed with Juan Manuel at the Castilians. He had the troops and they would enforce his wishes. He did not doubt that before long he would have Juana put right away finally and he himself would be accepted as ruler in very truth.

'In the meantime,' he said, 'we should celebrate our victories, my dear Juan. The Alcazar of Segovia has fallen into our hands; and now we might say that the same has happened to this palace of Burgos. Once we have rid ourselves of that interfering woman the place is ours. Do you not think that that is worthy of a little celebration?'

'Very worthy, Highness,' agreed Juan.

251

'Then see to it. Arrange a banquet, a ball; and I will show these Spaniards how the Flemings can beat them at all sport.'

'It shall be done.'

While they talked together a page arrived to tell Philip that an envoy from Ferdinand had arrived at Burgos.

'Let him be brought to me,' said Philip; and when the page had gone he smiled at Juan Manuel.

'What despatches are these my worthy father-in-law sees fit to send me, I wonder?'

'Oh, there is nothing to fear from him. The old lion has had his teeth drawn. He will find it a different matter being merely King of Aragon instead of Spain.'

'My mother-in-law kept the fellow in his place. She must have been a strong-minded woman.'

Juan Manuel looked serious for a moment. When he remembered the great Queen Isabella he could not help wondering what she would say if she could see him now, a traitor to her husband.

He shrugged aside the thought; Ferdinand's conduct would not have pleased her either, he reflected. It seemed to him that if the great Queen could come alive again she would be so saddened by her husband's conduct that she would have little thought to spare for Juan Manuel.

Philip was his master now, and it was Philip whose interests were his own.

'It will be interesting to see what despatches this fellow has brought,' went on Philip. 'You may remain, and we will study them together.'

A few minutes later the page returned with Ferdinand's envoy.

'Don Luis Ferrer,' he announced.

And Ferdinand's envoy was bowing before the man who was certain that before long he would be sole ruler of Castile.

*　　　*　　　*

The celebrations were magnificent. Juan Manuel had arranged them to appeal to his master. He wished to show his gratitude for all the benefits which had come his way since he had entered Philip's service; he wished him to know that he would continue to lay all his skill at his master's feet.

Juana was allowed to partake in the celebrations.

Juan had said: 'It would be unwise at this stage to shut her away completely. Wait until more fortresses have come into our hands.'

'Rest assured,' said Philip, 'there will be others as important as Segovia and Burgos.'

'Let her show the people that she is truly mad. Then they cannot complain.'

Philip agreed with this. But he had made up his mind that he was going to put her away in as complete a seclusion as that in which her grandmother had passed the last years of her life.

Juana joined in the feasting. There were days when she was very gay, and others when she was overcome by her melancholy. There were times when she calmly received the homage of all; there were others when she shut herself away in her apartments.

She called her father's envoy, Luis Ferrer, to her and demanded to hear news of her father, of whether he spoke often of her or any of her sisters;

of how he lived with his new wife.

Luis Ferrer was eager to talk to her of Ferdinand, and Manuel was afraid that he was trying to bring about a meeting between father and daughter which, he was sure, could only result in harm to Philip.

'We should watch this Luis Ferrer,' he said to Philip. 'It is my belief that the fellow is here for no good purpose.'

The peak of the celebrations was planned to take place on a warm September day. There was to be a banquet more lavish than any of those of the last few days, and afterwards there would be ball games, because Philip excelled at these and he was very eager to show the Castilians what he called his superior Flemish skill.

Juana was present at the banquet. She had rarely seen her husband so gay, and she thought how beautiful he was and how in comparison all others—men and women—seemed ugly and lacking in grace.

Beside her at the table was Luis Ferrer, and she was glad of this because she knew that it disturbed Philip to see them together, and that meant that, while she was with Ferrer, at least Philip was thinking of her.

As soon as the banquet was over the ball games began and here Philip certainly did excel, for he beat all his opponents. Yet how could one be sure, Juana wondered, whether his opponents felt it would be wise to let him win? Nevertheless he played with great skill and she was momentarily happy to see him flushed and taking a boyish pride in his achievements.

He was very hot when the game was won, and he

called for a drink. No one was quite sure afterwards who gave him that drink; one thing was certain: he drank deep.

During the dancing and pageantry which followed, several people noticed that he seemed a little tired. But then it had been a strenuous ball game.

When she retired that night Juana lay in her bed hoping he would come to her, although she knew he would not; in four months' time she could expect the birth of a child, so he would not come—unless of course he wished to placate her, which he seemed nowadays inclined to do at certain times.

There in the quiet of her apartment Juana began to think of the sadness of her life and to ask herself if there was not a curse on the House of Spain. She had heard such a legend at the time of her sister's death. Her brother, Juan, was dead and his heir had been still-born; her sister, Isabella, had died in childbed and her child had followed her to the grave. That left Juana, Maria and Catalina. Maria might be happy in Portugal, but Catalina certainly was not so in England. As for herself surely none was as unhappy as she was.

She thought sadly of Catalina's woes. Her sister had talked of them.

'But I did not listen,' whispered Juana. 'I could only think of my own miseries which I know are far greater than hers. For what greater tragedy could befall a woman than to have a husband whom she adores with a passionate intensity which borders on madness, but who cares so little for her that he is planning to declare her mad and put her from him?'

There were strange noises in the palace tonight.

She could hear the sound of footsteps and whispering voices.

'Shall I wake the Queen?'

'She should know.'

'She would want to be with him.'

Juana rose from her bed and wrapped a robe about her.

'Who is there?' she called. 'Who is whispering there?'

One of her women came in, looking startled.

'The doctors have sent word, Highness . . .' she began.

'Doctors!' cried Juana. 'Word of what?'

'That His Highness is in a fever and a delirium. They are bleeding him now. Would Your Highness care to go to his bedside?'

Juana did not wait to answer; she sped through the apartments to those of Philip.

He was lying on his bed, his fair hair made darker with sweat, and his beautiful blue eyes looked blankly at her. He was murmuring, but none understood what he said.

She knelt by the bed and cried: 'Philip, my dearest, what has happened?'

Philip's lips moved, but his glassy eyes stared beyond her.

'He does not know me,' she said. She turned to the physicians. 'What does this mean? What has happened?'

'It is a chill, Highness. Doubtless His Highness became too hot during the ball game and drank too much cold water. That can produce a fever.'

'A fever! So it is a fever. What are you doing for him?'

'We have bled him, Highness. But the fever

persists.'

'Then bleed him again. Do not stand there doing nothing. Save him. He must not die.'

The physicians smiled knowledgeably. 'Your Highness is unduly disturbed. This is but a slight fever. His Highness will soon be playing another ball game to delight his subjects.'

'He is young,' said Juana, 'and he is healthy. He will recover.'

She was calm now, because she felt exultant. It was his turn now to be at her mercy. She would let no one else nurse him. She would do everything herself. Now that he was ill she was indeed Queen of Castile and mistress of this palace. Now she would be the one to give the orders and, no matter whom she commanded, they must obey.

*   *   *

All through the rest of the night she was with him, and in the morning he seemed a little better.

He opened his eyes and recognised her sitting there.

'What happened?' he asked.

'You had a little fever.' She laid a cool hand on his brow. 'I have been sitting by your bed since they told me. I am going to nurse you back to health.'

He did not protest; he lay looking at her, and she thought how defenceless he seemed, with the arrogance gone from him, and his usually ruddy cheeks pale. She felt very tender towards him, and she said to herself: 'How I love him! Beyond all things. Beyond my children, beyond my pride.'

He was aware of her feelings, and even now, weak as he was, he relished his power over her.

'I shall nurse you until you are quite recovered. I shall allow no other woman in the room.'

His lips twitched faintly in a smile, and she thought he was remembering the early days of their relationship when he had found her more desirable than he did now.

He tried to raise himself but he was very weak and, as he moved, he grimaced with pain.

'It is in my side,' he said in answer to her question and, as he sank back, she saw the beads of sweat which had broken out on his smooth brow and across the bridge of his handsome nose.

'I will call the physicians,' she said. 'I will send for Dr Parra. I believe him to be the best in the country.'

'I feel safe . . . with you,' said Philip, and there was a wry twist to his lips.

'Ah, Philip,' she said gently, 'you have many enemies, but you need not fear while I am here.'

That seemed to comfort him and she told herself exultantly: He rejoices that I am here. My presence comforts him. He knows I will protect him. For a time he loves me.

She smiled almost roguishly. 'You do not think me mad now, Philip?'

She took his hand which was lying on the coverlet, and he returned the pressure feebly because he felt so weak.

She thought: When you are strong and well you will mock me again. You will try to convince them that I am mad. You will try to put me in prison because you want my crown all for yourself. But now . . . you need me and you love me, just a little.

She was smiling. Yes, he had taken all her pride. He loved her once for her crown; and now he loved her for the safety he could feel in her presence.

But I love him with all my being, she reminded herself, so that I care not for what reason he loves me, if only he but will.

She rose and sent at once for Dr Parra.

No one else should come near him. She would nurse him herself. She would forbid all other women to come into this sickroom. She would give the orders now. Was she not the Queen of Castile?

*   *   *

It was four days before Dr Parra reached Burgos, and by that time Philip's fever had increased. He was now quite unaware of where he lay or who tended him. There were days when he did not speak at all but lay in a coma, and others when he muttered incoherently.

Juana remained in the sick-room, clinging to her determination that no one but herself should wait on him. He took no food but occasionally sipped a little drink, and Juana would allow no one to offer this but herself.

None could have been more calm than she was at that time. Gone was all the hysteria; she moved about the sick-room, the most efficient of nurses, and all the time she was praying that Philip would recover.

But after seven days of fever his condition grew rapidly worse, and Dr Parra ordered that cupping glasses be applied to his shoulders and purgatives administered. These instructions were carried out, but the patient did not rally.

He had now fallen into a lethargy from which it was impossible to waken him; only now and then

259

would he groan and put a hand to his side, which indicated that he suffered pain.

On the morning of the 25th September of that year, 1506, black spots appeared on his body. The doctors were baffled, but there were strong suspicions now throughout the palace that Philip had drunk something more than water on that day when, overheated by the sport, he had asked for a drink.

There were whispers now of: 'Who brought the drink?' None could be sure. Perhaps Philip remembered, but he was too weak to say.

Philip had many enemies, and the greatest of these was Ferdinand, who had been forced to surrender his rights in Castile. Ferdinand was far away, but men like Ferdinand did not do such deeds themselves; they found others to do the work for them.

It was remembered that, shortly before Philip had been taken ill, Ferdinand's envoy, Luis Ferrer, had come to Burgos. But it was well not to talk too much of this, for, if Philip died and Juana were proved mad, then Ferdinand would undoubtedly become the Regent of Castile.

So it was only in secret that people asked themselves who had poisoned Philip the Handsome. In public it was said that he was suffering sorely from a fever.

*   *   *

He was dead. Juana could not believe it. The doctors had said so, but it must not be.

He was so young, only twenty-eight years of age, and he had been so full of vigour. It was not

260

possible.

They were surrounding her, telling her of their sorrow, but she did not hear them; she saw only him, not as he was now, drained of all life, but young, handsome, mocking, full of the joy of being alive.

He is not dead, she said to herself. I will never believe that. I will never leave him. He shall stay with me always.

Then she thought: I can keep him to myself now. I can send them all away. I am the ruler of Castile, and there is none to stand beside me and try to snatch my crown from me.

They were weeping; they were telling her they suffered with her. How foolish they were! As if they could suffer as she suffered!

She looked regal now. There was no sign of wildness in her face. She was calmer than any of them.

'He shall be carried to the hall, and there he shall lie in state,' she said. 'Wrap him in his ermine robes and put a jewelled cap on his head. He will be beautiful in death as he has been in life.'

They obeyed her. They wrapped him in his ermine robe, which was lined with rich brocade; they placed the jewelled cap on his head and they laid a diamond cross on his breast. He was put on a catafalque covered with cloth of gold and carried down to the hall. There a throne had been set up and he was seated upon this so that he looked as though he were still alive. Then the candles were lighted and the friars sang their dirges in the hall of death.

Juana lay at his feet, embracing his legs; and there she remained through the night.

And when the body was embalmed and placed in its lead coffin she refused to leave it.

'I shall never leave him again,' she cried. 'In life he left me so often; in death he never shall.'

Then it seemed that the madness was with her once more.

*   *   *

They carried her to her apartment from which all light was shut out. She was exhausted, for she would neither sleep nor eat. It was only because she was weak that they were able to remove her from the coffin. For several days she sat in her darkened room, refusing all food; she did not take off her clothes; she spoke to no one.

'Assuredly,' said all those of her household, 'her sanity has left her.'

While she remained thus shut away, the coffin was taken from the hall of the Palace of Burgos to the Cartuja de Miraflores and, when she heard that this had been done, she hurriedly left her darkened room.

Now she was the Queen again, preparing to follow the coffin with all speed, giving orders that mourning should be made and that this was to resemble the garb of a nun, because she would be remote for ever from the world which did not contain her Philip.

When she arrived at the church she found that the coffin had already been placed in a vault, and she ordered that it should immediately be brought out.

She would have no disobedience. She reminded all that she was the Queen of Castile and expected

262

obedience. So the coffin was brought from the vault.

Then she cried: 'Remove the cerecloths from the feet and the head. I would see him again.'

And when this was done, she kissed those dead lips again and again and held the feet against her breast.

'Highness,' whispered one of her women, 'you torture yourself.'

'What is there for me but torture when he is no longer with me?' she asked. 'I would rather have him thus than not at all.'

And she would not leave the corpse of her husband, but stayed there, kissing and fondling him, as she had longed to during his life.

She would only leave after she had given strict orders that the coffin should not be closed. She would come again the next day and the next, and for as long as the coffin remained in this place she would come to kiss her husband and hold his dead body in her arms.

And so she did. Arriving each day from the Palace of Burgos, there she would remain by the coffin, alternately staring at that dead figure in the utmost melancholy, and seizing it in her arms in a frantic passion.

'It is true,' said those who watched her. 'She is mad . . . This has proved it.'

CHAPTER XIII

KATHARINE, THE AMBASSADRESS

After her meeting with Juana, Katharine realised that she could hope for no help from her own people. Her father was immersed in his own affairs, and indeed was far less able to help her by sending the remainder of her dowry than he had been when her mother was alive. As for Juana, she had no thought of anything but her own tragic obsession with her husband.

That month had arrived during which, Katharine believed, she would know what her fate in England was to be.

Her maids of honour chatted together about that important day, the twenty-ninth; she listened to them and did not reprove them. She knew they would talk in secret if not before her.

'He will be fifteen on the twenty-ninth.'

'It is the very month, this very year.'

'Then we shall see.'

'When they are married it will make all the difference to our state. Oh, would it not be wonderful to have a new gown again!'

Katharine broke in on their conversation. 'You are foolish to hope,' she said. 'The Prince was betrothed to me, but that was long ago. Do you not realise that if we were to be married we should have heard of it long ere this? There would surely be great preparations for the marriage of the Prince of Wales.'

'It may be that the marriage will be announced,'

said Francesca. 'Mayhap they are saving the announcement, that it may be made on his fifteenth birthday.'

Katharine shook her head. 'Does the King of England treat me as his future daughter-in-law?'

'No, but after the announcement he might.'

'You are living in dreams,' said Katharine.

She looked at those faces which had been so bright and were now often clouded by frustration and disappointment.

She knew that the betrothal of herself and Henry would be forgotten, as so many similar betrothals had been, and that his fifteenth birthday would pass without any reference to the marriage which was to have taken place on that day.

Katharine caught the despair of her maids in waiting, and she sent for Dr de Puebla.

The doctor arrived, and the sight of him made her shudder with disgust. He looked so shabby; he seemed to wear a perpetually deprecating expression, which was probably due to the fact that he was continually apologising to Henry for Ferdinand, and to Katharine for his inability to improve her lot. He was infirm nowadays and almost crippled; he could not walk or ride the distance from his humble lodgings in the Strand to the Court, so travelled in a litter. He was in constant pain from the gout and, since he had received no money from Ferdinand for a very long time, he was obliged to live on the little which came in from his legal business. This was not much, for Englishmen were not eager to consult a Spaniard and he had to rely on Spaniards in England. He dined out when he could and, when he could not, he did so as cheaply as possible; and he was a great deal shabbier than Katharine and her maids of honour.

He was unfortunate inasmuch as he irritated Katharine; she was by nature serene and compassionate, but the little Jew, perhaps because he was her father's ambassador in a Court where she needed great help, exasperated her almost beyond endurance and she began to feel—wrongly—that, if only she had a man more worthy to represent her father and to work for her, her position would not be so deplorable as it was and had been for most of her stay in England.

'Dr de Puebla,' said Katharine, as he shuffled towards her and kissed her hand, 'have you realised that the fifteenth birthday of the Prince of Wales has now come and gone and there has been no mention of the marriage which was once proposed between us?'

'I fear I did not expect there would be, Highness.'

'What have you done about this matter?'

Puebla spread his hands in a well-remembered gesture. 'Highness, there is nothing I can do.'

'Nothing! Are you not here to look after the interests of my father, and are they not mine?'

'Highness, if I could persuade the King of England to this marriage do not doubt that I should do so.'

Katharine turned away because such bitter words rose to her lips, and the sight of the sick little man made her feel ashamed of her anger towards him.

'Is nothing ever going to happen?' she demanded. 'How do you think I live?'

'Highness, it is hard for you. It is hard for me.

266

Believe me, I am well acquainted with poverty.'

'It goes on and on and on,' she cried. 'There is no way out. If I could return to Spain . . .'

She stopped. In that moment she had made a discovery. She did not want to return to Spain, because all that she had wished to return to was no more. She had longed for her mother, but Spain no longer contained Isabella. Did she want to be with her father? There had never been any great tenderness between them, because his affection for his children had always been overlaid with hopes of what they could bring him. Maria was in Portugal. Juana had grown strange. Did she want to go to Spain then to be with Juana and her husband, to see their tempestuous relationship, did she want to see that handsome philanderer gradually driving her sister over the edge of sanity?

Spain had nothing for her. What had England? Nothing apart from the dazzling prospect of marriage with the Prince of Wales.

Katharine realised in that moment that she must marry the Prince or remain all her life an outcast from Spain, the unwanted stranger in a foreign land.

She needed brilliant diplomacy to bring about the marriage, and all she had was this shabby, gouty Jew.

He was saying now: 'Highness, I have done everything I can. Believe me, I will not spare myself . . .'

Katharine shook her head and murmured: 'Mayhap you do your best, but I like not the way these matters go. You may retire now. Should you become further acquainted with the King's mind, I pray you come to me, for I am anxious.'

Puebla shuffled out, and he was surprised, when he had left her presence, to find his cheeks were wet.

I am worn out, he said to himself, with all the work which has come to nothing. I suffer pain; I can no longer amuse and entertain. I have outlived my usefulness. That is why old men shed tears.

And, left alone, Katharine wrote to her father. She told him that his ambassador in England was no longer able to work for her good or the good of Spain. She implored him to give this matter his attention and appoint a new ambassador to the Court of the Tudor King, for the sake of Spain and for his daughter, who was beside herself with misery.

$$* \qquad * \qquad *$$

Eagerly she awaited news from her father. Each day during that summer seemed more trying than the last. The maids of honour did not attempt to hide their dissatisfaction. They were continually longing to be back in Spain.

There were perpetual quarrels in the household, and Katharine almost wished that Doña Elvira was back with them to keep them all in order. Francesca was more restless than the others and she seemed to find a wicked delight in accusing each member of the household of intriguing to keep them in England. There could be no greater sin in the eyes of Francesca.

The fact is, thought Katharine, they need to be married. If Arthur had lived, they would all have worthy husbands now, and rich, full lives.

It seemed to her that each month it was

necessary to rifle her store of jewels and plate. She felt guilty when she sold or pawned these pieces, but what could she do? Her expenses had to be met, and disposing of her plate and jewellery was the only means of doing this.

At last news came from Spain, and when she read of the death of Philip she could not help but rejoice.

He was my father's enemy, she told herself; he turned him from Castile and he would have taken the crown from Juana. She is miserable now, but it is a good thing that he has gone.

She imagined her father's secret delight, for if Juana were incapable of ruling it was certain that Ferdinand would come back to Castile and the Regency.

She realised what this would mean. Ferdinand would be of more account in Europe than previously, and the manner in which the King of England treated her depended largely on what was happening to her father.

So could she consider this sudden and mysterious death of her handsome brother-in-law good news? She believed she could.

There was a letter from her father in answer to that which she had sent asking for a new ambassador.

'Why should you not be my ambassador?' wrote Ferdinand. 'You have been at the English Court for some years. You know their ways; you speak their language. In due course I will send you an ambassador, but in the meantime you may consider yourself as such. Listen to Puebla; he is a clever man, perhaps cleverer than you realise. Be guided by him. He has worked well for Spain and will, I hope, continue to do so.'

When Katharine had stopped reading there was a faint colour in her cheeks. She felt more cheered than she had for a long time. Now she would have an interest in life; now she would have more power, and she would try to serve her father faithfully and at the same time bring about a happier state for herself. And how could she achieve such a state? There was one answer: Only by marriage to the Prince of Wales.

*   *   *

The King of England requested the pleasure of her company. She went to his apartments, her hopes high, wondering what news he had to impart to her.

He was alone and he received her with graciousness, as though, she believed, he considered her of greater importance than he had when they had last met.

When she had been formally greeted she was allowed to sit in his presence and, cupping his face in his hands, the King said: 'This is a matter which I believe I can entrust to your hands more readily than I could to any other.'

'Your Highness delights me,' she answered.

Henry nodded, his lower lip protruded, his expression more pleasant than usual.

'I shall never forget the day when your sister, the Queen of Castile, arrived at Windsor. What grace was hers! What charm!'

Katharine was puzzled. She too would never forget that day, but had been struck more by Juana's melancholy than her grace and charm.

'I have not forgotten her from that day to this,' said the King. He paused and then went on: 'You now act as your father's ambassador, so I am going to entrust this matter to you. I want you to tell your father that I am asking for the hand of the Queen of Castile.'

Katharine caught her breath in astonishment. Juana . . . the wife of the King of England! She, who had adored that handsome, golden-haired philanderer, to become the wife of this ageing man with the cold, hard face and the uncertain temper! It was impossible.

But was it? Royal marriages could be incongruous. And if this one were to become fact, she would have her sister in England, the Queen of England. Surely the sister of the Queen of England could not be humiliated. Surely she would be able to live in a state worthy of her relationship to the Queen.

And what joy to have her own sister in England!

Katharine's busy thoughts were halted suddenly. But to be married to the King. She remembered her own feelings when it had been suggested that he should be her next bridegroom. She had shuddered with distaste, and yet she had felt delighted at the thought of Juana's taking the place she despised.

But this could not be. Juana was mad. She had begun to believe that there was little doubt of this, since she had heard further rumours of her sister's strange behaviour.

The King was watching her intently. She must learn to guard her expression. She hoped that she had not allowed distaste to show itself.

He seemed not to have noticed and was smiling

almost vacuously, as a country yokel might smile at the prospect of a bride. It was almost as though he had fallen in love with Juana. Oh no, no! Henry VII could never fall in love . . . except with a crown. That was the answer. He was falling in love with the crown of Castile.

She must be wily. She must not tell him that she thought this marriage would be quite distasteful because he was an old man and her sister was mad.

If she listened to his plans, if she worked with him, he might be prepared to reward her in some way. She was not a foolish young girl any more. She was a woman who had suffered great hardship and deep humiliation, and there was little that could make an Infanta of Spain suffer more.

She said calmly: 'I will inform my father of your request.'

Henry nodded, still smiling that smile which sat so oddly on his harsh features.

'You should write to your sister and tell her of the delights of the English Court. Tell her that I have been a faithful husband to one Queen and would be so to another. You will plead my cause; and from whom could that plea come more effectively than from her sister?'

So Katharine, in her new role of ambassadress, prepared herself to open the courtship between that incongruous pair—Henry Tudor, King of England, and Juana, Queen of Castile, who was now becoming known as Juana the Mad.

CHAPTER XIV

THE STRANGENESS OF JUANA

When Juana received the invitation to state her views as to a marriage with Henry Tudor she shrugged her shoulders and immediately dismissed the matter from her mind. She was concerned only with one thing, which was to keep Philip with her now that he was dead.

She would sit for hours alone in her darkened room, wearing the mourning garments which were like a nun's and included a great cowl, the purpose of which was to hide as much of her face as possible.

She would mutter to herself: 'Women . . . Let no women come near me. They are seeking now to take him from me. It was always so. Wherever he went they sought him. He could not escape from them even had he wished . . . but of course he did not wish. Now they shall not take him from me.'

Sometimes her attendants heard wild laughter coming from her apartments. They never heard sobs. She had not shed a tear since his death. When the melancholy moods were with her she would sit silent for hours at a time.

She ate scarcely anything and her body was pitiably thin beneath the flowing nun's robes. But there were times when she would have musicians play to her, for only music could soothe her. She would send for her minstrels and they would play to her in the darkened room until she tired of them and sent them away.

There were no women now in her household, except one, her washerwoman.

'And even that one, I must watch,' she often murmured to herself. Then she would send some of her men-servants to see what the washerwoman was doing, and have her summoned to her presence.

'Wash the clothes here,' she would cry, 'that I may see what you are about.'

And water and tubs would be brought to the royal apartments while the poor bewildered washerwoman washed the clothes under the suspicious eye of the Queen.

It was small wonder that rumours of her madness were growing.

She was heavy with her child now, and sometimes she would talk of it.

'It is not so long since he was here,' she would say, putting her hands on her body that she might feel the movement of the child. 'He was happy to see his family growing. I hope I shall be able to tell him soon that we have another boy.'

There were occasions when certain grandees came to her and implored her to take an interest in state matters, reminding her that she was the Queen.

But she only shook her head. 'I shall do nothing more, until I die, but pray for the soul of my husband and guard his dead body,' she said. 'There is time for nothing else.'

They could only shake their heads and wait for the return of Ferdinand.

The year was passing and December came. In January her child would be born, and those who wished her well told themselves that with the coming of the child she would forget this obsession with her husband's dead body.

It was one cold December day when she set out to hear mass at the Cartuja where Philip's body lay. Soon, it was said, she would be unable to make even the short journey from the palace, encumbered as she was with her pregnancy. She went through the usual ceremony of kissing the lips of her husband and embracing his feet; and then suddenly she announced: 'It was his wish that he should be buried in Granada. He has tarried long enough here. I shall take him to Granada. Pray prepare to leave at once.'

'Your Highness,' she was told, 'this is winter. You could not cross the steppes of Castile at this time of the year.'

She drew herself up to her full height and her eyes flashed wildly. 'It was his wish that he should go to Granada, and it is my desire to take him there.'

'With the coming of the spring . . .'

'Now,' she said. 'We leave today.'

This was indeed madness. She proposed to cross the snowy wastes between Burgos and Granada in the bitterly cold weather, and she herself in her eighth month of pregnancy!

The monks did their best to dissuade her. She grew angry; she reminded them that she was their Queen.

'He shall stay no longer in this place,' she cried. 'It is unworthy of him. Prepare at once, I say.'

'But the weather, Highness . . .'

'He will not feel the weather. He never cared for the heat. He loved the open air. The cold winds invigorated him, he said.' Then she suddenly

275

screamed: 'Why do you hesitate? Do not dare disobey me. If you do it will be the worse for you. Prepare at once. We are taking him to Granada this day.'

* * *

Across the snowy tablelands the procession slowly made its tortuous way. The wind penetrated the garments of the bishops, the choristers, the men of the Church and the men-servants. The only person who did not feel the cold was the Queen who, in her nun's robes, was carried over the rough land in her litter.

There was not a person in the retinue who did not hope that the Queen's child would be born before the middle of January when it was expected. They prayed for anything which could put an end to this nightmare journey.

Beside the litter, and covered with a velvet pall, was the hearse, so that it should never be out of the Queen's sight. As they walked it was the duty of the choristers to chant their mournful dirges.

At dusk the Queen reluctantly allowed the cortège to halt at an inn or a monastery, and there each night the coffin must be opened that the Queen might throw herself upon the dead body, kissing those silent lips again and again.

Those who looked on at this ritual asked themselves how long they could expect to be at the mercy of a madwoman's whims.

One night the coffin was carried into what was believed to be a monastery; and there, before entering the buildings, by the light of torches the coffin was opened and the gruesome ceremony began.

While it was in progress a figure appeared from the building followed by two others.

One of the bishops said: 'We come, with the Queen, to rest here a night.'

'I will make ready to receive Her Highness,' was the answer. But at the sound of that high, musical voice Juana leaped to her feet, her eyes suddenly blazing.

'That is a woman!' she cried. 'Come here, woman. No . . . no. Stay where you are. I will come to you. You shall not come near him.'

'I am the Abbess, Highness,' said the woman.

Juana screamed at her bishops: 'How dare you bring me here! There are women here. That place is full of women. You know I will let no woman come near him.'

'Highness, these are nuns . . .'

'Nuns are women,' she retorted. 'I trust no women. Close the coffin. We are going on.'

'Highness, the night is cold and dark.'

'Close the coffin!' She turned to the Abbess. 'And you . . . go back into your convent. Do not dare to set foot outside until we have gone. No woman shall come near him, I tell you.'

The Abbess bowed and retired, thankful that the mad Queen was not to be her guest.

The coffin was closed; the procession left the convent precincts and went on, in the hope that the next place of refuge would be a monastery.

So the dreary journey continued with painful slowness.

It was a great relief when it reached the village of Torquemada, for here Juana's warning pains began, and even she realised that she could not go on. They had come only thirty miles in some three weeks.

The coffin was set up where she might see it and make sure that no woman came near it; and on the 14th January in that year 1507 her child was born.

It was a girl and she called her Catalina after her sister, about whom now and then her conscience troubled her. She was unhappy, even as I am, she thought; and yet I did not listen to her tale of suffering.

She lay in melancholy silence, the child in her arms, while she kept continual watch over all that was left to her of her gay and heartless Philip.

*　　　*　　　*

In England Henry was waiting impatiently for news of his proposed match with Juana.

He sent for Puebla, and the gouty old man was carried to Richmond in his litter.

'I hear nothing from Spain concerning my proposals,' he began. 'It would seem that they are unwelcome.'

'Nothing, Your Grace, would be more welcome to Spain than a match between Your Highness and Queen Juana.'

'Then why do I hear nothing?'

'My master is still in Naples, and there is much to occupy him.'

'And the Queen of Castile herself?'

'Has been so recently widowed, so recently brought to bed of a child . . .'

Those words increased Henry's impatience. There was a woman who had borne several children. If she were his wife he need have no doubt that he could beget many boys. She had already borne two healthy boys and she was only twenty-eight. Certainly she was capable of bearing more. She had given proof of her fruitfulness. Had not her husband left her pregnant when he died? And it was said that he had given the greater part of his attention to other women.

Puebla, accustomed now to Henry's irritable temper, reminded him that Juana was considered to be somewhat unstable of mind.

'I saw her here in England, and I was impressed by her charm and beauty,' said the King. 'I did not see any signs of insanity. And yet . . . if it should be that she is insane I should not consider that an obstacle to marriage, for she has proved that this mental illness does not prevent her from bearing children.'

'I will tell my master what Your Grace has said.'

Henry nodded, and a familiar grimace of pain crossed his face as he moved in his chair.

'There is one other little matter,' he went on. 'His Highness Ferdinand may well return to the position he occupied immediately after the death of Queen Isabella. He will return to power as Regent of Castile and ruler of Spain—that is if his daughter is indeed unfit to take her place on the throne. He has made no effort to pay the remainder of his daughter's dowry. Say this to him when you write: If he does not soon pay this long overdue account there will be only one course open to me. I shall be obliged to consider the match between his daughter Katharine and the Prince of Wales broken off.'

Puebla felt a lifting of his spirits. This was an indication that a match between Katharine and young Henry was still possible. Henry's terms were: the rest of the dowry which had not been paid after Arthur's death, and marriage with Juana.

*   *   *

Juana did not recover quickly from the birth of her daughter Catalina. Those who had accompanied her on the thirty-mile trek from Burgos hoped that when she was well again her interests would be concentrated on the child, and she would give up this mad project of taking her husband's corpse to Granada in this way.

While Juana lay in her apartments, the cradle of her daughter beside her, and the coffin placed in the room so that she could gaze at it at any hour of the day or night, one of her servants came to tell her that a friar, who had heard she was in Torquemada, had travelled far to see her. He had important news for her.

Juana was not interested in any news which could be brought to her; but she agreed to see the Friar, and when the man stood before her she looked at him with melancholy eyes clearly showing her indifference.

The man was travel-stained; his eyes were wild. As he bowed, his gaze went at once to the coffin and stayed there; and watching him, Juana lost her listlessness and found herself gripped by excitement.

'Highness,' cried the Friar, 'I have had a vision.'
'Of whom?'
The Friar indicated the coffin.
'I saw him rise from it. He came out, all shining

and beautiful.'

Juana sat up in her bed that she might see the Friar's face more clearly.

'He rose from the dead!' she whispered.

'Yes, Highness. He threw off the cerecloths and there he was, whole and well; and there was great rejoicing.'

'This came to you in a dream?'

'As a vision, Highness. I had fasted many days and spent many more on my knees in humble seclusion. Then this vision came to me. He left his coffin and walked from this place into the streets. I saw him clearly in these very streets . . . and I knew that it was in Torquemada that the Queen's consort had risen from the dead.'

'Here in Torquemada!' cried Juana, clasping her hands together in ecstasy. 'Then it was by divine will that we left Burgos . . . that we came here and were forced to rest at Torquemada. Oh, glory be to God and all His saints! Here in Torquemada my Philip will rise from the dead.'

'I came with all haste to tell Your Highness.'

'I thank you with all my heart. You shall be well rewarded.'

The Friar closed his eyes and bowed his head.

Excitement gripped the village of Torquemada. All were waiting for a miracle. Outside the house in which Juana lodged people gathered; they were coming in from the neighbouring villages to wait for the miracle.

Juana had changed completely; all her melancholy was thrown aside; she was gay—not hysterically so, but with a quiet contentment. She was certain that the Friar was a holy man and that Philip was about to return to life.

281

She kept her vigil by the coffin, determined that she would be the first to welcome him back to life. He would hear then how she had kept him with her, and he would be so much happier to awaken from the dead by her side than he would have been to awaken in the gloom of some dismal vault that he would be grateful to her. If ever he had needed proof of her love he would have it now.

The Friar, well rewarded, left Torquemada, but the sightseers continued to come in. The summer was hot and the village had never contained so many people; and as the houses were filled, many were forced to sleep in the street and the fields.

In the heat of the afternoon one of the sightseers collapsed suddenly and lay groaning in a high fever. He died almost immediately, and that very day three more people were stricken in the same manner. Before the next day came, the crowds in and about Torquemada realised that someone had brought the plague among them, and were terrified.

News was brought to Juana that there was plague in Torquemada.

'Highness,' said one of her bishops, 'we should prepare to leave this place with all speed.'

'Leave it!' she screamed. 'But it is here that my Philip will come to life again.'

'Highness, every hour you delay you put yourself and the child in danger.'

'Our faith is being tried,' she answered. 'If I leave Torquemada now there will be no miracle.'

Again and again efforts were made to persuade her. Juana remained stubborn.

So, while the plague raged in Torquemada, Juana stayed there with her newly born daughter

282

and the remains of her husband, waiting for a miracle.

* * *

All through the summer Juana remained in Torquemada. The plague abated with the passing of the hot weather, and still Juana watched over the coffin, waiting for a miracle.

There were occasions when she believed that Philip had indeed risen from the dead, and her servants would hear her murmuring endearments or loudly upbraiding him for his infidelities. It was a strange household that rested in the village of Torquemada. There was the Queen of Castile, living humbly with no women in her household except the washerwoman, a young Princess who thrived in spite of the conditions in which she lived, and the remains in the coffin which were regularly kissed and embraced.

Then one day there was great rejoicing in Torquemada. The news spread rapidly, and all in that grim household knew that the days of waiting were over.

Ferdinand had arrived in Valencia. Now there would be some law and order throughout Castile.

* * *

'I must go to meet my father,' declared Juana. 'He will expect it of me.'

She had either forgotten the Friar's prophecy or given up all hope of its coming true, for it was almost with relief that she prepared to go.

She had no wish to see the sun, she said. She was

283

a widow and her life would therefore in future be lived in darkness. She would travel only by night and by the light of torches, and wherever she went there would her husband go with her.

In vain did those who cared for her comfort seek to dissuade her; any opposition to her will sent her into paroxysms of rage. She would be obeyed. She would have them remember that, although she was the most unfortunate widow in the world, she was their Queen, and from them she expected obedience.

So once more the cortège set out. Beside her went the hearse so that she never lost sight of Philip's coffin. They travelled by the light of torches and the going was rough and very slow. The choristers sang their dismal funeral dirges as they went; and Juana, riding or carried in her litter, travelled always in melancholy silence.

It was at Tortoles that Ferdinand and his daughter came face to face.

When Ferdinand saw her, he was horrified. It was years since they had met, but the lapse of time did not entirely account for the great change. It was almost impossible to believe that this sad woman, with the melancholy eyes in which madness lurked, was his gay daughter who had often shocked her mother by her wildness.

Juana also was not unmoved. She found herself in those first moments of reunion remembering the days of her childhood, when she, her brother, sisters, father and mother had all been together.

She went on her knees and gripped her father's hands, while Ferdinand, astonished at his emotion, knelt too and, putting his arms about her, held her tenderly.

'My daughter, my daughter,' he murmured, 'what has happened to bring you to this?'

'Oh, my father,' she murmured, 'I have suffered as few are called upon to suffer. I have lost all that I love.'

'There are your children. They can bring great comfort.'

'They are his children too,' she said, 'but when he died the sun went from life. Now there is only darkness, for it is perpetual night.'

Ferdinand rose from his knees, his emotion evaporating. If Juana was really as mad as she seemed, then the way would be easy. He could now be sure of taking the Regency.

'I will care for you now,' he said, and she did not notice the glint in his eyes; nor did she see any hidden meaning in his words.

'It is a joy to me that you have come,' she said.

Ferdinand pushed back the black hood and kissed her brow.

He thought: She is indeed mad. There can be no doubt of it. Regent of Castile until Charles is of age! There were many years of government ahead of him.

'We cannot stay here in Tortoles,' said Ferdinand. 'We should travel to a place where we can live and discuss matters of state in comfort.'

She did not demur and he was delighted that she appeared ready to agree with everything he said; but he soon discovered how stubborn she could be.

'I only travel by night,' she told him.

He was astonished.

'Travel by night! But how is that possible? The journey would take four times as long.'

'That may be so, but I am in no hurry. I am shut

285

away from the sun and the light of day. My life from now on will be lived in darkness.'

'Certainly we cannot travel by night. You must end this foolishness.'

Then he saw it, the flash of obstinacy, and he remembered that she was Isabella's daughter. Similar conflicts came to his mind; he remembered how often his will had pulled against that of Isabella, and how Isabella had invariably won because she was the Queen of Castile and he but her consort. Now here was Isabella's daughter reminding him that she was the Queen of Castile and he but her father.

Ferdinand determined then that all Castile must know that Juana suffered from periodic insanity, that she could not be relied upon; and the only way in which Castile could be satisfactorily ruled was by a Regent while the Queen spent her life in seclusion.

Let her travel by night. Let her carry the coffin of her husband about with her; let her fondle the corpse when she liked. All this would enable the people to understand that the Queen was in truth a madwoman.

So Ferdinand travelled by day, and Juana by night; and when Juana realised that they were taking the route to Burgos, that town full of the most poignant memories—for it was there that Philip had died—she refused to travel further.

She stopped at Arcos and took up her residence there. In vain did her servants protest that she had chosen the most unhealthy spot in Spain. She retorted that she did not care for the weather. The cold meant nothing to her; she no longer felt anything but sorrow.

Ferdinand made no protest. He could wait.

She was making it easy for him to convince the people that their Queen was mad, and then he would cease to fear anything she might do. With great vigour he set about putting his affairs in order.

He read the despatches from Puebla. Puebla was growing old; he would send a new ambassador to England; he must try once more to bring about the marriage of his youngest daughter with the Prince of Wales.

CHAPTER XV

FUENSALIDA AT THE KING'S COURT

It was a bleak February day and a chilly mist enveloped the countryside. The elegant foreigner clearly found the weather distasteful, and his retinue, being fully aware of his choleric temper and his habit of speaking his mind, whispered together that it was to be hoped the weather improved before they reached London.

The journey from the coast had taken them several days and they had come to rest for the night in an inn still some miles from the capital. Their coming had aroused a certain flutter of excitement within the hostelry, for it was known that the party must be on their way to the King's Court, and there was speculation even among the scullions as to whether this meant a marriage for the Prince of Wales with his brother's widow, and perhaps a bride for the King.

This was not the first party of Spaniards they had seen; but the nobleman who was clearly the most important member of the party was certainly a very touchy gentleman. He complained of this and that, and although he was too haughty to speak to them they were fully aware of his fastidiousness.

Don Gutierre Gomez de Fuensalida was however in far from an ill mood. The weather might be distasteful and he hated the discomforts of travel, but he was quite certain that he was going to complete a mission, over which that fool Puebla had been stumbling for so many years, and complete it to such satisfaction to his master that great honours would be showered upon him.

The futility, he said to himself, of allowing such a man as Puebla to handle these delicate matters! A Jew of no standing! Diplomacy should be conducted only by members of the nobility.

Don Gutierre was complacent. He himself belonged to a family which could trace its glorious ancestry back through the centuries; he was wealthy; he was not in the diplomatic service of his country for financial gain but for honours. He had recently come from the Court of Philip the Handsome, and previously he had represented Ferdinand at that of Maximilian. He was fully aware of the intrigues of traitors such as Juan Manuel and he had never swerved from the cause of Ferdinand. Now that Philip was dead and Juana recognised almost universally as mad, Gutierre Gomez de Fuensalida was coming into his own; his would be the rewards of fidelity and, when he had satisfactorily arranged the marriage between Ferdinand's daughter and the Prince of Wales, Ferdinand would indeed be grateful to him.

While he mused thus a visitor arrived at the hostelry; he came riding in with a few servants and asked immediately of one of Gutierre's servants if he might be taken to his master.

'I have ridden from London,' he said, 'for the sole purpose of greeting Don Gutierre Gomez de Fuensalida and that I might have the pleasure of returning with him to the capital.'

Gutierre, delighted when he heard that a gentleman of distinction had called to see him, although it was no more than courtesy demanded and it was certainly what he expected, ordered that the visitor should be brought to him immediately.

'I am Dr Nicholas West, Bishop of Ely,' Gutierre was told. 'I heard that you had arrived and have come to usher you into Court circles, on the express command of His Highness the King.'

'It gives me great pleasure to meet you,' answered Gutierre.

The innkeeper, a little flustered by such distinguished guests, provided a private room in which refreshment was served to the two gentlemen.

And when they had talked of the perils of sea journeys and the weather in England, they reached the real purpose of the meeting.

'The King has not enjoyed such good health during this winter as he has hitherto,' explained Dr West. 'Indeed, his physicians are in constant attendance.'

'What ails His Grace?'

'He has been plagued by pains in his body for some years, and his limbs have become so stiff that it is often painful for him to put foot to the ground. These pains are always more severe during the winter months. But this winter he has suffered more than usual. He has had rheums and coughs which have kept him to his bed for many weeks. His physicians do not allow him to spend long at a time with his ministers, and there are days when they implore him not to see them at all.'

'I understand,' said Gutierre. 'This will mean that there may be some delay in his receiving me?'

'It may well be so.'

'Then I must perforce wait until he commands me to his presence. In the meantime I will call on the Infanta. I doubt not she will be eager to have news of her father.'

'That is something of which I must warn you. It is the etiquette of the Court that ambassadors should not visit anyone belonging to the royal household until they have been received by the King.'

'Is that so? That is going to make my position somewhat difficult . . . unless I have an early interview with the King.'

'You may rest assured that as soon as His Grace's health has improved he will receive you. He is eager to have news of his friend and brother, King Ferdinand.'

'He cannot be more eager for these negotiations than my master is.'

'Had you any plans as to where you would lodge?'

'Yes. I thought of staying awhile in the house of Francesco Grimaldi, who, as you know, is the London agent of the Genoese bank.'

Dr West nodded. He understood that this was significant. There was no doubt in his mind that Ferdinand was now preparing to pay the remainder of Katharine's dowry and that Grimaldi would be called in to conduct the business.

'I cannot think of a more satisfactory arrangement,' he said.

The conversation continued in the pleasantest manner. Dr West informed the new Spanish ambassador of affairs at Court. He spoke of the popularity and charm of the Prince of Wales, who was becoming more and more important to the people as his father grew more infirm.

The eyes of the Spanish ambassador glinted

with pleasure.

There could be no doubt that his main purpose in coming to London was to bring about the marriage of his master's daughter and the Prince of Wales.

*   *   *

Francesco Grimaldi was delighted to welcome the Spanish ambassador. Grimaldi was well past middle-age, but he lived well and he was fond of gaiety, and any form of excitement was welcome. He was an astute business man who had built up a considerable fortune, and was therefore able to entertain Don Gutierre Gomez de Fuensalida in a manner to which even he was accustomed.

Excellent food and wines were served at Grimaldi's table, and Gutierre was not the most discreet of men.

So the dowry which had brought so much trouble to the Infanta was at last to be paid? How many years was it since she had arrived in England a hopeful bride? It must be nearly seven. And what a sad life the poor lady had led since the death of Prince Arthur!

Gutierre found Grimaldi not only entertaining but useful, for he was able to supply that kind of Court gossip which never appeared in the state papers.

He did not see why he should change his lodgings since he was perfectly comfortable in the house of Grimaldi, which was within easy reach of the Court.

On the day of his arrival in the banker's house a young man called to see him. He humbly announced himself as the son of Dr de Puebla, who deeply regretted that he was unable to call on the ambassador as he was confined to his bed with an attack of gout.

Gutierre looked down his long aristocratic nose at the humble son of a humble father. He was eager to show these people that he, Knight Commander of the Order of Membrilla, scion of an ancient house, was quite determined not to listen to the babbling of upstarts, who were of humble origin and *marranos* at that.

'Give your father my regrets and wishes for his speedy recovery,' he said coldly.

'My father hopes you will call on him at the earliest time Your Excellency finds agreeable. He wishes me to say to you that this matter, which is the reason for your coming to England, is a very complicated one and, as the English are extremely shrewd, he would like to make you acquainted with all details as soon as possible.'

Gutierre bowed his head and murmured that he would bear the matter in mind.

He would make no appointment to call at the residence of his fellow ambassador, and the young man was forced to retire in some bewilderment.

When he had gone, Gutierre let his anger burst forth.

Does that Jew think that he can teach me Court manners? he asked himself. He would show Dr de Puebla—and their master, Ferdinand—that the only ambassadors worthy of the name were those of noble blood.

*   *   *

293

The news was brought to Katharine that her father's ambassador was in England, and she rejoiced. She was optimistic. Her father's affairs were becoming prosperous once more and she knew that, on the rise and fall of her father's power, her own future prospects would fluctuate.

She wept bitterly when she heard the news of Juana's strange conduct and of how she kept the dead body of her husband with her and refused to relinquish it. She had become accustomed to hearing her sister referred to as the mad Queen; but she was still endeavouring to bring about a marriage between Juana and Henry because Henry so desired it and, she told herself, if Juana were to come to England, I could help to look after her; and surely she could not bring the body of her dead husband here. Katharine believed that once Juana could be persuaded to bury Philip, she would begin to regain her sanity.

She was not unconscious of the fact that, as a result of Juana's madness, Ferdinand was a greater power in Spain than he would be if Juana were sound in mind and able to rule; and, since it was due to the rising power of Ferdinand that she herself was treated with more respect, she could not help reflecting sadly that they appeared to be a house divided against itself, since Juana's misfortune could work to her, Katharine's, good.

She was all eagerness to meet Gutierre Gomez de Fuensalida, for she would be delighted to dispense with the services of Puebla.

Her maids of honour—and Francesca de Carceres in particular—were continually complaining about the little man. They were sure it was due to his mismanagement of affairs that they were still living in this unsatisfactory way, while the years passed, they grew older, and no husbands were found for them.

Francesca was particularly bitter, as she loved gaiety more than did the others. Maria de Salinas and Inez de Veñegas were resigned, and she believed these two very dear friends of hers suffered more on her account than on their own.

Katharine lost no time in telling them of the arrival of the new ambassador.

Francesca was frankly delighted. 'And Don Gutierre Gomez de Fuensalida!' she cried. 'He is a very grand gentleman. He will know how to deal with your father-in-law, Highness.'

'I do not believe my father-in-law will care whether he has to deal with the nobleman or the lawyer Jew. His great concern will be the payment of the dowry.'

'I shall make our sad state known to the new ambassador,' declared Francesca. 'Something must be done for us before we are too old to be married at all.'

Poor Francesca! thought Katharine. How she longed for marriage! She should be the mother of several children by now.

'I am a little anxious,' she said. 'I am wondering what will happen when my plate and jewels are valued. The value will be found to be a great deal less than when I arrived. And these were to be part of the dowry.'

'But what could Your Highness do?' demanded Maria de Salinas. 'You had to live.'

'There are times,' Katharine murmured, 'when I believe that kings and ambassadors do not think that it is necessary for a princess and her

295

household to eat. She is merely a figure to be used when the state needs her. She can marry. She can bear children. But eat! That is not considered at all necessary.'

Maria de Salinas was startled to hear the bitterness in Katharine's voice. It was well, she reflected, that the new ambassador was here and that it was possible he would bring the negotiations, which had been going on for so many years, to a satisfactory end.

*　　*　　*

When Henry received the Spanish Ambassador, the King was wrapped in a long robe and sat huddled near a blazing fire.

'My dear Ambassador,' said Henry with more warmth than he usually displayed. 'You find me in ill health. I cannot move easily, so you must sit beside me and give me news of my dear brother, the King of Aragon.'

'My master sends his greetings to Your Grace,' answered Fuensalida, bowing with courtly grace.

'I pray you be seated,' said Henry; and, his alert eyes looking out from the wrinkles which pain had set about them, he summed up the character of the new ambassador. Here was one of the Spanish grandees, a man with a great opinion of himself. That was not displeasing. Henry liked weakness in the ambassadors of other countries.

When Fuensalida was seated, Henry said: 'I know that you have come to see me on two matters of great importance and interest to me. They are also matters of great happiness: marriages. How much better it is for Kings to unite through such

296

alliances than to quarrel together! What news do you bring me of Queen Juana?'

'There is no King to whom Ferdinand would rather see his daughter married than yourself.'

'Then why delay . . . why delay?'

'It is on account of the strangeness of the Queen of Castile.'

Henry frowned. 'I have heard of this strangeness, but what does it mean? She has recently been brought to bed of a fine daughter. She has borne sons. I would ask nothing more of a wife than that.'

'It is said that the Queen of Castile is insane.'

'Insane! Bah! She is fertile. We in England would have no objection to a little insanity if a Queen were fertile, as I have already explained.'

'Then the negotiations should go forward.'

'And with speed,' cried the King. 'You see me here . . .'

He did not finish, and Fuensalida spoke for him: 'Your Grace is no longer in your first youth. A speedy marriage is a necessity for you that you might get sons before it is too late.'

Henry was astonished. No one had ever dared refer to the fact that it was possible he would not be long for this world. And here was this stranger calmly telling him so. He felt very angry, the more so because he knew the truth of the statement. Had they told Juana that he was an old man and that his eagerness for their marriage was not his regard for her but the immediate and desperate need to beget a son before the grave claimed him?

Surely this ambassador must be the most tactless man Ferdinand could possibly have sent him.

'And there is a matter of great importance to us

both,' went on Fuensalida who, since he never considered the feelings of others, was never conscious of wounding them, 'and that is the marriage of the Infanta and the Prince of Wales.'

Impudence! thought Henry. He dares to change the subject! Where are his manners? Or does he think that a Spanish grandee takes precedence over a King of England?

Henry did not show his anger when dealing with foreign diplomats. He said calmly: 'I have a great regard for the daughter of the King of Aragon. I find her gracious, charming and beautiful. It has grieved me that she must live so long in such uncertain state.'

'Your Grace remembers that he promised that she should marry the Prince of Wales?'

'I do not forget it and I see no reason why this marriage should not take place, providing certain questions can be amicably settled between my friend the King of Aragon and myself.'

'It is precisely that such matters should be settled that I am here with Your Grace.'

'Is that so?'

Still Henry showed no sign of the fury he felt. It was not the marriage of Katharine and the Prince of Wales he was eager to discuss, but his own marriage with Juana.

'Why,' he went on, 'I remember full well that these two were betrothed. I am not a man to break my word. I should tell you that the Prince of Wales has had many offers . . . many brilliant offers of marriage.'

'There could scarcely be a more brilliant marriage, Your Grace, than with a daughter of Spain.'

298

Insolent fellow! thought Henry. He would see that Ferdinand realised his folly in sending such a man to England. Henry greatly preferred little Dr de Puebla—a man who lacked this arrogance and certainly realised that the best way to serve his master was not to antagonise those with whom that master wished to make new friendships.

'I am weary,' he said. 'My doctors warned me. You will be received by my councillors, and you can lay the terms of the King of Aragon before them.' The King closed his eyes. Gutierre Gomez de Fuensalida was dismissed.

*   *   *

The Council were far from helpful. Fuensalida did not know that the King had already told them of his dislike for the new ambassador, and had hinted that no concessions should be made to him.

As for Fuensalida, he was afraid that certain members of this Council were not of sufficient nobility to be on equal terms with him, and he was disgusted that the King was not present that he might address himself to him.

The Bishop of Winchester, who with the Bishop of Ely and the Earl of Surrey formed part of the Council, showed no grace or finesse in dealing with this delicate matter of Katharine's dowry. They wanted to know how the money was to be paid.

'As previously arranged,' said Fuensalida. 'There will be sixty-five thousand crowns and the remainder in plate and jewellery.'

'You have presumably brought the plate and jewels with you?' one of the members of the Council enquired.

'You know full well that the Infanta brought her plate and jewels with her when she arrived in this country.'

'That,' said Surrey, 'was in the year 1501; quite a long time ago.'

'You knew that this plate and these jewels were intended for her dowry?'

'How could that be,' asked Winchester, 'when the Infanta has been wearing the jewels and using the plate?'

'And disposing of them if my information is correct,' added Surrey.

The Bishop of Ely added slyly: 'On the marriage of a husband and wife, the wife's property becomes that of the husband. Therefore it would seem that the Infanta's jewels became the property of Prince Arthur and consequently the property of the King.'

'Does Don Gutierre Gomez de Fuensalida then seek to pay the King the remainder of the Infanta's dowry with the King's own plate and jewels?' Ely wanted to know.

'This is monstrous!' cried Fuensalida, who had never learned to control his temper.

Winchester was delighted, for he knew that the best way of scoring over the Spaniard was to make him lose his temper.

He went on: 'This is the King's property, into which over a number of years the Infanta has been breaking, selling a piece here, and a piece there, so that much of that which should be in the King's coffers is now in those of the Lombard Street merchants!'

'This is a matter for your shame!' shouted Fuensalida. 'You have treated the Infanta as a beggar. You have dared behave so to a daughter of

Spain.'

'Whose dowry was never paid in full,' put in Winchester.

'I shall not remain to hear more of such insolence!' cried Fuensalida; and he left the council chamber to the delight of the English.

CHAPTER XVI

IN THE HOUSE OF GRIMALDI

Francesca de Carceres was determined on action. Something had to be done, and she guessed that the marriage negotiations of the Infanta and the Prince of Wales were as far as ever from reaching a satisfactory conclusion.

Until the Infanta was married, none of her maids of honour would be.

And thus, thought Francesca, the years will pass until we are all dry old spinsters whom no one would take in marriage even if we had big dowries.

Francesca was never one to wait for opportunity; she went out to seek it.

She had met Don Gutierre Gomez de Fuensalida and recognised in him a nobleman such as Puebla could never be. Being suspicious of Puebla and believing that he worked for the King of England rather than for Ferdinand, she wished that he should be recalled to Spain; it seemed that he never would be, because Ferdinand for some strange reason trusted him. And in any case the old fellow was now so infirm that he would be of no use in Spain. It was characteristic of Ferdinand that he should not recall him. It was so much easier to keep the ailing old man in England, pay him no wages and let him work for Spain.

Francesca pinned her hopes on Fuensalida.

She decided therefore that she would see him in private. This was not an easy thing to do at Court because when he came he was not alone; and in any case what chance had a maid of honour of a private interview without calling a great deal of attention to herself to obtain it?

There was plenty of freedom now in Katharine's entourage, so Francesca had planned that she would slip away one afternoon and call on the ambassador at his lodgings, which she knew to be in the house of the banker, Francesco Grimaldi.

She wrapped herself in a cloak, the hood of which did much to conceal her face, and set out. When she reached the banker's house she was taken into a small room and the servant who had brought her in went away to discover whether the Spanish ambassador was in his apartment.

While Francesca waited she examined the rich hangings and the fine furniture in this small room. She had been struck by the grandeur of the house as soon as she entered it. Perhaps this appreciation was the more forceful because she thought of the poverty in which she and the Infanta's maids of honour had lived for the last few years.

Banking must be a profitable business, she reflected; and it was brought home to her that people such as bankers must live in more affluent circumstances than many a Prince or Princess.

The door was opened and a rather plump man stood in the doorway. Francesca noticed at once that his jacket was made of rich velvet and that his stomacher was most elegantly embroidered. His hanging sleeves were somewhat exaggeratedly long and there were jewels at his throat and on his fingers. He gave an impression of elegance and wealth and his corpulence and air of general well-being indicated a man who lived most comfortably. His eyes were warm brown and very friendly.

303

When he bowed low over Francesca's hand on which his lips lingered slightly longer than Court etiquette would have considered necessary, she discovered that she was not displeased.

'I am happy to see you in my house,' he said. 'But alas, Don Gutierre Gomez de Fuensalida is not here at this time. If there is anything I could do to help you, depend upon it I should be greatly honoured.'

'That is very kind of you,' Francesca replied, and she told him who she was.

'This is a happy day for my house,' answered the banker, 'when one of the Infanta's ladies call. And that she should surely be the most beautiful adds to my pleasure.'

'You are very gracious. Will you be so kind as to tell Don Gutierre Gomez de Fuensalida that I called? I should have told him I was coming.'

'Pray do not leave so soon. I cannot say when he will return, but it is possible that he may do so within the hour. If in my humble way I could entertain you during that time, I should be most happy.'

Francesca said: 'Perhaps I could linger for a little while.' And she was gratified to see the look of bemused pleasure in the face of the banker.

'Allow me to offer you refreshment,' he said.

Francesca hesitated. This was most unconventional, but she was known to be the most adventurous of the Infanta's maids of honour and she thought how she would enliven them all when she returned by telling them of her adventures at the home of the Genoese banker; so she succumbed to temptation and sat down; whereupon Grimaldi summoned a servant and gave his orders.

Half an hour later Francesca was still in the banker's company; she was amusing him with stories of Court life, and he was amusing her equally with stories of his own world. When she expressed her admiration for his beautiful furniture he insisted on showing her some of his more elaborate pieces, which resulted in a tour of this very fine house of which he was clearly—and justly—proud.

Fuensalida had not returned when Francesca decided that she really must leave; Grimaldi wished to escort her back, but she refused to allow this.

'We should be seen,' she said. 'And I should doubtless be severely reprimanded.'

'What a mischievous young lady you are!' murmured the banker rapturously.

'One must bestir oneself in some ways,' retorted Francesca. 'I do admit the others are somewhat prim.'

'I shall never cease to bless the day you came to see Don Gutierre Gomez de Fuensalida, and I feel grateful to him for not returning, thus allowing me to enjoy your company and have it all to myself.'

'Are bankers always so gallant?' asked Francesca almost archly.

'Even bankers cannot fail to be in the presence of such overwhelming beauty,' he told her.

It was all very pleasant and Francesca had enjoyed the encounter; and when he said goodbye his lips lingered even longer on her hand. We are so unused to such attentions, she told herself; and even when they do not come from the nobility they are not without their attractions.

'If you should ever desire to do me this honour again,' he said earnestly, 'I should rejoice in my good fortune.'

She did not answer, but her smile was provocative.

She hurried back to the palace, telling herself how she would enjoy explaining her little adventure to the others; she imagined herself imitating the banker's voice as he paid her the most extravagant compliments. How they would laugh! And who among them had ever had such an adventure?

Then suddenly she decided she would say nothing. What if she were forbidden to visit the banker's house again? Not that she intended to go again; but suppose she wanted to, it would be most irritating to be forbidden to do so.

No, for the present her encounter with Francesco Grimaldi should remain her secret.

*   *   *

When Katharine heard that Fuensalida had quarrelled with the Council she was disturbed and commanded Puebla to come to her at once.

The old man sent for his litter and, as he was carried from his lodging to the palace, he reflected that he would not make many more such journeys, for he was well aware that the end was in sight for him. It was sad that he had worked so hard and un-failingly to bring about this marriage without success, and now that Ferdinand had sent his new ambassador the position had rapidly worsened.

He did not expect to be appreciated. When had he ever been appreciated? He was a Jew by birth,

306

and he had become a Christian. Such as he must become accustomed to injustice. He should think himself lucky that he was not in Spain, where he might so easily commit some mild indiscretion and be taken before the tribunal of the Inquisition and charged with heresy.

At least, he thought, I shall die in my bed; and the reward for my services will be merely neglect and general ingratitude.

As he dragged himself painfully into the Infanta's apartment Katharine felt an immediate pity for him.

'Why, you are ill!' she said.

'I grow old, Highness,' he murmured.

She called for a chair that he might sit in her presence, and for this he was grateful.

She came straight to the point. 'I had hoped,' she said, 'that my dowry was to be paid and that I should be able to claim the fulfilment of my marriage treaty. It seems this is not to be so. When I came here it was understood that my plate and jewels were to form part of my dowry, and now Don Gutierre Gomez de Fuensalida informs me that the King will not accept this.'

'He must accept it,' said Puebla. 'It was part of the marriage treaty.'

'But Don Gutierre says that the Council refuse to admit this.'

'Then they must be made to admit it. I fear he has offended the Council with his quick temper and high-handed manners. He forgets that he is in England; and he will never bring matters to a satisfactory conclusion if he is going to offend the people whom it is necessary to placate.'

'You think that they can be made to accept the

plate and jewels?'

'I am sure they will. But the jewels and plate are much depleted, I believe.'

'I have found it necessary to have some money to live, and I have pawned or sold a considerable amount of the plate and jewels.'

'Highness, if your father will make up the discrepancy I feel sure we can come to an arrangement with the King.'

'Then you must see Fuensalida and make him understand this.'

'I will. And Your Highness should have no fear. The King will wish to come to this arrangement. He is eager for a match between your nephew, Charles, and the Princess Mary. He is even more eager to enter into marriage with your sister, Her Highness Queen Juana. I believe that a little diplomacy will settle these matters amicably.'

'Then I pray you go to Fuensalida with all speed. And, Dr de Puebla, I am concerned for your health. I am going to send my physician to see you. You must act on his advice.'

'Your Highness is gracious,' murmured Puebla.

He felt resigned. He knew that Fuensalida was the last man to handle this delicate situation with the right amount of tact and shrewdness. He knew also that when Katharine's physician saw him, he would be told to keep to his bed. That he knew was tantamount to receiving his death warrant.

*   *   *

Katharine was frustrated. She was aware that the King disliked the Spanish ambassador and made continual excuses not to grant the interviews he asked.

Puebla, who alone might have made some progress now that Ferdinand really seemed desirous of settling his daughter's affairs, had now taken to his bed. Too late Fuensalida learned how useful the little man could be.

The matter dragged on. Henry, who was beginning to see that he would never get Juana, was growing angry. He did not trust Ferdinand. Henry was becoming increasingly difficult to deal with because he was now in acute pain and the calmness which had been characteristic of him was deserting him. His skin was turning yellow and he was rapidly losing weight. There were whole days when he was invisible to any but his doctors.

Katharine was so eagerly watching the progress of her own affairs that she failed to notice the change in one of her maids of honour. Francesca had seemed to grow younger; she had come into possession of some beautiful pieces of jewellery. She did not flaunt these before the eyes of the others, it was true, but on one occasion when Maria de Rojas had called attention to a handsome ruby ring which she was wearing, Francesca had shrugged her shoulders, murmured, 'Have you not seen it before?' and hastily changed the subject.

Francesca was the only member of the Infanta's household who was not depressed by the way things were going; each day she contrived to slip away, and remained absent for several hours.

Fuensalida was making himself unpleasant to various members of the Infanta's household. He had quarrelled with Puebla many times, and only the little man's humility and desire to bring about a successful solution of the troublesome matter of the dowry made their association possible. His chief enemy in the household was Fray Diego Fernandez, who was Katharine's confessor and whose position gave him especial influence over her. This friar seemed to Fuensalida an arrogant young man because he did not show sufficient respect to the ambassador, and he had threatened to write to Ferdinand to the effect that Fernandez was not only incompetent but dangerous, as the Infanta placed too much trust in him.

Katharine was desperate, realising that when she needed as much support as she could get, her affairs were continually being obstructed by strife within her own circle.

One day Fernandez came to her in a state of great indignation. He had had a narrow escape, he told her. Fuensalida had made an attempt to have him arrested and shipped out of the country.

Katharine was angry, but there was nothing she could do. Puebla was confined to his bed and clearly was dying; now she reproached herself for not appreciating that little man before. It was only now that she could compare him with Fuensalida that she realised how admirable he had been. She could not ask her father to recall Fuensalida and send her another ambassador. The situation was too involved and, by the time a new man arrived, who could say what might have happened?

So she prayed constantly that her ill luck would change and that soon her affairs might be put in order.

*   *   *

What joy it was to escape to the house of the

310

Genoese banker! thought Francesca. How merry that man was, and how delighted that Francesca de Carceres should deign to visit him. It was true, of course, that she was of a most noble family and he was merely a banker; but how much more extravagantly he lived, and what great comfort he enjoyed!

She could not recall how many times she had been to his house, ostensibly to visit the ambassador, and how she arranged her visits to fall at those times when she knew Fuensalida would not be present.

She had meant to implore him to do something for Katharine's maids of honour, who should have marriages arranged for them, but she had found no opportunity of speaking of this matter to the ambassador.

There was so much of interest to see in the house, and her banker delighted in showing her. She had only to admire something, and he implored her to accept it. He was surely the most generous man in the world!

So it was fun to slip on her cloak and hasten to his lodgings.

On this occasion he was waiting for her, and he seemed more serious; as it was unusual to see him serious, she wondered what had happened.

They took wine together with some of those excellent cakes which his cooks made especially for her, and as they sat together he said suddenly: 'How strange that I should be Francesco, and you Francesca. It seems yet another link between us.'

'Yes,' she smiled, 'it is certainly strange.'

Then he became even more serious and said: 'How long can this continue?'

'You mean my visits? Oh, until the Court moves, or until I am discovered and forbidden to come.'

'That would stop you . . . if you were forbidden?'

'I might be tempted to disobey.'

He leaned towards her and took one of her hands. 'Francesca,' he said, 'would you consider becoming mistress of this house?'

She grew a little pale, realising the enormity of what he was suggesting. She . . . marry him! But her marriage was one which would have to be approved by the Infanta, by the Queen of Castile or by Ferdinand, and by the King of England. Did he not understand that she was not a little seamstress or some such creature to make a match on the spur of the moment?

'The suggestion is repulsive to you?' he said wistfully.

'No . . . *no*!' She was emphatic. She was thinking of how dull her life had been before these visits; and how it would seem even more dull if she were forced to give them up. She went on: 'Marriages are arranged for people in my position. I should never be allowed to marry you.'

'You have been neglected,' he argued. 'To whom do you owe loyalty? As for myself, I am no subject of the King of England. If I wish to marry, I marry. If you decided you did not want to go back to the palace one day, I would have a priest here who should marry us. I would place all my possessions and myself at your service. I love you, Francesca. You are young, you are beautiful, you are of noble birth, but you are a prisoner; and the only one of these attributes which can remain to you is your noble birth. Francesca, do not allow them to bury you alive. Marry me. Have we not been happy together? I will make you happy for the rest of your life.'

Francesca rose. She was trembling.

She must go quickly. She must be alone to think. She was terrified that she would commit some indiscretion which would decide the whole of her future life.

'You are afraid now,' he said gently. 'Make no mistake. It is not of me, Francesca, that you should be afraid. You would never be afraid of me. You are bold and adventurous. Not for you the palace prison. Come to me, Francesca, and I will make you free.'

'I must go,' she said.

He did not attempt to detain her.

'You will think of what I have said?' he asked.

'I cannot stop thinking of it,' she answered. Then he took her face in his hands and kissed her forehead tenderly. She knew that she was going to feel cheated if she did not see him again. Yet how could she?

CHAPTER XVII

JUANA AT TORDESILLAS

Juana in the town of Arcos knew nothing of the negotiations which had been going on to marry her to the King of England. She had settled in this most unhealthy climate, but she was quite unaware of the cold winds which penetrated the palace. Her little Catalina had become a lively little girl who seemed readily to accept the strangeness of her mother. Juana had also insisted that her son Ferdinand should be brought to live with her, and this wish had been granted. But little Ferdinand, who was nearly six years old, did not take kindly to his mother's household. He did not like the coffin which was always prominently displayed; nor did he care to look on his dead father and to see his mother fondling the corpse.

Juana went about the palace dressed in rags, and she did not sit at table but ate her food from a plate on the floor like a cat or a dog. She never washed herself, and there were no women-servants in the house except the old washerwoman.

Music could sometimes be heard being played in the Queen's apartment; otherwise there was almost continuous silence.

Young Ferdinand was very happy when his grandfather came to Arcos and took him away, although his mother screamed and shouted and had to be held by attendants while he rode away with his grandfather. Ferdinand loved his grandfather, who made much of him.

'We are both Ferdinands,' said the elder Ferdinand, and that delighted the boy, who decided that he would be exactly like his grandfather when he grew up.

Juana might have gone on in this state at Arcos but for the fact that revolt broke out in Andalusia, and it immediately occurred to Ferdinand that the rebels might plan to use her as a figurehead. He decided then that he was going to remove her to the isolated castle of Tordesillas, where it would be so much easier to keep her under restraint.

He came to the Palace of Arcos one day and went straight to those apartments where Juana was sitting, staring moodily at the coffin of her husband. Her hair, which had not been dressed for many months, hung about her haggard face; her face and hands were dirty, and her clothes hung in filthy rags about her gaunt figure.

Ferdinand looked at her in horror. There was indeed no need to *pretend* that she was mad.

Undoubtedly she must be removed to Tordesillas. He knew that there was a plot afoot to displace him and set up young Charles as King. As Charles was now nine, this arrangement would give certain ambitious men the power they needed; but Ferdinand was determined that the Regency should remain in his hands, and he would be uneasy until Juana was his prisoner in some place where he could keep her well guarded.

'My daughter,' he said as he approached her— he could not bring himself to touch her. As well touch a beggar or gipsy; they would probably be more wholesome—'I am anxious on your account.'

She did not look at him.

'Last time I was here,' he went on, 'I did not

315

please you. But you must realise that it is necessary for the people to see little Ferdinand; and what I did was for the best.'

Still she did not answer. It was true then that, although she had raged when he had taken her son, a few days later she had completely forgotten the boy. There was no real place in that deranged mind for anyone but the dead man in the coffin.

Ferdinand went on: 'This place is most unhealthy. You cannot continue to live here in this . . . squalor. I must insist that you leave here. The castle of Tordesillas has been made ready to receive you. It is worthy of you. The climate is good. There you will recover your health.'

She came to life suddenly. 'I shall not go. I shall stay here. You cannot make me go. I am the Queen.'

He answered quietly: 'This place is surrounded by my soldiers. If you do not go of your own free will, I shall be obliged to force you to go. You must prepare to leave at once.'

'So you are making me a prisoner!' she said.

'The soldiers are here to guard you. All that is done is for your good.'

'You are trying to take him away from me,' she screamed.

'Take the coffin with you. There is no reason why you should not continue to mourn in Tordesillas, as you do in Arcos.'

She was silent for a while. Then she said: 'I need time to prepare myself.'

'A day,' he said. 'You can wash yourself, have your hair dressed, change into suitable clothes in a day.'

'I never travel by day.'

'Then travel by night.'

She sat still, nodding.

And the next night she left Arcos. She had been washed; her wild hair had been set into some order; she wore a gown suited to her rank; and, taking little Catalina in her litter, she set out with her followers; as usual, beside the Queen's litter, so that it was never out of her sight, went the hearse drawn by four horses.

Through the nights she travelled and, as the third day was beginning to break, the party arrived at the old bridge across the Douro. There Juana paused to look at the castle which was so like a fortress. Immediately opposite this castle was the convent of Santa Clara, and in the cloisters of this convent she allowed the coffin to be placed. Then from the windows of her apartments she could look across to the coffin, and she spent the greater part of her days at her window watching over her dead. Each night she left the castle for the convent, where she embraced the corpse of Philip the Handsome.

So dragged on the long years of mourning, and each day she grew a little more strange, a little more remote from the world; only in one thing was she constant—her love for the handsome philanderer who had played such a large part in making her what she was.

CHAPTER XVIII

KING HENRY VIII

Katharine had now lost all hope. Her affairs were in the direst disorder. Fuensalida had quarrelled openly with Henry, and when the ambassador had gone to Court he had been told that the King had no wish to see him.

Fuensalida, haughty, arrogant and tactless, had even tried to force an entry, with the result that he had suffered the extreme indignity of being seized by guards and put outside the Palace precincts.

Never had an ambassador been submitted to such shame, which clearly indicated that Henry had no respect for Ferdinand's suggestions. Indeed Henry was boasting that he would marry Mary and Charles without the help of Spain.

Katharine was with her maids of honour when the news was brought to her of Puebla's death. This, she had at last come to realise, was one of the greatest blows which could befall her, for now there was no one to work for her in England but the incompetent Fuensalida.

'This is the last blow,' she said. 'I fear now that there is no hope.'

'But what will become of us?' asked Maria de Salinas.

'Doubtless we shall be sent back to Spain,' put in Maria de Rojas hopefully.

Katharine said nothing. She realised that to be sent back to Spain was the last thing she wanted. She would go back, humiliated, the unwanted

318

Infanta, the widow who was yet a virgin. Had ever any Princess of Spain been so unfortunate as she was? There was only one dignified course left to her, and that was marriage with the Prince of Wales.

That was hopeless, for the King had shown so clearly that he would not allow the marriage to take place. Whenever she saw the Prince he had kindly smiles for her, which was comforting, for his importance grew daily, one might say hourly.

Katharine noticed that Francesca was not with them.

'Where is Francesca?' she asked.

'I have not seen her, Highness,' answered Maria de Salinas.

'Now that I recall it,' pursued Katharine, 'she seems to absent herself often. What does she do when she is not with us?'

No one could answer that; which was strange because Francesca had been inclined to talk a great deal—often it seemed too much—of her personal affairs.

'I shall ask her when she returns,' said Katharine; and then they fell to discussing what would happen when Ferdinand learned that his ambassador had been refused admittance to the Palace.

Nothing would happen, thought Katharine wretchedly. Looking back over the years since Arthur's death, she saw that her position had changed but little. She could go on living in penury and uncertainty for the rest of her days.

*   *   *

'Highness!' It was Maria de Rojas, and her voice was trembling with excitement.

Katharine had left her maids of honour an hour before because she wished to be alone; she had felt she could no longer endure their chatter, which alternated between the desire to raise her hopes by improbable changes of fortune and sighing for their native land.

She looked at Maria quickly, eager to know what had happened to change her mood.

'This has been delivered at the Palace. It is for you.'

Katharine took the letter which Maria was holding out to her. 'It is in Francesca's handwriting,' said Maria.

'Francesca!'

Katharine's heart began to beat fast as she opened the letter, and she hastily scanned the words without taking them in the first time. Then she read it again. It was brief and to the point.

Francesca would never return. She had married Francesco Grimaldi, the banker from Genoa.

'It is . . . impossible!' breathed Katharine.

Maria was at her side; forgetting all ceremony, all discipline as she looked over Katharine's shoulder and read the words which the newly married bride had written.

'Francesca . . . married! And to a banker! Oh, how could she? How could she! A banker! What will her family say? Highness, what will *you* do?'

'It must be some joke,' murmured Katharine.

But they both knew that it was no joke; Maria's horror changed momentarily to envy. 'At least she *married*,' she whispered; her lips quivered and there came to her eyes the frantic look of a prisoner who has heard of another's escape, but sees no way out for herself.

'So this is where she has been,' went on Katharine. 'It is the man with whom Fuensalida had his lodgings. How could she, a Carceres, so far forget the honour due to her rank as to marry a banker!'

Maria was speaking as though to herself: 'Perhaps she fell in love with him. But it is more likely to be because he is very rich and we have been so poor. Francesca did not have an offer all the time we were here . . . perhaps she thought she never would have one.'

Katharine remembered her dignity. 'Leave me now,' she said. 'If she has left us we should make no effort to bring her back. She has chosen the way she wishes to go.'

'Your Highness will allow this?'

Katharine smiled bitterly. 'You do not blame her, Maria. I can remember, when I came to England, how eager you all were to come with me. It seemed such a glorious future, did it not? But how differently it turned out! Francesca has escaped . . . that is all. As you would escape, Maria, if the opportunity offered itself. Go now. Break this news to the others. I'll warrant they will share your envy of Francesca.'

Maria left her mistress and Katharine re-read the letter. Francesca was happy, she said. She had married the man of her choice. There was excitement in every line. Francesca had escaped.

It seemed to Katharine in that moment that she touched the depth of hopelessness. Gay Francesca had risked the displeasure of kings and a powerful noble family to escape from the dreary existence which she had been forced to share with the daughter of Ferdinand and Isabella.

*   *   *

It was the month of April. The birch and willow were in flower; the stitchwort threw a silvery sheen on the green hedges; and the meadows were bright with deep yellow cowslips.

In the Palace of Richmond, Henry VII lay dying, and in the streets the people rejoiced furtively. The old reign was passing and the new one would soon begin. People forgot that their King had brought peace to England. To most he had seemed unkingly because he hated war—not because of the misery it brought, it was true, but because of the waste of good money and lives which could be used to make the country prosperous. He had never spent lavishly on pageants for the people's pleasure, and there had only been rich ceremonies when there had been the need to impress other rulers with England's powers.

To the people he was a miserly King, insignificant in appearance; he had imposed cruel taxes on his subjects; he had shown little affection even to his family. They forgot that from 1485, when he had come to the throne, to this year of 1509 the country had lived in peace, and in place of a bankrupt state he had built up a rich treasury. They did not tell themselves that this was the first King who had lived within his income, who had laid the foundations on which could be built a major Power. They said: 'The old miser is dying. Old Henry is passing; this is the day of young Henry.' And when they thought of their laughing, golden Prince, they said: 'Now England will be merry.'

The excitement throughout the Court was growing to a feverish pitch. Courtiers gathered in little groups waiting for the cry of 'The King is dead.'

That young Henry should marry almost immediately was a matter on which all seemed to agree. Such a Prince needed a Queen. Who should it be?

There were many who favoured alliance with France. Let it be Marguerite of Angoulême, they said. There were others who believed that alliance with the Hapsburgs would be more advantageous. Let it be Eleanor, the daughter of Juana and Philip. Was Eleanor too young for their golden Prince? Well then, Duke Albert of Bavaria had a daughter. Maximilian would be delighted to sponsor such a match.

There was no mention of Katharine of Aragon, who had gone through a betrothal ceremony with the Prince of Wales some years before.

When Fuensalida came to visit Katharine he was gloomy. He was shut out from the Palace; he was useless as an ally. He told her that he was making arrangements to have her plate and jewels secretly shipped back to Spain.

He could not have said more clearly: The game is over, and we have lost.

*   *   *

The Prince of Wales waited in his apartments. Soon he would hear the stampede. They would come to acclaim him as their King. They, no less

323

than he, had been waiting for this day.

He would tower above them all; none could mistake him, with his great height and his crown of fiery hair; his big, beaming and benign countenance was known throughout the country.

His eyes narrowed as he thought of the years of restraint when he, the beloved of the people, had been forced to obey his father.

He was no longer a boy, being in his eighteenth year. Surely this was the threshold of glorious manhood. He could not be merely a man; he was a god. He had so much beauty, so much strength. There was none at Court who could compare with him; and now, as though not content with the gifts which had been showered on him, fate was putting the crown of yellow gold on that red-gold head.

From his window he could see the courtiers. They were whispering together . . . about him. Of course it was about him. The whole country was talking about him. They were saying he should marry soon, and marry soon he would, for he had a fancy for a wife.

Marguerite from France, who thought her brother the most wonderful man in the world? Little Eleanor who was but a child? They were daring to choose his bride for him!

He could scarcely wait for the moment when they would proclaim him King. One of his first acts would be to show them that he was their King in truth, and that, whether it was a bride or a matter of policy, it was the King who would decide.

They were coming now. So it was all over. The long-awaited moment was at hand.

He was ready for them as they came into the apartment. His eyes gleamed with appreciation, for

324

he quickly sensed the new respect, the subtle difference in the way a King was greeted.

They were on their knees before him.

'Then it is so?' he said. 'Alas, my father!'

But there was no time for sorrow. There was only triumph for the cry had gone up: 'The King is dead. Long live the King! Long live King Henry VIII!'

*   *   *

Katharine had come to pay homage with the rest, and kneeling before him, she looked appealing in her humility.

The young King turned to those who stood about him and said: 'You may leave us. I have something to say to the Infanta which she must know before all others.'

When they were alone he said: 'You may rise, Katharine.'

He was smiling at her with the expression of a boy who has prepared, for a friend, a wonderful surprise, in which he is going to find as much pleasure—or even more—than the one for whom it is intended.

'Doubtless,' he said, 'you have heard of many plans afoot to marry me to Princesses of Europe.'

'I have, Your Grace.'

'And I venture to think they have caused you some disquiet.' Henry did not wait for confirmation of that which he considered to be obvious. 'They need concern you no more. I have chosen my own bride. Do you think, Katharine, that I am the man to allow others to decide such a matter for me?'

'I did not think you would be, Your Grace.'

'Then you are right, Kate. I have chosen.' He took both her hands in his and kissed them. 'You are to be my bride. You are to be Queen of England.'

'I . . . I . . .' she stammered.

He beamed. No speech could have been more eloquent in his ears. She was overwhelmed by the honour; she was overcome with joy. He was delighted with her.

'I'll brook no refusal!' This was a joke. How could any woman in her right senses refuse the most glorious offer that could possibly be made? 'I have made up my mind. You *shall* be my bride!'

How handsome he was; his face creased in that happy, sunny smile. Yet behind it there remained the shadow of the sullen boy who had said: Nobody shall tell me what I must do. I make my own decisions.

For a brief moment Katharine asked herself what would have become of her if this boy had been told he must marry her instead of having been forbidden to.

Then she refused to consider such a thought.

Of what importance was what might have been, when she was being offered freedom from poverty and the humiliating position in which she had lived for so many years?

She knew the waiting was over. The neglected Infanta was about to become the most courted woman in England, the Queen, the bride of the most handsome, the most kingly ruler in Christendom.

CHAPTER XIX

QUEEN KATHARINE

Katharine rode beside the King through the streets of London.

A few days earlier they had been married in the Palace of Greenwich, for Henry, once having made up his mind, was eager for the marriage to be celebrated.

He was attentive to his bride; he was affectionate; he, who had never made a secret of his feelings, announced to his councillors that he loved her beyond all women.

So they must proceed from Greenwich to the Tower, and with them rode the flower of the nobility; through the streets they went, past the rich tapestries which hung from the windows to welcome them; and Cornhill, proud that all should know it was the richest street in the city, hung cloth of gold from its windows. The route was lined with young girls in white to indicate their virginity; all sang praises of their King and Queen.

There was Henry, and even he had never looked quite so magnificent as he did on that day; his enormous figure ablaze with jewels, his open countenance shining with good intentions and pleasure in his people and himself. The handsomest King ever to ride through the city of London, not excepting his maternal grandfather, Edward IV.

And there was the Queen looking radiant, with her beautiful hair streaming over her shoulders, on her head a coronal set with jewels of many colours. She was dressed as a bride in white satin exquisitely embroidered, and she rode in a litter of cloth of gold drawn by two white horses.

It was not easy to recognise in this dazzling bride the neglected Infanta of Durham House.

Happiness had brought beauty to her face.

She could only say to herself: It is over . . . all the humiliation, all the misery. Who would have believed it possible that it could have happened so quickly?

And there was another matter for rejoicing. She was in love. What woman could help but fall in love with the gay and handsome King who had rescued her from all her misery? He was the Prince of legend, and no such Prince had ever been so handsome as this young Henry VIII of England.

The people cheered her. They were ready to cheer anyone whom their King honoured, for they told themselves, the old days of parsimony and taxation were over; a gay young King was on the throne.

There were some in the crowd who remembered the day the Queen had married Arthur. Was a brother's widow the happiest choice? Was there not some allusion to this in the Bible which stated that such marriage was illegal?

But the sun was shining. The dour reign of Henry VII was over, and England was about to grow merry.

Away with such thoughts! This was the occasion of their King's wedding. He had married the woman of his choice. He was a radiantly happy bridegroom and a dazzling King.

'Long live King Henry VIII and his bride!'

shouted the people of London.

And so from the pleasant Palace of Greenwich came the dazzling cavalcade, through the gaily decked streets into the precincts of the Tower of London.

The grey fortress looked grim, the stone towers menacing; but Katharine only saw the golden beauty of her bridegroom, only heard the shouts of the people: 'Long live the King's bride! Long live our Queen, Katharine of Aragon.'

BIBLIOGRAPHY

Aubrey, William Hickman Smith, *The National and Domestic History of England*

Bertrand, Louis and Petrie, Sir Charles, *The History of Spain*

Burke, Ulick Ralph, *A History of Spain from Earliest Times to the Death of Ferdinand the Catholic*

Fisher, H. A. L., *The Political History of England (1485–1587)*

Hume, Martin A. S., *Queens of Old Spain*

Hume, Martin A. S., *Spain: Its Greatness and Decay (1479–1788)*

Hume, Martin A. S., *The Wives of Henry VIII*

Mattingly, Garrett, *Catherine of Aragon*

Prescott, William H., *History of the Reign of Ferdinand and Isabella the Catholic*

Quennell, Marjorie and G. H. B., *A History of Everyday Things in England (1500–1799)*

Salzman, L. F., *England in Tudor Times*

Sedgwick, Henry Dwight, *Spain*

Strickland, Agnes, *Lives of the Queens of England*

Wade, John, *British History*

CHIVERS
LARGE
PRINT
–direct–

If you have enjoyed this Large Print book
and would like to build up your own
collection of Large Print books, please
contact

Chivers Large Print Direct

Chivers Large Print Direct offers you
a full service:

• Prompt mail order service

• Easy-to-read type

• The very best authors

• Special low prices

For further details either call
Customer Services on (01225) 336552
or write to us at Chivers Large Print Direct,
FREEPOST, Bath BA1 3ZZ

Telephone Orders:
FREEPHONE 08081 72 74 75